"*Roadside Sisters* is a powerful, intense exploration into the raw, complicated bonds of sisterhood. In this journey of love, betrayal, and unhealed wounds, we follow Molly, Penelope, and Scottie as they navigate the ruins of their fractured relationships—a legacy from their parents' broken marriage. When Molly is diagnosed with cancer, past traumas resurface, and the sisters are forced to confront the secrets and pain they've kept buried for years. This gripping novel is wrenching at times, but the sisters' path to reconciliation and healing will strike a deep, enduring chord."

-Carla Damron,
award-winning author of *The Orchid Tattoo* and *Justice Be Done*

"*Roadside Sisters* is a raw, poignant novel about the human need for connection, forgiveness, and love. Written with compassion and honesty, Matthews tells the tale of three sisters brought together under devastating circumstances, and their journey to heal what's broken between them . . . before it's too late."

-S. G. Prince,
author of *To Poison a King* and *The Elvish Trilogy*

"*Roadside Sisters* is a deep dive into the family dynamics, the heartache, the love and affection of three complex women. Matthews' second novel is brilliant and will leave you wanting more!"

-James Shipmen,
bestselling author of *Before the Storm, Beyond the Wire,* and *Irena's War*

Roadside
Sisters

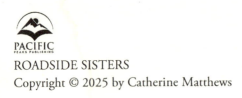

ROADSIDE SISTERS
Copyright © 2025 by Catherine Matthews

All rights reserved.

No part of this publication may be reproduced, distributed, or transmitted in any form or by any means, including photocopying, recording, or other electronic or mechanical methods, without the prior written permission of the publisher, except as permitted by U.S. copyright law. For permission requests, contact catherine@catherinematthewsauthor.com.

NO AI TRAINING: Without in any way limiting the author's and publisher's exclusive rights under copyright, any use of this publication to "train" generative artificial intelligence (AI) technologies to generate text is expressly prohibited. The author reserves all rights to license uses of this work for generative AI training and development of machine learning language models.

The story, all names, characters, and incidents portrayed in this production are fictitious. No identification with actual persons (living or deceased), places, buildings, and products is intended or should be inferred.

Contact Info: www.catherinematthewsauthor.com

Book Cover by Damonza
Author Photo by Starla Shaulis Photography

1st edition 2025

ISBN
979-8-9898840-4-9 (paperback)
979-8-9898840-3-2 (eBook)

First Edition: 2025

Roadside Sisters

A NOVEL

Catherine Matthews

PACIFIC
PEAKS PUBLISHING

To Judy
Thanks for all the miles of love, laughter, and sisterhood, and thanks for taking me to see the largest wine bottle and the tiniest Notre Dame (the life-sized Acropolis was pretty cool, too).

Chapter One

Scottie

Scottie latched the door on a melancholic Great Dane who, after two days, still refused to play with the other dogs. She just lay there like Clara Bow with a case of the vapors. No amount of belly scratching or kibble would move her. Scottie respected her refusal to feign joy after being unceremoniously dumped in the middle of nowhere with complete strangers. The dog had clearly amassed more self-respect in her three short years than Scottie had in forty-two. Still, whether her owner deserved it or not, genuine tail-wagging glee was sure to dominate their reunion. Scottie envied the canine ability to forgive and forget.

In between abandonment and reunion, it was her job to make the animal feel at home. She took that job seriously. Discarding several ideas, including smearing a thin patina of bacon grease on a particularly active West Highland Terrier that the Dane had no chance of ever catching, Scottie pulled down a box of training aids her father had saved from his duck-hunting phase. The contents were damning evidence of his many schemes to catapult the kennel from a reliable boarding enterprise to a championship bird dog facility.

She grasped a fishing reel attached to the dismembered end of a rod. As she tugged on the line, like a puppeteer with a marionette, decoys jerked about until they revealed a knobby orange bumper. Midway through formulating a plan based loosely on something she saw Wile E. Coyote do, the phone rang.

"I'll get it," she shouted down the aisle.

Through the open door to the exercise yard, her dad returned something halfway between a growl and a grunt, his standard preamble to a lecture on how he was perfectly capable of running the kennel, not to mention answering his *own damn phone*. She'd welcome that apoplectic tirade every night for the rest of her life if she never had to deal with another injury he could have avoided by tamping down his pride and asking for a little help.

Like father, like daughter. His last had been a twisted ankle that put him in a boot for a month and resulted in the One-Big-Ass-Dog-At-A-Time Rule. A docile Saint Bernard and an aging Newfie got a wild hair as he was moving them to the play area. Such a small thing, guaranteed to heal if he would just stay off it. Like a river wearing down boulders, time was taking its toll on him. He'd hidden the shame of helplessness behind a mask of anger. Scottie knew firsthand the power of anger to defy what doctors claimed to be inevitable, so she'd let him have his. She would take care of him. She certainly owed him that much.

"Casey's K-9s. Scottie speaking."

"Hey, Scottie! Thank God! I was worried Dad would answer." Molly, like the Great Dane, had a flair for the dramatic, though her style leaned more toward a Yorkie triggered by a doorbell.

"Well, I'm not sure why it matters, but do you know how you can ensure, with one hundred percent accuracy, he won't?" Scottie paused, but the middle Casey sister didn't bite. "Call my cell."

"What would be the fun in that? It's part of the thrill of calling. A little telephone roulette."

"And how is Sin City?"

"I think Vegas is Sin City. Reno's the Biggest Little City."

"Catchy slogan." Scottie toed the mud building up in the crevice where the cement floor met the kennel door and made a mental note to pressure wash it when the dogs were out to play. She pictured Molly sitting on a wrought-iron chair at a tiled bistro table on her balcony, warming her hands around a cup of coffee as she eased into the day. Though Scottie had never visited her apartment in Reno, she imagined it as a tidy, demand-free oasis. How nice it must be to put thirteen hundred miles between you and your family for a few months each year.

"So, what's up?" Scottie asked.

"I need a favor."

"From me?"

"Why do you sound so surprised?"

"Princess Penny lives closer." Scottie loved Molly, and she knew Molly loved her too. But she had no illusions. They would never be as close as Molly and Penelope were. After all, they shared a complete childhood and DNA from the same parents. Scottie couldn't break through those bonds with a battering ram.

"She hates it when you call her that." The playfulness drained from Molly's voice.

"I'm sure she has a special name for me." Letting her jealousy bubble to the surface was careless. It only provoked a protective response that pushed Molly away.

"She doesn't."

"Fine. What did you forget, and where is it?" She mentally rearranged her schedule to make room for spending a half day in traffic between Snoqualmie and north Seattle and at least an hour in line at the nearest post office.

"I didn't forget anything. Thanks for your faith in me, by the way." Molly huffed. "I need you to bring me home."

"Kind of early in the season for you, isn't it? There's still got to be enough snow for your rock skis." When Molly didn't answer,

Scottie conceded. "OK. Fine. I'll get Meaghan to come stay with Dad. What time does your flight get in?"

"Why does my favorite niece have to stay with Dad? What happened to him?"

"He got old, Molly. And like his age and the number of times he gets up to pee every night, the sheer volume of bad ideas Hank Casey has each day has increased exponentially. He cannot be left alone." Without thought, Scottie reached behind her, snaking her hand beneath her waistband to rub the muscles tensing around her hip. She let her fingers follow the ache nearly to the center line. As always, she stopped before they reached her spine where the results of Hank Casey's worst idea were carved indelibly in scarred flesh.

"Did he have an accident?" Molly asked.

"Yes. About a million of them. Last week, I caught him halfway up a ladder to the roof." Scottie stopped herself. It was a betrayal to talk to Molly about him like this. "Anyway, flight schedule? What time do I pick you up?"

"You don't. I mean, I need you to come to Reno and drive me home."

"Is there something wrong with your car?"

"No. I'm getting rid of it. Look, just come get me. It'll be fun."

Scottie leaned her forehead against the cold metal of the kennel gate and closed her eyes. "Molly, that's ridiculous. Get on a fricking plane."

"Scottie, just say the word. Fake swearing is pathetic."

"Get on a damn plane."

"Well done. We'll work up to the F-word."

"Molly, get serious. It's a thirteen-hour drive each way."

"I am not flying."

Scottie banged her head on the chain-link. How hard would

she have to hit it to require stitches or, better yet, an overnight observation?

"Are you there?" Molly asked.

"Yes," said Scottie. "This is nuts. Just get on a plane. It's not going to drop out of the sky." The request was absurd. Still, stitches or not, she would cave and do whatever Molly asked. She always did.

"You don't know that. I saw a preacher on TV who said he needed his own jet because the commercial ones are filled with sinners and demons. I'm not even asking for my own airplane. I just want you to drive me home." Molly paused. "What's that banging noise?"

"Nothing." Scottie touched her forehead, checking for blood. "Since when are you opposed to traveling with sinners and demons? I thought some of your best friends fit that category."

"You're hilarious. I'm opposed to hurtling thirty thousand feet in the air at six hundred miles an hour in a metal tube with people God might smite at any moment. Smite? Smate?" Molly paused. "Whatever. I don't want to be collateral damage in His mission to rid the world of evil."

"Maybe you'll be on a flight filled with saints who've devoted their lives to feeding the hungry and healing the sick." *Do not give in.*

"Great, then I can get caught up in their Rapture moment. No thanks. We'll all feel better if you just come get me."

"I won't feel better. It's a two-day drive for me. My back will be screaming." At the thought, her muscles clenched. Twenty-five years had done little to dull the pain. Like a child anxious to be let out to play, she stepped forward and back and side to side, trying to disengage the muscles.

"Maybe you don't have to drive it alone."

"If I do come, and I'm not saying I will, I won't be alone.

Burnie will come with me. So, pack accordingly. He's shedding his winter coat. Black or brown is your best bet."

"I was thinking more of a two-legged traveling companion."

"Dad?" she scoffed.

"No." Molly paused. "Penelope."

Scottie fell back against the wall and looked up at the clock over the office door. The second hand jumped forward and stopped. She breathed in, tick, tick, tick. She breathed out, tick, tick, tick. *Twenty-six hours in a car with Penelope. You must be out of your mind, Molly.* The second hand passed the number five, encircled in red ink as clear as the day Hank drew it. It indicated the morning feeding, which he'd assigned to her ad infinitum after catching her sneaking into the house in the middle of the night. Hank's punishment, like his memory, was long and harsh.

Maybe if Mary had sent all three daughters away to live with him, it would have been easier. Maybe having three chances to get the whole parenting thing right would have taken the pressure off Scottie. Or maybe Hank always felt some responsibility to raise her to be perfect, since he was raising someone else's child. In the end, it wasn't her mischief but his negligence that had kept her from perfection.

Breathing wasn't helping.

"OK. What's really going on here?"

Molly didn't answer. The crescendo of paws and nails on concrete was growing with each passing second. If she didn't get moving, her dad would start taking the dogs out on his own. More and more, he would forget to check the buddy sheet. They didn't need another vet bill. She didn't have time for this.

"Look, this seems like a longer conversation, and I need to get these dogs fed before they stage a revolt. Can I call you tonight?"

"I have cancer."

Molly's words slammed into her.

"Scottie, it's not the kind that can wait."

Chapter Two

Molly

"How'd that go?" The right side of George's mouth snuck up from beneath the unruly beard to meet the corner of his clenched right eye.

Molly knew his grimace held back words he couldn't bear to say and she didn't want to hear. She forced a smile. "Scottie's all business in a crisis. She'll try to back out to avoid Penelope, but in the end, she'll come. Her maternal instincts run deep, ironically. The next one will be the hard one."

"Do you want me to stay?" he asked.

The cancer had telescoped their relationship from casual buddy to dependable friend. It hadn't been planned, but he was the first person she told. On a ride, like hundreds before, she was overcome with the sheer joy of the cold air slipping between her helmet and jacket to clasp her neck as her wheels pulled miles of open road beneath her. Her eyes welled, and soon mist fogged her visor. She pulled onto the shoulder just as the tears began to fall. Exuberance and grief took up the battle in her chest. It was like she couldn't feel the true pain of the loss of this until every part of her being was electrified by the beauty of it.

Though she'd waved the others off, George refused to leave her there alone. Fearing her sobbing might drown her, she was forced to pull the helmet off. The weight of her sadness weakened her knees, and she sank to the grass. He didn't ask what was wrong. He didn't try to hold her. He didn't tell her it would be OK or she was making a mountain out of a molehill. He just sat beside her on the side of the highway and waited for the wave to recede.

Hugging her knees, as the damp grass wicked rivulets in the dust on her boots, she told him how she'd watched her mother decay—how her ability to ride would die long before her will. That wanting was the worst pain. How she'd never seen a snow-dusted peak as beautiful as the one before them today, though she'd ridden by this very one a hundred times. From the corner of her eye, she saw him nod. He understood the words she could not find.

And here he was, all these months later, offering to do more.

"No. But thank you." Molly was saying those words a lot more often. "They'll be here in a couple of days. I appreciate your help getting the boxes in the mail. All I have left is the cleanup. I don't want to leave this place a mess for Angie."

Picking up the last box, he nodded on his way out the door. He wouldn't be back. Like most of the tough guys in her circle, George stunk at goodbyes. She wanted to hug him, but that would give her away. She wouldn't be back, either.

Molly surveyed her progress and rewarded herself with a break. At the table on her balcony overlooking the courtyard, she stared at the deserted pool below. Without people, the concrete patio was institutional. She remembered the glossy brochure that had lured her in. Stylish thirtysomethings tipped their heads back in laughter while balancing wineglasses and appetizers.

She'd never been to a party on the patio. Once the ski season ended each year, she headed back to Seattle. Here, the thirtysomethings were busy burning up their remaining days of freedom and building their earning potential with an eye on transferring to a bigger city. Most had moved up and out by the time they were fortysomethings. Molly had been happy right where she was up until a year ago, when she'd learned there might not be many more days of powder for her.

Staring through the window, she thought of the hundreds of people living in the complex. They would wake up just like they did every day. Their lives were on autopilot. The same routine seven days a week, minus the wake-up alarm on Saturday and Sunday. For each one that stepped onto a steeper treadmill, a fresh face appeared to replace them. At forty-five years old, Molly was a senior citizen and, she guessed, a bit of a joke. But what was more pathetic, working yourself to death to pay for a future of adventures that might never come or working just enough to fund your adventures and dying anyway? Molly knew the answer, though she was sure Penelope would disagree.

In a few hours, she would call. To avoid interrupting her at the law firm during work hours, which were excessive at best, Molly had trained her to call at least every other day by 6:00 p.m. On the third day, Molly would call her at precisely 9:00 a.m. Penelope would try to ignore her, but she was like a raven on roadkill. Though fiercely independent, Molly played on her dysfunctional need to take care of her, which had been honed to a fine point by their mother's intermittent incompetence. She participated because she feared Penelope was wasting her best years storming the castle in pursuit of the partnership that would prove she deserved to be at McArthur Kane LLP, that she was smart enough and good enough. Molly did her best to divert that campaign every other day at 6:00 p.m. What Penelope needed, what all the sisters did, was a friend. Scottie was too pigheaded to admit she needed anyone. Penelope was too busy convincing her bosses she was not an imposter. Somehow, Molly had to get them to stop looking inward and see each other.

❧

Molly pulled out the kitchen garbage can. Like a million other things in the last six months, she looked at it—really looked at it. That same plain brown plastic bin had been in the apartment when she moved in ten years ago. She began sorting through the first of her junk drawers. A decade of rubber bands formed a ball. She chuckled at the thought of adding each but never taking off a single one. Habits were hard to break, and this drawer overflowed with generations of habits. Her grandma had a rubber band ball. Her mama too.

An envelope held coupons she always meant to use but never had with her when she needed them. She didn't bother to check the expiration dates. It wasn't like she could take them with her. Spare keys to forgotten locks sat in a layer atop contact paper printed to look like weathered pine. *Why did the fake stuff always outlive the real thing?* Mismatched pens and broken pencils lay like Pick Up Sticks strewn throughout. In the end, she kept a blue ballpoint and a mound of keys. The rest she dumped into the garbage. Then she moved on to the next drawer.

The second drawer was in her office, once a guest room she'd dreamed Penelope and Scottie would share on long weekends. In her imagination, being together would chip away at the wall of ice between them. One day, a festering hurt would slip across a tongue. Accusations would fly. *You didn't care she sent me away. Well, you obviously didn't want to stay. You never came back.* Offenses would be taken. Even if the small room couldn't contain their animosity, where could they go beyond the walls of the apartment in the dead of winter so far from home? They would run out of steam and see their ridiculous feud for what it was, nothing more than misunderstandings and unspoken hurts. Then they would laugh and hug and be real sisters.

But none of that happened, despite the many invitations. After the second season of coding alternately on the sofa and kitchen table, she named the crick in her back Scottie and the ache in her knee Penelope. Then she accepted they were never going to come down for a healing sisters' ski weekend. She denied her own hurt and resentment and redecorated.

Her desk drawers were full of papers she'd thought important, not important enough to put in a file but important enough to keep. Warranties for things she no longer had. User manuals she never referred to. Bills she paid online but never bothered to cancel the paper copies of. Penelope would lose her mind if she opened these drawers. Molly smiled at the thought. Scottie would pretend it was no big deal, but only because Penelope would be ranting about identity theft and organization and *how can you be a successful web designer and file literally nothing*. Chaos and shouting made Scottie twitch, but Molly loved seeing Penelope decompose into their mother. Would she live long enough to hear them both admit they were acting like their parents?

Stowed in the back of the top drawer was a white lacquered music box. Delicate rosebuds, muted in color and translucent, framed the top. When she opened the lid, a plastic ballerina popped up and lurched in a circle around one toe to the "Dance of the Sugar Plum Fairy." *Da di da, da da, duh duh duh.* Her mother, Mary, had brought it home from Woolworths. Molly saw it now for what it was, a purchased apology because her mother could never bring herself to say the words.

Mary, her bouffant hair coated in a shellac of Aqua Net and neck adorned with a gold cross as thin and straight as she, had taken her three girls to Seattle at Christmastime to see the Pacific Northwest Ballet Company's *Nutcracker*. In their Sunday best, they sat in a row, six patent leather Mary Janes swinging to the beat of Tchaikovsky's masterpiece. Molly marveled as each note lifted the ballerina's limbs until they pivoted and floated back to earth. Placing her tiny fingers on the back of the seat in front of her, she stood and flexed her ankles forward until her weight steadied on her tiptoes.

Just as Molly grasped the ballerina's tiny waist and lifted her out of the Mouse King's path, Mary leaned forward and grabbed her wrist. "Sit down, Molly Molloy Casey. Do not embarrass me." Her mother glanced to her right and left, no doubt to be sure no one had taken notice of Molly's offense. She smoothed her woolen skirt and tugged the hem to her knees—Mary's sign that order had been restored.

At the bottom of the music box, a small crucifix and a rosary lay tangled on a bed of cheap pink satin. Though she could not remember wearing the plated gold cross, patches of silver told her she must have. Five groups of ten white beads were strung in a circle. A small pewter pendant separated each group. Molly rubbed the beads between her thumb and forefinger, and without thinking, recited the prayer. *Hail Mary, full of grace, the Lord is with thee. Blessed art thou among women, and blessed is the fruit of thy womb, Jesus.* The words flowed, though she didn't feel them. She still prayed, but not to her mother's emissaries, who demanded repentance for something she could not reject.

She dropped the beads onto the shiny cloth. Careful to tuck the tiny ballerina away, she closed the lid. After placing it in one of the boxes by the door, she found two large manila envelopes and sat down at the desk. *This will be the hardest part. You're ridiculous. You probably won't even be around when they get them. Lord, not even death frees you from the horror of sharing your feelings in the Casey clan. It isn't just that, Molly Molloy Casey. You let it seep into your life. Your most honest relationship is with the apartment manager.*

Molly let her anger propel her and yanked the bottom drawer

open. It was packed so tightly, though, that it ground to a halt not halfway out. Bracing her foot against the desk leg, she pulled with all her strength. The chair tipped back and, before she could right it, the drawer flew out. Its contents spilled onto the floor at her feet. Molly turned the drawer over, emptying the remnants on the rug. There, on the carpet, lay a collage of their youth—evidence of a family that no longer existed, photographically documented in black and white and fading Kodacolor. Molly sank to her knees, tears spilling down her cheeks. Reaching with both hands, she spread the pictures out.

On top of the pile, three little girls stood in front of a fading blue Grenada. Their Easter dresses exploded with crinoline from their hips—minty antebellum ballgowns cut off at the knees. Molly could almost hear her mother. *Smile pretty for the camera, my Casey girls!* Two heads taller than the others, Penelope held a glossy clutch purse in one hand and Scottie's outstretched hand in the other. Scottie's eyes and mouth were open wide in adoration of her older sister. Molly stood on the other side, their shoulders touching as she leaned in to make sure she was in the shot. Penelope's face strained to minimize her lips as she flexed every muscle to hold in her laughter behind the dam of a proper smile. Molly, in contrast, stared into the camera, her smile forced but true. Teeth jutted up from her chin like she wanted every one of them in the picture. These are the sisters she remembered. *It will do in a pinch, but there must be a better one.*

Like a psychic at a seance, divining just the right image, Molly's hand drifted over the chaotic stack. On the periphery, she spied the corner of a black-and-white photo of Chimney Rock. Hope bloomed in her chest as she brushed away the others. It died just as quickly. Could she have been wrong? *No, this has to be a one-off. It must be that picture at the end of the day when everyone is tired of posing and smiling and just wants dinner.* Molly lifted the picture to her eyes.

On a dusty path, Penelope leans on one leg. Bell-bottoms fan out from her slender waist to hide her shoes. One hand is planted defiantly on her hip. With the other, she shades her eyes from the sun as she sneers. If not for the tableau, she might be mistaken for a captain searching the seas, desperate for land. Instead of open blue water, though, Penelope surveys a dirt path, dying sedge in the background. Behind her, Chimney Rock looks more like the remnants of a house fire than a majestic monument to the pioneer spirit. Ten feet away, Molly's butt has sunk to her heels. Wedged between her knees and chin, her forearms keep her head aloft. Scottie is the only one making no effort to look into the camera. Hand shoved deep into the pocket of her overalls, she bends her knees as if she might launch herself. Though only half her face is visible, that half is smiling at Penelope.

Hope restored, one by one she sorted the photographs into two piles, careful to be sure they were even. If she'd had time, she would have made copies and given them each a full set. But there wasn't the time or the need. Maybe she wouldn't need them at all. But if she wasn't around to remind them of what they once were, this would do the trick. She pulled two pieces of paper from her printer and began to write.

Though the message was the same, Molly considered the audience in her approach. Penelope liked to be in charge. She would have to discover what was lost on her own, but Molly would have to make her take a hard look first. The truth was in the details. Scottie was skittish. She wouldn't want to look at all. Molly would have to treat it like holding an apple out to a deer. No sudden moves and definitely no pursuit. Scottie would come to it in her own time, but only if she held perfectly still. They hadn't been in the same room without Molly in years. Left to their own devices, they never would again. Her heart clenched at the thought of loneliness for the sake of holding on to ancient wrongs.

When the packages were complete, she placed them at the bottom of her suitcase. Moving to the closet, she rolled the door open and eased herself to the floor. She snickered at the cavernous feel of the space that had never been quite big enough for her liking. Maneuvering her body to the small safe on the floor, she recited the numbers sixty-seven, thirty-seven, seventeen. As she did every time, Molly spun the dial too far on the first try and made a mental note to warn Angie it was touchy. She signed the title, fished out the keys, and placed them both in an envelope. On the outside, she wrote the address of the garage and placed it back in the safe.

Angie would protest. Her friendship was a precious gift. An old muscle car was a cheap token in comparison. She'd take it and say she was keeping it safe. Molly knew better. Removing the papers from the top shelf, she thumbed through them to make sure they were all in order. Satisfied, she added them to her suitcase.

Stopping by the bathroom, she took the remaining clean towels from beneath the sink. Molly laid two on the counter for Scottie and Penelope in case they wanted to shower before they left. She took the last one back to the closet. After checking to see that her handgun was not loaded, she wrapped the cloth around it and a box of bullets and slid them into the front pocket of her suitcase.

Chapter Three

Penelope

Penelope glanced at the clock on her phone as she straightened the folders and slipped them into her briefcase. She calculated all the scenarios. She discarded the first, not to call at all, because she had back-to-back meetings the next day and could not be distracted by her sister, who would hit redial until she answered. The second, to call Molly now and be late for the client dinner, would relegate her to sit next to some trophy wife with oh so many words and oh so little to say. She pictured herself smiling and nodding as she tried to keep tabs on the high-profile cases being doled out at the other end of the table. She blamed her breasts. It wasn't that she didn't like them. She did. They were lovely. They were also a prominent reminder she was the only person in most meetings that had them. She would not allow them to be the impediment to making partner.

The third option was to race down the stairs while talking on the phone. A tempting choice, but then she would be sweaty and ruin her makeup. Fixing that would delay her and move her farther down the table, past the trophy wives, to the grandmother wives. The elder matriarchs were always happy to talk about what they hadn't been able to do with their lives and how lucky she was to be born at a time when she could have it all—sit at the executive table and set the dinner table. They were oblivious to the fact that sitting with them was evidence her place at the table was tenuous at best. Penelope's temple throbbed just thinking about it. Luck had nothing to do with it. She worked her ass off. Michael's life insurance might have paid the tuition, but she'd earned that too. She was sitting at this table despite him, not because of him.

The fourth was the best choice. Head for the elevator, hop in her car, and call Molly while driving. It was efficient. It ensured she would arrive at the dinner early enough to stake her claim, and her little sister, who apparently had nothing else to do, would not ping her all day.

By the time she made it to the garage, it was 6:10 p.m. She hoped Molly would answer. Sometimes, she wouldn't pick up this late. Penelope, convinced it was the adult version of her hideous childhood tantrums, pictured her sitting by the phone with her arms crossed and her face scrunched up, tapping her foot.

Molly picked up on the second ring. "You're late." To an outsider, she would surely appear petulant. Penelope knew Molly preferred to live unanchored, but when she drifted too far, she got angry with the shore. Her weekly calls were a test of her distance.

"Yes. But I'm here now, though I can't talk long. I'm on my way to a business dinner. I just wanted to check in."

"Well, I need to talk to you. It might not be a short conversation. Do you want me to call tomorrow?"

Penelope rested her forehead on the steering wheel. Her unfortunate shoe choice momentarily distracted her—high heels on slender women threatened short men. Molly cleared her throat, bringing Penelope back to the more important question—what would be worse, being interrupted tomorrow or being late tonight? A horn blared behind her, signaling the green light she had missed.

"Dammit," Penelope snarled.

"We can talk tomorrow."

"No, sorry. It's not you. I missed the light. Let's talk now. What's going on?"

"Do you have any vacation time?"

"Yes. I have loads of vacation time. When do I have time to take a vacation?" She shook her head at the absurdity of arguing about vacation with a woman who was perpetually on one.

"Penelope, that's terrible. You need a vacation. It's not healthy. Also, I read an article about how taking a vacation actually makes you more productive."

"It also ensures someone else is meeting the needs of your clients until you no longer have any. Is this what couldn't wait until tomorrow? My favorite ski bum admonishing me for working too hard?"

"Hey, I'm not a ski bum. I'm a web designer. I just have a life and I'm not spending the whole thing working."

"I have a life too. And I'm happy with it. You have fifteen city blocks. Start talking."

"Fine. Jeez. You'd make a terrible negotiator."

"I am, in fact, a brilliant negotiator. Fourteen blocks."

"Stop counting! I need you to come to Reno and bring me home."

"Wait, what? Why?" Penelope swerved to miss the car in front of her who made a last-minute decision to parallel park.

"You're not going to tell me to get on a plane?"

"Yes. I am. But I still want to know why, since one, there must still be snow somewhere in Nevada and two, you're a grown-up woman who can get herself home."

Penelope glanced at the map on the dashboard and then at the clock. Seven blocks to go. She had plenty of time to get inside before the guests arrived, if she could just wrap up this conversation. *Shit, what if I show up and it's some kind of prank? Like they want me to serve drinks or something.* Her neck reddened with humiliation. *Penelope, pull yourself together. That's nuts. That is Mary Casey level nuts. You might only be an associate, but they wouldn't have invited you if you didn't have something to offer.*

"Hello. Are you there?" Molly asked. "I'm not hearing a no."

"You're not hearing a yes, either. Why am I coming to Reno to take you home?"

"Not just you. Scottie too."

"That's not a why. But great, then you don't need me." *There's no way in hell I'm spending two days in a car with Scottie Casey.*

"I do need you. I can't drive from Reno to Seattle with just Scottie. She'll do it in one sitting and never let me stop to pee. She definitely won't stop for road snacks. It's the only time I get Bugles and Oreos."

"And yet, they're carried in every grocery store. Look, then fly. I won't even send a car. I'll pick you up myself at the airport. Hell, I'll buy you a first-class ticket to avoid crossing three state lines with Scottie."

Penelope searched for a parking space. Looking to the sky, she didn't see any stars, so she circled the block and drove into the garage. Concentrating on finding the safest spot nearest the restaurant entrance, another problem that came with breasts, she missed most of what Molly said.

"—cancer treatment center in Seattle."

Penelope stepped on the brakes. "Say that again."

"I am not flying. I hate flying."

"No. Not that. The sentence that had cancer in it." A vision of their mom flashed across Penelope's mind. Not the lacquered-bouffant, life-of-the-party version but the gaunt one who all but disintegrated in her arms.

"I have cancer. I need to come home because I have an appointment next week in Seattle."

Penelope jumped at a knock on her window.

Jackson—*don't-call-me-Jack*—Carter leaned down to peer at her. "Are you going to park?" His raised voice was muffled through the glass, but his condescending look was crystal clear. He didn't wait for a response. In one practiced motion, he unfolded his arms, pulled his jacket flat, and straightened his tie. With a smirk, he took the hand of a wispy blonde and led her in front of the car. Penelope shook her head. *Tool.*

"Molly, this is a lot to process." *There is no crying in public, Penelope Casey.* "I can't talk about this now."

She felt the familiar pull, tearing her in two directions and leaving nothing of herself in the middle. Mom or Dad. Michael or her family and friends. Work or relationships. Something always won. She'd managed to hold on to Molly. She thought she had, anyway.

"But we will," Penelope continued. "I promise. Can I call you later? I really have to get to this dinner." She pulled down the visor and looked in the mirror. Without Molly, she'd be well and truly alone.

"Sure. But first, promise me you'll come. I need to get back to Seattle in the next couple of days."

"I'll figure it out. Don't worry."

"That's not a no."

"It's not a no." Penelope dabbed at the tear clinging to her lower lashes. "I love you."

Clutching the wheel, she wanted to back out of the garage and head to Reno right then, but she knew she wouldn't. She could feel the wobble setting into her spin and righted it. Jackson had seen her. He was, no doubt under the guise of supporting a colleague, making excuses for her. *Penny will be right in. She seemed to need a moment. Nearly ran me over.* She would not let them see her upset. *Lock it down, Penelope. You have shit to do.* As she strode toward the entrance, she started her list—dinner, doctor's appointments, guest room, real food. The stifling, medicinal air of her mother's convalescence bubbled to the surface of her memory, but she tamped it down just as fast. *No. Dinner. Dinner first. Then Molly.*

Chapter Four

Molly

MOLLY EXPECTED RELIEF to flood through her. But telling them was only the first step. Her sisters hadn't agreed to come get her. Not really. Standing in front of the mirror, she pulled the T-shirt over her head, yanking the hem down to hide her bony hips. Her fingertips grazed the skin slackening on her legs. Worn cotton that had once hugged her hips and bunched at the curve of her rump now draped mid-thigh, undeterred. She may have overestimated how much meat would still be on her bones to fight Penelope's urge to take charge and fix everything and Scottie's penchant for shutting down and disappearing. She looked in the mirror and vowed to force herself to eat. Her stomach contracted at the thought. Once they saw her, it was going to take some serious calories to prevent them from reenacting the Cold War and ruining her plans.

Molly ran her fingers across the raised letters on her chest. She no longer wore concert tees in public. It was the one concession she'd made a decade ago toward acting her age. Still, she bought them to sleep in. With her hand on the only physical remnant of her memory, the night came back to her. The Lumineers, Cleopatra, Sacramento. It had been a birthday present for Angie. Molly's days of crushing crowds and dancing her way to the stage were long over, so she splurged for tenth-row seats. Despite Angie's protests, she'd paid for the babysitter so they wouldn't have to drive home from Sacramento after the concert.

Her body rocked to the faint echo in her head, O-O-phelia. The night had been perfect. Music pulsed thick in her chest. The way Angie's head tipped back when she laughed, as if it might capsize from the weight of joy, tugged at Molly's heart. She added that to the growing list of things she would miss.

Dragging her fingers through her bangs, she pulled back the wisps and searched her face for lines. Though her cheeks had hardened and hollowed, not the faintest crease marred the smooth surface.

"Whoever said it's best to die young and leave a beautiful corpse was full of shit," she said to the stranger in the mirror.

The brunette strands fluttered back to cover the widow's peak her grandma had given them. Penelope didn't even try to hide hers. The arrowhead of hair anchored her sleek ponytail, unapologetically front and center. Though only by happy coincidence, Scottie had one too. As children, the small triangle gave them all a reprieve from the stinging curiosity about Scottie's origins which adults made no effort to quell.

As her palm slid across her belly, she cringed at the swelling. She loved her curves, but this one was alien. Molly and Scottie both had muscular frames. She knew for a fact she'd inherited this from her father. She assumed Scottie's dad had been stocky too. For a time, in adolescence, Molly envied Penelope's long, delicate limbs. She soon realized her body held her hostage. Molly wanted to run, and climb, and jump, and those things brought bumps and breaks and scars, things their mom would never allow Penelope to have.

A wicked smile spread across her face, and Molly closed her eyes. She could feel the fat limb of Mr. Rossellini's apple tree beneath her feet, one hand on the trunk as she reached for a higher branch.

"Don't you take one more step, young lady!" Her mother stood, manicured hands splayed on her hips, mouth aimed skyward. "I mean it. Not one more step, Molly Molloy Casey."

Getting caught made her faster, not repentant. If Molly didn't fall off it, she jumped off or got knocked off. Either way, she did not regret one scar. Reveling in her mother's fury, she was oblivious to the underlying terror. This, Molly did regret, but not as much as realizing it was too late to make it right. Time was running out on making things right.

Angie always told her things work out in the only way they can. Molly believed it too, but then things had worked out mostly in her favor until now. In the end, the body she loved had failed her. She pressed a finger into her abdomen. Concentric circles of white rippled outward. When she pulled the digit away, a pit remained in the flesh. She counted the seconds. The fluid building up in her belly was just the outward sign. What grew inside was far more insidious.

On her way to the bathroom, she pulled on a pair of discarded shorts. Her boldness was replaced in part with shame. Though her doctors had assured her she'd done nothing to land herself in this place, she felt responsible somehow. Like, if it wasn't some negligent action, it was a sin she was paying for at full price. Like everyone else, except maybe Penelope, she'd committed all the big ones—pride, greed, lust, sloth, envy, wrath, and gluttony—to some degree. None so completely as to warrant this painful demise, though.

Perhaps it was the cumulative effect. One big sin would definitely kill you. Could a serving of each add up to enough sin to do you in cell by cell? Angie said God doesn't work that way. He wasn't up in heaven measuring your sins in some cosmic recipe for damnation. He was on earth sweeping them out of your path.

Aside from herself, Angie was the worst Catholic Molly knew. The priest would ban her if he knew all the scriptures she bastardized in the name of a lenient and loving God. Penelope might disagree with both of them. After all, God had given her Michael, but he'd also given Michael a weak liver and a thirst that could only be quenched with bourbon.

She scanned the medicine cabinet, selecting the evening pill bottles. One for impact, the others to counteract its complications. With her stash, she headed to the balcony and took up her post, perched in her rattan chair facing the hills. Molly refused to call them mountains. Rainier was a mountain. Baker was a mountain.

As she watched the shadow slink down the peaks, cold air bit into her legs. She closed her eyes and pulled it into her lungs until they could hold no more. When the burning began, she opened her mouth and let it seep past her lips. Covering her hand with her sleeve, she buffed the dust from the glass tabletop before spilling the contents of the bottle. Molly lined the pills up. The doctor had only given her enough for two weeks to hold her over until the appointment she had no intention of keeping. She ran a finger over the line of pills, stopping on the last one and placing it in her mouth. Sliding the tip of her nail along each one, she counted them out. Thirteen. Such an unlucky number.

Chapter Five

Scottie

A MOSSY FOG HOVERED just above the fields. Scottie slowed the pickup as she neared the kennel's drive and searched the shoulders for the resident elk herd, prone to materialize from the early morning mist. She hadn't slept much and probably shouldn't have been on the road. Taking a day off, even sleeping in, would have raised a red flag with Jason, though. A normal person would have talked it out with their spouse and then gone to sleep unburdened. Scottie wished she could open her mouth and let all her fears spill out. Instead, she'd lain frozen next to her husband of twenty-three years as her mind raced.

She saved some time by resigning herself at the outset to the worst possible outcome. Molly was going to die and, no matter when, it was going to happen too soon. The rest of the night, she imagined the moment and every possible iteration. With every pass, her mental roller coaster picked up another passenger and her stomach dropped. *Everybody is going to die. What will I do when Jason dies? Or my children. If anything happened to Meaghan or Justin . . . or worse, what will happen to them when I die? Oh*

God, my dad. He's going to lose his child. The cycling thoughts burrowed into her head until the wee hours of the morning. Before she left for work, she kissed her sleeping husband because he would have stayed up all night listening to the circus in her head, if only Scottie could have asked.

She slid the seat back and opened the truck door. In the short drive, from her house to the kennel, the cab hadn't warmed up. She grabbed the steering wheel with her right hand and hauled her body toward the door. Locking her knees together, she unfolded them and slid to the ground. It always took a few minutes on cold mornings to straighten out after driving. She preferred to do it alone in the darkness, away from her father's guilt-laden brow.

Burnie barreled past her to the nearest bush to pee. Scottie chose to think of this as evidence of a complete lack of pity, rather than the more likely full bladder. Hiding her broken parts exhausted her, physically and mentally, but bearing someone's pity blistered her pride. She pushed her hips forward and her shoulders back, forcing her spine to straighten. The pressure built, but experience had shown her that the relief of the vertebrae snapping back into place would be worth it. In the beginning, the doctors scolded her for interfering with the fusion, but they only had X-rays. Scottie could feel the fingers of scar tissue choking the nerves as they tried to escape her spinal column. Arthritic bone adhered to her vertebrae like a coral reef growing upward from her tailbone. She knew how good breaking all that loose felt. Pop, pop, pop.

Burnie sat staring at her as she rocked her hips from side to side until the muscles gained confidence and freed her legs. Though she was not cold, she zipped her coat to keep the early spring air from drifting up her back.

Light shone through the row of windows below the eaves of the kennel. The fog contained the rays in diaphanous boxes, fading before they reached the ground. She wondered what pain had pushed her dad from his warm bed so early. Whatever it was, she wasn't going to add to it until she knew what was really going on with Molly.

Scottie veered down the path that circled the building, checking that none of the dogs had been let into their runs. Burnie waited by the door, front paws bouncing on the gravel. She needed to spend more time training him, but there were no more pieces left in her pie. Scottie stopped and caught his eyes. He sat. As she put her hand on the knob, he lifted his butt off the ground. She held still.

"Sit."

He sat.

She opened the door, and he brushed past her down the aisle. Scottie shook her head. "Progress, I guess."

Burnie trotted to the end of the hall and worked his way backward, taking inventory with his nose. With the exception of the Great Dane, now moping jowls-skyward on her bed, the dogs barked as he passed. Scottie wondered what the other dogs thought of Burnie's freedom.

"Nice job." She patted his head, and he followed her to the first kennel. Scottie pulled the clipboard from where it hung on the chain-link fence. Cleopatra "Cleo" Harrington had eaten all her meals. She pooped regularly and walked without coaxing. When it came to playing with the other dogs, Cleo slumped to the ground and closed her eyes. Scottie understood the inclination.

Before the kennel door was fully open, Burnie pushed past Scottie and stuck his nose in the business end of the Dane. Cleo shot up on her gangly legs and turned nose to nose with the intruder. Burnie craned his neck upward and held his ground. Cleo lost interest in the stalemate, did her best downward dog, and returned to her bed.

"Progress," Scottie said with a smile.

Hank was making coffee when she walked into the kitchen. Bent at the hips, one leg in front of the other, he pressed his hands against the edge of the counter. If you couldn't see his face, you might think he was stretching. Scottie knew he was giving his right hip a brief reprieve before the workday began.

He handed Scottie her favorite cup. Thin white letters whispered from the matte black finish, *I love your dog. I don't care about you.* Her dad hated the mug. He'd thrown the first one in the garbage. A new one arrived a couple of days later. Scottie had it shipped to the kennel, a subtle example of her silent defiance and the slow erosion of their hierarchy—both of which she should have long grown out of had she not missed her rebellious phase strapped into a halo. They agreed she could have her morning coffee in the mug, but then it had to be put away for the day so as not to offend the owners, who she'd *absolutely better care about.*

"You're up early." Hank reached down to scratch Burnie's head. As all dogs did, he sat perfectly still and firmly planted on his butt for her dad. Nobody got a head-scratching if they didn't behave.

"I was going to say the same to you. How are you feeling?" The coffee verged on scalding, just how she liked it. Her dad always heated the cream for her. When she was little, he heated it before pouring it on her oatmeal. Scottie cherished that act because he'd never done it for her sisters. She pretended it was intentional and not simply a lack of opportunity. Oatmeal was a school-day breakfast, and they hadn't spent a school day with him since the divorce.

"I'm feeling just fine. You gotta stop worrying about me, kiddo." He gave her a sad smile. The lines around his eyes crinkled downward to meet those climbing from his mouth.

"Somebody's got to worry about you, old man." She raised her mug to him. She made light of it, but they both knew there was no end to the worries bottled up inside her. Though he couldn't have known them all, she guessed he knew the biggest one—that she would lose him one day—if for no other reason than she was still working at the kennel with him forty-two years later.

"Who're you calling old? I can keep up with you."

Scottie didn't have to look at him. Regret punctuated the sentence. She knew he was being playful, so she gifted him a smile and hoped he knew she didn't blame him anymore for the accident.

"Well. Let's get to work then." She pulled the dishes from the shelf. "Have we got many new dogs coming in this weekend?"

He slid the cart out from beneath the counter. "Just one. We'll have more, once spring break starts."

They'd been doing this dance for more than thirty years. In the beginning, she'd wanted nothing more than to be close to him. Back then, though she could have stayed in bed, she woke when she'd heard him moving around. Every morning, she'd rolled on her tummy and slid out of bed. After pulling on jeans and a T-shirt, just like her dad, she'd plodded downstairs to get her coat and his hand to walk the path to the kennel. She'd said almost nothing in the beginning, so he prattled on to her and, when she wouldn't answer, to himself.

"Did you brush your teeth? I bet you forgot. We can do that after breakfast. I bet you're excited about school. What's your favorite subject, and don't say recess?"

He could wait forever, but the words would still be lodged in her throat for fear her answers would make him discard her like her mother had. She extended her fingers, sinking them into the dense chocolate fur. She'd wanted to stay there all day helping her dad. She missed her sisters. Anger and sadness churned in Scottie's tummy every day before school. If her dad knew the terrible thoughts she had, he wouldn't love her anymore, either.

Best not to speak at all. She ran her hand across the velvet ear and was thanked with a slobbery tongue.

"Hey, Scottie. Wake up. We need to get moving. The troops are getting restless." Hank tossed an empty can in the sink.

On cue, the Great Dane let out a woof. Scottie lined the bowls up on the counter and began scooping dry food into each one from the containers lined up against the wall. A plastic sleeve taped to each lid held a card with feeding instructions. To ensure they were accurate, each owner completed the card and slipped it into the sleeve.

Most made perfect sense to Scottie. She pictured the owner of the German Shorthair Pointer strangling the pen as he meticulously printed instructions in architectural script. The cocker spaniel's owner, who looked like she used the same groomer as her dog, wrote in careless cursive. Then there were the surprises. The five-foot-three ex-cheerleader, pristine in every way, save for the clumps of long black hair covering her pants, bouncing in with her lumbering Newfie. The printing on her card periodically jerked off the page like she wrote it while simultaneously holding the furry beast back from trying to make friends with or dinner out of a smaller dog, and let's face it, they were all smaller dogs. All so different and yet they shared something so elemental you couldn't distinguish them if the lights were out.

Scottie turned to her dad and took a deep breath to steady her voice against the lie that was coming. "I was thinking I would take a couple of days and go see Molly."

Hank locked another can into place and pushed down on the trigger. It spun halfway round before he answered. "I'd think she'd be spending all her free time skiing right about now."

"The snow must not be very good. She's coming home early." Scottie took the can from him and mixed the contents into a bowl of kibble.

"Why don't you just wait until she comes home then?"

"I thought it would be fun to drive back with her. Do you mind if I take a couple of days off? Meaghan can cover for me."

"You don't need to bother Meaghan."

"Dad, it's no bother. Besides, you could stand to spend some time with your granddaughter."

"If she wanted to spend time with me, she would come out here without being asked."

"Dad, she's a college student. She loves you and she loves the dogs, maybe even more than I do. But she's got a lot going on."

"All the more reason not to bother her. And, again, I don't need the help."

"It's done. She's coming. Don't send my baby away, Dad. She loves you." It was a cheap shot, but she knew he would not be able to refuse.

"We can talk about it later. You better get moving with that food or you're going to have a mutiny on your hands."

"Nothing to talk about, Dad. It's decided."

He was never one to back down. Scottie had taken years to learn that lesson. Ask first, but don't take no for an answer or the answer will always be no.

"I'm going to let the dogs out and get started hosing down the floors." He said it without anger, though not completely lacking in emotion. Then he walked out in the methodical way he walked everywhere, intention in every footfall.

Scottie knew the stinging powerlessness of relying on another to do something that had come easily in the past. While she did not want to make him feel less than he was, she couldn't risk leaving him alone. His body was showing the full wear and tear of his seventy-three years, despite the fifteen-year reprieve pushing a pencil in his father-in-law's insurance office between being a farmer and a kennel owner. She wished they could talk about it, but she had forgotten how to start.

After her accident, the acrid taste of anger threatened to

sneak past her lips with each breath. She'd blamed her father for keeping the recalled three-wheeler. She'd blamed herself for racing through the woods on it. She'd hated Jason for walking in on his own two legs and sitting there day after day as she seethed. She'd hated her mother for not having the courage to do what even a sixteen-year-old boy knew was the right thing to do.

Scottie had summoned every bit of energy not devoted to healing her broken parts to hold those bitter words in. The sheer injustice boiled just below the surface. Sharing that with her father would have taken away some of its power, and the power of that anger propelled her. It propped her up on weak legs and made her focus on moving them forward, step after agonizing step. She'd been ashamed of the drama that played in her head. All the words hitting her father like a blast furnace, sucking the air out of the room so he could not speak, not even to beg forgiveness. That satisfying moment had been fleeting, and in its place, disgrace lingered. After all, he had warned her.

Scottie waited until she heard the rush of water on concrete to dial the number. With any luck, Penelope would be working on an important case and unable to break free. It rang three times.

"You've reached Penelope Casey. I'm unavailable at this time. Please leave a message and I, or my assistant, will contact you."

Her sister's voice was commanding, and Scottie felt a pang of jealousy for all she'd accomplished. Scottie's college dreams were crushed under the weight of medical bills and a plummeting GPA.

"Penny, this is Scottie. Hoping Molly called you. I'm going to drive down tomorrow. Let me know when your flight gets in and I'll pick you up. No reason to rent a car. We can figure all that out when we get there. OK, well, call me back and tell me what you're doing." She started to hang up. "Wait. Don't call the kennel. Call my cell. I haven't told Dad yet." Scottie kicked the wall with the heel of her boot. *Shit, why did I tell her that?*

"You haven't told me what yet?"

Scottie jumped at his voice. "Damn it, Dad. You scared me."

Undistracted by her deflection, he stared at her. "Well?"

He would spot a weak attempt at fabrication before the second word slipped past her lips, so she tossed in an inconsequential truth instead. "I'm taking Burnie with me."

Chapter Six

Penelope

SCOTTIE'S NAME FLASHED on the dashboard screen.

"Oh, hell no. It's way too early for you." Penelope sent the call to voicemail. She glanced in the rearview mirror and then snuck into a slice of I-5 left by a rookie rush-hour commuter. Penelope pretended his gesture was a wave and waved back.

There had to be a way to extricate Scottie. With the Ashbridge negotiations mere weeks away, she needed to get Molly sorted out quickly and get back to work. What was Scottie going to do other than complicate decision-making? She certainly didn't have the means to support Molly. That alone should disqualify her from asserting her opinion. Besides, the best doctors were in Seattle, not some backwoods town.

Penelope tapped the connect button on the dash. "Call. Victoria. Office." A robotic voice confirmed her request. It rang once.

"You're going to be late."

Penelope raised her eyebrows and looked at the phone. "Is this how you answer my phone?"

"My apologies." Victoria cleared her throat. "You've reached the office of Penelope Casey, Attorney at Law. You have reached her loyal and contrite assistant. Why are you calling, as you cannot possibly afford her?"

"Nice." Penelope rolled her eyes. The firm's clients could more than afford her, not to mention every other cog filling the partners' coffers. Penelope's hourly rate would never live up to Victoria's assessment of her.

"Don't get spicy. I have caller ID. Everyone else is treated to my most regal greeting on your behalf. To which I will have to add, she is unavailable because she is running late."

Penelope let the sarcasm slide. "Cute. I need you to clear my calendar for a couple days."

"Intriguing." Victoria paused, her nails clicking across her keyboard. "Don't get me wrong, you deserve a vacation, but you never take one. Certainly not in the middle of closing a deal."

Penelope kicked herself for passing over the young and ambitious applicant who had an obvious dysfunctional need to please and an irrational fear of termination. Instead, she had selected Victoria, the more experienced candidate who exceeded every claim on her resume. Her efficiency and quasi-psychic ability to predict what she needed disconcerted Penelope. She was putting a lot of faith in someone who was only tied to her by a paycheck. People with much stronger bonds had betrayed her for far less.

"Molly needs me to bring her back from Reno. I'm hoping I'll only need two days."

"What's wrong?"

"Nothing's wrong. Why should something be wrong?" Penelope had managed to keep most of her personal life private. Michael's rules made that easy when he was alive. Now the price of misplaced trust was too high, so it was one of the few freedoms she hadn't reclaimed at his death. One-off casual dates and business lunches would never be permitted to take root and bloom.

Like a weed in a sidewalk crack, though, Victoria managed to get a foothold.

"Because adults don't usually have to be brought home. They get on a plane and come home."

"She doesn't fly."

"Or drive or take a train? You get my point."

"Just work on making some space on my calendar, please." Penelope took a deep breath through her nose and let it escape from her mouth, the way her limber and serene yoga instructor had taught her. She had yet to experience the promised blissful release of tension, though her desire to headbutt people was showing signs of fading.

"Of course. I'll take care of it today." Victoria wiped the words of all emotion, like she was reciting the Act of Contrition.

Penelope mentally whipped herself for being curt. *Dammit, Penelope, you're turning into Mom.*

"I'm sorry, Victoria. She's sick." The words lodged in her chest. She had to force the rest out. "She says cancer."

"What does that mean, she says cancer? Is it not cancer?" And just like that, Penelope's barb was forgiven.

"Molly leans toward the dramatic. It's entirely possible she googled her symptoms and diagnosed herself." *Survival rule number one—do not panic. Survival rule number two—do not trust; verify.* "I don't have all the details yet." *Scottie probably does, though.* "I'll get her back here and we'll figure it out. Meanwhile, clear my calendar for a couple of days. And stall any prying partners. I don't need them accusing me of choosing family over firm."

"I'll take care of it. Don't worry about a thing. I can get you on a flight this afternoon. I'll have a rental waiting. Do you have a preference for a model? If she's not feeling good, you might want an SUV."

Penelope could tell from the conspiratorial tone of her voice that Victoria knew all too well the sacrifices she'd made to get where she was. The partners were no match for her sleight of hand. There was a good chance no one would even notice she was missing.

"I won't need a car. I'm sure Scarlett will insist on driving her four-bedroom SUV down. I'll drive back with them."

"Scarlett?"

"Scottie. My youngest sister."

"Interesting. I don't recall you mentioning her." Victoria hit the tender edge of Penelope's personal bubble. "Why don't you drive down with her? It might be nice to have some sister time."

"There's a reason you've never heard of her before." Penelope never quite knew how to describe Scottie. Most of the time, she simply omitted her. From the moment she arrived in the Casey household, people seemed fascinated with Scottie's origins and oblivious to the jaw-clenching tension it caused their mother.

"I see. Well, if you rode down with her, you'd have about ten hours to work. It might be nice to have some uninterrupted time to work on the Ashbridge deal and catch up on some cases you've had to sideline. Unless Scottie is a talker, that is."

"She is not. When she has words, I'm the last person she spends them on." Penelope squeezed the fob on her keychain and waited for the gate to retract. "Got to go. I'm in the garage. I'll be up shortly."

"Make it quick. The Ashbridge meeting is starting."

"Dammit." *What is wrong with me?*

Penelope pulled into her spot, grabbed her bag and jacket, and ran for the stairs. At the top, she took a moment to catch her breath before entering the conference room. All eyes turned to her.

"Well, now we can get started. Ms. Casey has arrived," Jackson—*not Jack*—Carter announced from his place at the right hand of the managing partner.

Though a hurricane was building steam inside her, Penelope calmed her exterior to meet the needs of the partners. With a penitent smile, she said, "My apologies." But offered no excuse. What excuse could there be?

The senior partner acknowledged her with the slightest of nods. As Penelope pulled her notes out, he turned to Jackson and said, "Why don't you start, Jackson? I don't think Ms. Casey has had a chance to hear your ideas about the Ashbridge case. It will give her a chance to get settled."

Penelope could feel the mask disintegrating. The muscles between her eyebrows carved two sharp trenches in her forehead. She willed them to relax.

He turned to her, letting his eyes linger for the smallest acceptable time, before speaking to the middle of the long table. "Of course, it will still be your case. It is our belief that Jackson's strategy may yield the best resolution for the client. I'm certain you will welcome his ideas."

Though the other partners nodded in agreement, Penelope ignored the signal.

"Absolutely. However . . ." she said.

"Let's just listen, shall we?"

Penelope snapped the mask back in place. "Of course," she said. *Dammit, Molly. Why can't you just get on a plane?*

Chapter Seven

Molly

MOLLY SLID HER index fingers along the cracked loops and pulled on her boots. She'd been pinching the straps for months, hoping to keep them from ripping in half. Years of wear made the leather forgiving. Even with her thickest wool socks, they didn't hug her feet like they used to.

Though dew replaced the early-morning frost, a chill still hung in the air. Even before the cancer hijacked her pancreas, which to this point had been an organ she barely knew existed, she hated cold feet. The irony was not lost on her. She closed her eyes and imagined that first bounce into the powder. The explosion of snow, *poof,* etched in her muscle memory, signaling her to move forward or sink. *The story of my life.* Tears slid from the corner of her eyes, creating a frozen trail to her ears. Hot breath frosted the surface of her gaiter. Knees pistoned to split the moguls. Nothing registered but the sheer radiance of speed and power, whipping past evergreens buried neck deep by the snowpack, a trailing wake of powder, perfection on the knife's edge of disaster. Until she hit the bottom when, unless she headed right back up the mountain, the chill would catch up to her and bleed into her soles, creeping through her veins to her core. *So painful but I keep coming back for more.*

She filled her coffee and poured in real cream. Penelope's judgy face flashed through her mind, and she wiped it away with a blink of her eyes. Indulging was a consolation prize. A little fat wasn't going to kill her—not first, anyway.

At the end of the hall, Angie was locking her door when Molly walked out of the apartment. Mateo broke free from his mother's grasp and ran to her full force. He rocked side to side on his short legs as he pattered down the hall. With his winter coat, he looked like a colorful penguin.

"Ma-wee!"

Molly crouched, readying for impact. Though he weighed less than one of her legs and stood half its length, his hugs packed the punch of a linebacker. Molly took every ounce. As the wave spread through her, she hoped it would bounce off a memory and send an echo out. All the hugs the Casey girls shared would blanket her. If she could remember, they could too.

"Hey, little man."

He wrapped his arms around her neck, and she lifted him to her hip. Molly stared at Mateo's face, studying the unreserved grin. She took a deep breath and tried to memorize every molecule. As she tickled his belly, he gifted her his giggles. Closing her eyes, she collected the sound. That was what she wanted to fill her last moments with. Mateo's laughter. Unembarrassed, unrestrained, unapologetic joy.

Her shoulders began to burn from holding him against her. She set him on the ground. Unwilling to surrender the connection, Molly crouched down and took his hands in hers.

"Have you been practicing the L song?"

His lips pursed like he was holding on to a secret with all his might.

"Yes. Maw-Lee!" He punctuated each syllable with a grin.

Molly scooped him into a bear hug.

"Do you want a lily-livered lollipop?" she sang. "If you do, you have to ask for one."

"I want a lily-livered laweepop!" He frowned.

"So close! You're almost there. You must be working really hard." She kissed his forehead. The scent of green apples filled her nose. Though she knew it was from the only shampoo he would use, she preferred to think of it as new-kid smell.

"Morning." Angie smiled at Molly. She crouched down and straightened Mateo's coat. "Mateo, you can't run from me, even for Auntie Molly. You have to be safe. OK?" He nodded, and she rewarded him with a kiss.

She took hold of his free hand, and they set off for the steps. The women lifted Mateo off the ground and carried him down the stairs. His laughter filled the stairwell.

"He's never going to learn to walk downstairs." Angie warned Molly of this daily.

"He'll learn. In a year, he'll be too heavy for us to carry him." *In a year, I won't be here to try.*

Molly didn't have to say it out loud. Angie had been the first to notice her weight loss. She wasn't fooled by the explanations everyone else bought. In the end, Molly had told her everything. Though she could see the plea in Angie's eyes, it never left her lips. Molly needed one more winter undiminished. No matter what happened, she knew she would never be as strong and free again. So, Angie put her chin up, painted on a smile, and went about life like tomorrow was promised.

They waited with the other parents at the bus stop. Molly wondered if they thought she and Angie were a couple. Angie didn't care to make friends with them, so it hardly mattered what they thought about anything. The idea of her with one less friend in the world saddened Molly, though. Her circle was already too small.

Angie learned early to do for herself. When she didn't have a prospect and her biological clock turned into a time bomb, she took matters into her own hands and became a mother. Grateful she could stay home with Mateo, she never complained about giving up the lucrative tips she'd raked in bartending for the thankless job of building manager. Now that kindergarten filled his days, she filled hers with business classes. Molly was in awe of her strength and determination. Like one of those museum statues of a goddess in marble, Angie was as glossy as fine silk on the outside. Underneath, she was solid rock.

During those moments waiting for the school bus, Molly touched the faintest sense of what it would feel like to be a family. Like the spices Angie added to a dish, the taste faded from Molly's tongue before she knew what it was. She knew the score. It didn't keep her from pretending, though, as long as she didn't give herself away. Angie loved her, not in the way that Molly wanted, but in the way she needed. She'd resigned herself to it. Now, it didn't matter. Hope was for future-Molly, and there wouldn't be one.

"Do you have time to talk?" She half-hoped Angie would say no.

"Of course. What's up?"

Molly loved her natural optimism, like nothing bad had ever happened to her and everything would always work out. Of course, that wasn't true, which made it all the more magical to be around her.

"I called my sisters. They're coming, probably tomorrow or the day after at the latest. I need to go over the apartment with you."

"I wish you wouldn't do this. It's going to be hard to find you a unit next winter, especially one so close to us."

Lying would be like putting a bandage on a dirty wound. Molly wanted to be here when she faced the truth. "We talked about this. I won't be back next winter."

Angie took furtive swipes across her eyes and nose as they climbed the steps. "Why are you giving up? You haven't even met with the specialist in Seattle." Angie landed a half-hearted slap on Molly's shoulder when she didn't answer.

"Hey, that hurt!" She rubbed her arm.

"Oh, it did not. Quit being a baby."

"You can't hit a dying woman. Who does that?" Molly opened the door to Apartment 245.

"Don't joke about that. God is listening."

"Well, since He knows how this is going to turn out, I would think He would appreciate my good-natured kidding and my acceptance of the situation."

"Maybe it's a test."

"Well, if it is, I'm going to fail miserably." Molly sat at the table, steadying her breath. All these decades later, she still had that tightness in her chest, same as sitting in a pew listening to a priest proclaim that what was in her heart was a sin—that she was a sin. "That's enough of God's will—let's talk about mine."

Angie shoved her hands in the pockets of her coat and tightened it around her. She toed the only other chair away from the table. Perching on its edge, she scanned the room like a caged animal searching for escape. Tears welled in her eyes.

Molly opened the manila envelope and sorted the paper into two piles. With both hands, she picked up a stack of papers stapled together with machine precision. Lawyers were expensive, and she hoped the one she could afford had done this right.

"This is my will." She held the papers out to her.

"Don't give me that. I don't want it."

"Angie, this is hard on me too. It's important to me. Please." She waited until Angie took her hands from her pockets and opened them on the table. Tipping the stack forward until it rested in her outstretched palms, Molly let go. Angie caught them.

"I put a copy of this in my bag as well. I don't have much, so it's simple. I'm leaving the condo in Seattle to Penelope and Scottie. I'm leaving you my car and . . ."

"I don't need your car." She dropped the papers on the table and pushed the chair back.

"It's not about need. I love my car, and I want you to have it. Keep it for Mateo, if you want. Don't sell it to some muscle-bound Mopar junkie who gets off burning tires. Sell my bike, though. I don't want you or Mateo riding it." Molly reached across the table. With the tips of her fingers, she pushed the papers slowly back toward Angie.

"You don't need to worry about that." As she spoke, Angie's eyes darted across the wall above Molly's head.

"George hauled the junk away. I'm going to leave the good furniture. You can have it or sell it. Keep the money. I won't need it."

Angie stood up and went to the sink. She looked like she might throw up. "Is that all?" She ripped a paper towel off the roll and blew her nose.

"No. Please come back." Molly waited, but when Angie didn't move, she picked up the second stack and stood to face her. "I have a life insurance policy. It's not huge, but it will easily pay for the rest of your college tuition and Mateo's." She shuffled through the papers until she found one with a business card stapled to it. "This is the policy and agent information. My sisters can't contest. They don't need it, anyway."

"I don't need it, either." Angie's hands flew up to block the transfer.

"Don't be stubborn." She leaned back against the counter. "I know you can do it on your own. Why not let me do it for you? Please?"

Angie's tears spilled out. "Why are you doing this? I don't deserve it."

"Because I love you. I love Mateo. It's a gift. You don't have to deserve it. That's how gifts work. Why would you think you were undeserving, anyway?"

"Because I don't love you."

"Of course you do."

"But not the same way you love me."

"That doesn't matter. It never has. You've been my best friend. That's love too. Let me do this for you. You've done more for me than you'll ever know."

Angie shuffled over and put her arms around Molly's waist. She laid her head on her shoulder. Molly held her tight as she cried. This was grief. Knowing the feel of her. Wanting to take care of her. Causing her pain.

"Why can't you just fight this?" Angie's voice cracked as she said the words.

"There's nothing to fight. It's a treatment, not a cure, and a painful one at that." Molly pulled her in. "And I have something I need to do before I go."

Chapter Eight

Scottie

Scottie waited until after lunch to try again. Killing three birds with one stone, she walked Cleo down the gravel drive to check the mail while rehearsing the call. Pine sentinels lined the road, letting little sunlight through. Though the canopy was dense, and predators lurked, she wasn't afraid to walk down that road. In the beginning, though, the woods terrified her, with their limbs looming thick above. Even the deadfall dwarfed her.

Hank, I can't stand to look at this kid one more second. Come get her. What was it about her that had made two women send her away? Since the recipe eluded her, a universal dread settled in and held her close. Had Molly and Penelope seen in her what their mother had? Would her father? She felt like a package that had arrived broken and was returned, forgotten. Only there was nowhere else to send her. She must be a good girl, or she might end up in the woods where it was dark and damp and even the berries might kill you. So, Scottie watched her father for signs she had angered him, that she was stepping out of line.

As she did, she learned to walk with his confidence—chin up, shoulders back, deliberate steps. Outwardly, it hid her deepest fears. *Man or beast, they size you up and look for your weakness*, he'd said, *but a dog is special.* He told her if you loved them well, they would die protecting you, and unlike a gun, they couldn't be turned on you.

Scottie looked down at the gangly beast vacuuming the salal and waterleaf as they ambled by. She wasn't convinced Cleo would step in front of a cougar for her, but Burnie would, and he was never far away. Though the forest no longer frightened her, some threats still whispered in her ears.

She steeled herself and rehearsed the words. *Hi, Penny. What's your flight number? When do you get in? Shall I pick you up outside baggage claim?* Her head and shoulders curved into a question mark. Scottie hated how Penny made her feel small, like a stray circling the fringe for scraps. Had it always been that way? Surely they had played together when they were little. Before they knew she was adopted? Before the divorce? Before she was kicked out? Molly didn't seem to care that Scottie was a mongrel, but it kept her solidly out of the pack with Penny. Though she never said it outright, Scottie could feel her sizing her up, like an imposter. With Molly, she felt like a real sister. Her smile made you feel like you belonged. Penny's said, *Prove yourself!*

Cleo strayed into the underbrush to pee on a fern as Scottie prattled on. *Hi, Penny. Would you like me to pick you up at the airport? Hello, Penelope. It would be an honor to serve as your chauffeur. I shall endeavor to be on time. Penny, if you don't call me back, you can find your own damn ride.* Lost in her thoughts, Scottie didn't notice the giant had stopped until she reached the end of the slack in the lead. The dog, still evacuating her bladder, was rooted to the earth. Cleo jerked Scottie off her feet, dislodging her from the mental roller-coaster ride.

"Oh hell, Scottie, just make the damn call," she said to herself.

Cleo concurred with a mighty woof, which brought Burnie to heel.

"Fine. You're right." She reached down and scratched behind the big dog's ears. "I need to fish or cut bait. Time's running out." She took a step, but the Dane didn't budge. Burnie and Scottie turned to face her. "Let's go." Cleo stared at her, immobile. "Don't you judge me. I'll call when we get to the mailbox. There's better reception there. Yeesh, you would pick now to engage." Cleo waited a beat and then started down the drive.

When they arrived at the mailbox, Scottie made the call. A wave of relief flowed through her when the voicemail came on.

"Penny, please call me back. I'm leaving for Reno early tomorrow morning. Once I hit the pass, cell service will be spotty the rest of the way there. If I don't talk to you before that, I guess you can leave me a message about your flight. I'm sure you can find a direct flight." *Of course she can. She's a lawyer, idiot. She can figure it out. Stop talking.* "Anyway, I'll plan to meet you at the airport. OK, well, hopefully you'll get this and call me back before I leave."

The familiar pang hit her chest. An echo of bad things past coming around again. She imagined Molly ceasing to exist. Not like Scottie had with Mary, but worse—really and truly gone. Panic flooded her. And so, she did what she had done her whole life. She put it in a box and buried that box so far from her heart and mind that the pain turned to mist. She dusted herself off and got on with it. Scottie excelled at that. Her father loved that most about her. She was a hard worker. She didn't entertain self-pity or regret. She put her nose to the grindstone and got to work. And Scottie was happy to let her dad believe that. He wouldn't like the belly full of boxes she was hiding.

After she finished all her afternoon chores, she sat in the office and made a list of things to pack. Then she called Jason who told her to do what she needed to do. Scottie knew she should be grateful to have such a supportive partner. But inside, there was an inkling of anger that proved she was broken. It prodded her like a finger to the chest. His compassion made her itch inside. She wanted to pick a fight. *Dammit! Why would you just let me leave and put all this work on you? Doesn't it matter that I won't be here? Why are you being so nice? I hate that about you.*

But she didn't say it. Even in her head, she knew it was too ridiculous to express. She loved him, had for twenty-six years. The depth of it scared her, though she was sure he was unaware. It was like their life was a seesaw and he always found a way to balance her out so she never went flying off. She didn't understand what he got out of it. Deep down, with the boxes of foreboding and fury stowed in her belly, she worried one day he would step off the teeter-totter and send her crashing to the dirt, alone.

She made arrangements with Meaghan to work at the kennel. It wasn't a hard sell to a college student with bills to pay, though she would have done it for free. She and Justin were mysteries. When Justin came along, Jason was so happy, but then he didn't know about her moms and how it could end. When she held his tiny body, she knew she was holding the one being she would love without condition or restraint or even the need for reciprocation. Of course, she was wrong. Justin wasn't the only being. Meaghan came along and Scottie felt the same.

"Everyone's fed." Hank stood in the doorway, worry lines crawling across his forehead. "I'll come back and let them out tonight. You get some sleep. It's a long drive to Reno." As Burnie brushed by him, he leaned over and let his hand sift through the thick fur.

"I'll be OK, Dad. Back in a couple of days, tops. Meaghan will be here in the morning. You can always call Jason if you need anything." Burnie lay down next to her chair and rested his head on his paws.

"I won't. Need anything, that is. We'll be fine. You girls have fun."

"Thanks." She smiled, though she wanted to tell him fun was not on the agenda. She dreaded the drive and the inevitable confession of her lie.

"You know I love you, kiddo."

And she did. She knew he loved her. But her heart was like a breaker in the surf. Waves crashed and stopped. All she let in was the errant spray that breached the wall.

"I know. I love you too, Dad." And she did. She loved him so much it scared her because she knew it would end. It had to. When it did, that box would fill her belly. It would crush everything else beneath it.

※

Scottie's phone vibrated in her pocket as she pulled the key from the lock. Burnie headed for the truck, and Scottie let out a shrill whistle for him to stop as she answered the call.

"Jeez, Scarlett." Penelope's voice came on the line. "Don't whistle in my ear like that."

Scottie flinched.

"Sorry, I had my hands full. I nearly dropped the phone. I was closing up the kennel for the night and Burnie made a run for it because he had to pee." *OK, stop talking. You sound like a moron.*

"I got your message. What time are you picking me up tomorrow?"

So much for the pleasantries. I'm doing great, Penny. Thanks for asking. How've you been? Scottie's shoulders tensed and climbed toward her ears. She forced them down.

"Scarlett? Are you there?"

"Yes. I guess that depends on when your plane gets in."

"I'm not flying."

Apparently, you did not listen to my message. "What do you mean? How are you getting there then?"

"Scarlett. I'm not flying. I'm driving down with you."

Do not let her wind you up. You are not a child. She is not in charge of everything.

"Penny, it's at least a twelve-hour drive." *Which will feel like twenty, if I have to listen to your nails clicking on your laptop the whole time.*

"Don't call me that."

"Penelope, it's twelve hours by car under the best conditions." *I wonder how fast my truck can go.*

"So, I can help you drive, Scarlett."

"Don't call me that." *And 'oh hell no' to you driving.*

"Look, I have a meeting in ten. Just tell me when you're picking me up."

"Picking you up? I'm not. If you're driving with me, you need to be at the kennel at 5:00 a.m."

"Five in the morning? Are you nuts? It's not even light out."

"You can always fly."

"Why don't you pick me up in Seattle at, say, seven?"

"Because one, I will lose two good driving hours waiting for you to wake up. Two, I would be backtracking twenty miles which adds another hour. I'm going through eastern Oregon."

"That's nuts. It's all back roads. It'll take forever."

"It's a highway, Penelope, not some dirt road."

"Oh, trust me. That route is seared into my memory."

"I'm sorry you had a bad experience . . ."

"I didn't have a bad experience, Scottie. We all did. You weren't too little to remember. So don't play the baby card."

"Maybe I wasn't there. Maybe it was you and Molly and Mary."

"You were there."

"Whatever. It was forty years ago. I hate the corridor and I-5 traffic. I'm driving. Feel free to fly." *Please just bail on the trip. We do not need you.*

"Fine. I'll meet you at your house at seven."

"If we leave at seven, we won't get there until maybe nine. Come at five, and meet me at the kennel."

"Why the kennel? Your house is closer." Penelope groaned.

"Because I need to drop something off, and besides, your fancy car will be safer there."

"Five? Fine. But we need to just get on the road. I don't want to hang around and have coffee."

"Fine by me." Scottie waited for her to beg off for her meeting, but silence grew in the space. She wanted to ask the question, but she didn't want proof that Molly was telling Penelope more than her.

"Did she tell you what's wrong?" Penelope's words came out stilted.

"No. You?"

"No."

Scottie hesitated. Could that be true? "To be honest, I didn't ask for details. I figured it must be serious for her to ask us to come. I thought we'd talk on the way back."

"Captive audience. Good idea. We'll force her to tell."

"If she wants to. I mean, it's her life. She has a right to keep it private." Scottie remembered those first days back at school after the accident. She couldn't hide her injuries, but she didn't have to share it with them, either. It was one of the few choices she had.

"Not from her family. She'll need help," Penelope said, "and I can't help her if I don't know what's going on."

"Maybe that's not what she wants."

"Sometimes people don't know what they want. That's what family is for. To do what you can't do for yourself. To do what you need even when you think you don't need anything."

"Is that what you would want us to do?" Scottie asked.

"Molly would know what to do if I was in the same position."

"But not me."

"Here we go. I'm just saying Molly knows me better. She would know the right thing to do."

"Well then, I guess for your sake, I hope Molly isn't that sick."

"Don't be like that," Penelope said.

You don't have a clue. Maybe if you'd visited me even one time when I was in the hospital you'd have a little empathy.

"I'm not being like anything. Look, I have things to do to get ready for tomorrow. If you're riding with me, be at the kennel at five. If you aren't there, I'm leaving without you."

Scottie didn't say goodbye. Neither did Penelope.

Chapter Nine

Penelope

AN OPEN SUITCASE overflowed on the bed. Despite her strict adherence to the roll-and-tuck packing methods she'd learned from a man on TikTok, who might be the only person on the planet to make Penelope feel disorganized, there was no room for her makeup, moisturizers, or mousse. They lay on the comforter in two quart-sized bags, packed in order of decreasing volume. She'd wedged the hair dryer in early so she would not be forced to join Molly parading around the house for hours wearing an As-Seen-On-TV magical hair-drying turban. Penelope's cut required precision drying with a ceramic hair dryer and a boar bristle brush. Molly didn't know those things even existed.

Penelope dropped to the side of the bed. The list whirled through her head. *Pack. Identify doctor and hospital with best success rate. Get insurance approval. Get a second opinion. Determine stage. Chemo. Radiation. Hospital bed. Home nursing.* She'd blocked out Molly and her announcement until she was safely ensconced in her apartment at night. In the daytime, when the terror of losing her crept in, she fought it back by focusing on work. It had been easier to do at the client dinner. Corporate wives were skilled at making conversation. She had been relegated there for showing up late. It turned out to be a blessing, though she chastised herself for making room at work for any feeling other than ambition. It was the second strike in two days. *You cannot show weakness at work. Weasels like Jackson will sense it a mile away and then step in to collaborate you right out of your own project. Get it together, Penelope, or you are going to be out on your ear.* Meanwhile, her mind was filling with all the things she had to do to prevent losing the last family member that mattered, leaving only a sliver to ward off a good old boy coup or process the inane chatter of upcoming tropical vacations well enough to nod at the appropriate time.

Her watch beeped a warning, jarring her back to her current predicament. *Damn you, Scarlett. Do we really have to leave before dawn?* She stared at the deluge on the mattress. Adding another suitcase was out of the question. Scarlett, who hardly needed one suitcase since she only ever wore a T-shirt and jeans, would never let her live it down. She was already inviting disapproving looks for her style choice, which Scarlett called her costume: riding boots, tights, and a sweater. *Screw her.* Penelope wasn't putting any outfits back. How could she predict what she'd want to wear tomorrow? There were events, weather, and social norms to consider. She scooped up the bags of makeup and lotions and slid them into the briefcase next to her laptop. Lucy hopped on the bed and claimed the vacated real estate.

"Don't get comfortable. We need to leave in exactly five minutes. Your Auntie Scarlett runs a tight ship." She zipped her luggage. "On the upside, Molly is a pushover. So, we just have to survive the next thirteen hours." Thirteen hours to wrestle the Ashbridge case out of Jackson's clutches so she could give Molly what she needed—her undivided attention, a commodity in scarce supply even before her announcement. She could suffer Scarlett Casey Dunn that long to save her career.

Unlike every other being Penelope spoke to, Lucy was unmoved. To make that point, she walked in tight circles, pausing only long enough to look Penelope in the eye each time she came around, until the comforter made the perfect nest for her to lie on. As she dropped, her hair floated behind her like a wedding train. Penelope loved the dog's silky hair and furry paws. When she was a puppy, Penelope would cradle her in the crook of her neck. As Lucy's breath tickled her jawline, she would close her eyes and try to feel the pup's heartbeat next to hers.

"Pretty cocky, little mop." She tousled the puff of hair that sprang from the pink bow on the top of the dog's head. "You better be in your carrier before I get to the front door or I'm calling the dog sitter." It was an empty threat, but Lucy didn't know that.

Penelope pulled the suitcase to the floor, attached her briefcase, and grabbed her scarf and jacket. Before her hand hit the doorknob, she heard the tapping of tiny nails on the hardwood. In a blur of blond, Lucy hopped into her carrier.

"Smart girl. Just like your mom." Penelope took one last look around, mentally reviewing her list. Her alarm clock, backlit with manufactured sunlight, pronounced 4:25 a.m., mocking her. Scanning the sea of cream, taupe, and the palest of pinks, she confirmed everything was in its place. The faintest vibration of impending chaos built in her belly. Familiar as she was with the sensation, she pushed through. She had scheduled five minutes to get to the garage, load her bags, and secure Lucy. She would leave the garage at four thirty. That gave her thirty minutes to drive to Snoqualmie. If her calculations were correct, and they always were, she would be there early enough to miss her dad and still be on time for Scottie. If they were late, she would leave without her. Of that, Penelope had no doubt. No time to worry about chaos she couldn't prevent.

❧

Lucy lay clipped into her carrier on the passenger seat. As she waited for the security gate to go up, Penelope glanced at her. The dog reminded her of a swirl of frosting on a cupcake. Penelope reached over to stroke the hair made silky by the dog walker's daily brushing. Feeling the strands sifting through her fingers relaxed her. She took a deep breath in through her nose. As she opened her mouth to let it out, the sedan behind her sounded its horn.

"Dammit. Just breathe and you will experience peace, my ass. This is why there are no city-dwelling, corporate-lawyer Zen masters. It's going to take a lot more than oxygen. Seriously, deep breathing? I can't believe I paid for that advice." The driver honked again. "Really? You're in a hurry at four thirty in the morning?" She eased through the gate and paused to check for pedestrians. The last thing she wanted to do was run over someone looking for a warm place to sleep. Her caution bought her a double toot of his horn. "Jackass." Lucy sat up and looked around. Baring her tiny canines, she let out a cartoon growl. "That's right, give him the what for, you ferocious beast."

The freeway was clear heading east. Though she rarely drove past Bellevue anymore, crossing the bridge still tightened her jaw. Back then, when the courts deemed her too little to decide for herself, she was stuck. The only good reason not to visit her father would have required revealing she knew his secret. She couldn't cause her mother more pain, so she practiced smiling through clenched teeth. Gripping the window crank, she'd fantasize screaming at him, pounding his chest and, without dropping a single tear, telling him she knew everything.

She blamed him for her mother folding herself into her chair each morning and staring into the darkness with a sadness that covered them all like fog. If it were up to her, Penelope would never go back. And he would hurt like she did. He would be sad too, and then Scarlett would have to live in a house of sadness and anger. That would be fair. She shouldn't get to live with the happy parent. In a way, she blamed Scarlett too. Though she'd been old enough to know she had not chosen any of this, Penelope couldn't shake her anger. Things would have been different if Scarlett hadn't been born. She hated herself for the thought. Father Joe would make her confess it if he knew she had such awful thoughts. But she wouldn't be the only one confessing, then.

As if conjured from her memory, Penelope's phone rang, and Scarlett's number flashed on the screen.

"Are you on your way?"

"And good morning to you too, Scarlett."

"Sorry. I'm used to talking to dogs. Good morning, Penny. How are you? Are you on your way?"

Penelope could feel the eye roll on the other end of the line. "You don't greet the dogs?"

"Penny, are you on your way?"

"Could you please stop calling me that? And yes, I just passed Issaquah. I'll be there in ten."

"OK. Park on the left side of Dad's truck. That way it won't have to be moved."

"Why is he there?"

"Well, he owns the place. What do you mean?"

"I mean it's early, and I didn't think he would be in."

"He's doing the morning feeding. Plus, I'm sure he'll want to see you."

Penelope didn't know what to say to that. A candle flickered in that needy place in her heart where she wanted her dad to sweep her up in a bear hug, tell her how much he missed her, and beg her forgiveness for screwing everything up. She quickly extinguished that childish feeling. More likely, he was there to make sure Penelope was kind to Scarlett, which pissed her off, though she had to admit it wasn't unwarranted.

"I'll see you in ten." She disconnected before Scottie could say goodbye.

※

A wooden sign her dad had built marked the road to the kennel. On cedar, in high relief, he'd carved the body of a German Shorthair Pointer on alert. Its proud face was fixed on the words engraved above the horizon, Casey's K-9s. A shoreline, replete with reeds and cattails, framed the bottom of the sign. Though an impressive monument to his post-divorce enterprise, Penelope thought the waves in the water were unrealistic. She wondered how long it had taken him to create the sign. He'd never carved anything before it, and as far as she knew, he'd never carved anything after it.

She admired that about him. Hank was energized by a challenge when most people were deterred by the effort required to meet it. If he needed a place to sit, he didn't look for a furniture store. He went to the lumberyard. It wasn't enough to open a kennel; he had to be the one to build it. That made the hurt cut a little deeper, though. With everything else, he defied the problem. When his own home was breaking apart, he didn't even try to cobble it back together. He left the cracks widening in the foundation and walked away.

Penelope turned the coupe into the driveway and stopped. Her father had paved the road since her last visit. She tried to remember when that was. High school? Earlier? No doubt some awkward holiday that Molly roped her into in her relentless pursuit of reconciliation. Releasing the wheel, she placed her hands in her lap and drew in a deep breath through her nose. She held it and began counting.

Five, four, three—

A splash of fur grazed her arm as the dog popped to attention. Yip! Yip! Yip!

"Et tu, Lucy? The universe clearly does not want me relaxed."

She stood in the carrier, her furry paws pressed on the edge, raising her head almost above the dashboard. "Yip!"

"OK. OK. I'm going. I don't know why you're in such a hurry. Where we're headed, I'm pretty sure they'll think of you as an hors d'oeuvre." Penelope eased the car forward. "I'll protect you, though. You have nothing to worry about. I won't let anybody hurt you."

Scottie was pulling a box out of the back of her Suburban when Penelope pulled in. The fact she had to stand tiptoed to reach her target was proof she was not genetically related to Penelope Casey. Scottie was a shrub in a family of pines. As predicted, she wore jeans and work boots, and Penelope suspected she'd find a T-shirt beneath her coat. Scottie turned and waved with the enthusiasm of a road construction flagger.

Penelope parked in the first open spot. Scottie knocked on the window. "Do you want some help with your gear?"

"Thanks. My bag is in the back." She unlocked the trunk for Scottie and then walked around to the passenger side to collect her briefcase and Lucy.

"Why did you bring that?" Scottie asked.

"I thought I'd do some work in the car while you're driving. Don't worry, I'll do my share." Penelope hoisted the strap over her shoulder.

"Not that. Your dog."

"What did you want me to do, put her in a kennel?"

"What's that supposed to mean? And yes—I happen to know

an excellent kennel." Scottie turned to point at the building behind her.

"Scarlett, I'm bringing Lucy."

"Well, I hope you brought a crate."

"I'm not putting her in a crate. She has a car carrier, or she can sit on my lap. I don't understand why this is a problem. You allegedly love dogs."

"Not allegedly. I do love dogs. That is not a dog. That is a cat dressed up like a dog." Scottie walked over to the Suburban and opened the back door. "Besides, Burnie might get hungry." A mass of black, white, and tan hair barricaded the entrance.

"You're not serious. There's no reason to bring that animal." Penelope clutched Lucy.

"There's just as much reason to bring him as your ankle biter." Scottie scratched the big dog's ears. "Promise me you won't eat the small animal." She kissed his head and gently moved him back to close the door.

Penelope clenched her jaw and stared at Scottie, who lifted the corners of her lips long enough to say, "I'm joking. Lighten up."

Shit-show trip and we haven't even made it out of the parking lot yet! What the hell have you done, Molly?

"Well, this is a nice surprise." Hank walked up to Scottie and handed her a travel mug. "I thought you might want some coffee for the trip. You should have told me I'd need two." He walked over to Penelope and gave her and the dog a hug.

Though his embrace was delicate, tentative, the stun swallowed her breath. She froze like a rabbit faced with the unexpected, sure it must be a threat. She was grateful her arms were occupied protecting Lucy from Scarlett's behemoth. The little dog gave her heart some space.

"It's good to see you. I'm glad you girls are all getting together. Gosh, even when you were little, Molly planned the tea parties. Some things never change, huh?"

It dawned on her that Scarlett had kept more than her travel arrangements from their father. She considered telling him the real reason for their trip, as he seemed on the verge of scolding her for her omission, and Penelope was only too happy to give him a little push. There were two things she learned the hard way early in her career—never ask a question you don't know the answer to, and information is a precious commodity. She tucked it away instead. *The why of the lie is what leads to the truth*, a professor once told her. *What was the why behind Scarlett's lie?*

"Yes. It will be nice to see Molly." She forced a smile.

"Do you have time for coffee? I could make some pretty quick. Scottie bought us one of those coffee makers with the pods. Just takes a few seconds." Hank looked hopeful.

"No. I'm sorry. We have to get on the road. Maybe when we get back."

He smiled at her and opened the passenger door. Penelope looked at the big dog hanging his head over the front seat.

"You might as well get in," Scottie said. "Or you could head to SeaTac and I'll pick you up in Reno."

Penelope didn't move.

As if he knew her fear, Hank said, "They'll work it out. Burnie's a good dog. Your Lucy will be fine."

Surprised he knew Lucy's name, Penelope smiled at him without thinking. He gave her another hug, which she returned, this time with a weak, one-armed pat. As he stepped back, he took the dog from her and helped her into the SUV. Placing the animal in her arms, he pulled the seat belt around her, giving it a tug at the end to see that it was latched. Penelope stilled. She felt like the kid who fell into the gorilla enclosure at the zoo and was swept into the primate's paternal grasp, aware his compassion was capricious at best. Though she knew Hank would never physically harm her, experience had taught her you could take a beating without ever being hit. He looked into her eyes but said nothing.

Scottie gave her dad a hug with both arms, and he returned the same. He signaled the end with two heavy pats on her back that reverberated as waves of sadness in Penelope's chest.

Burnie let out a deep woof, and Scottie hurried to the cab. "OK. Settle down. We're on the road." Burnie hung his head over her seat and rubbed his snout on her cheek. She reached up and scratched his ear. He didn't move when she put the truck in gear and pulled away. "That's enough. Time to lie down." Lucy agreed with a yip. "You tell him, Lucy."

With a flourish, the dog broke free of Penelope's hold. She strained against the chest strap. Trying to get hold of the dog, her fingertips grazed the feathered ends of her fur as Lucy scampered over the headrest and landed next to Burnie.

Chapter Ten

Molly

THE CHIRP OF her cell phone flowed through Molly's consciousness into the stream of beeps emanating from the device hooked up to her chest. She looked down at the twisted rainbow of wires and followed them to their source. A white light hopped up and down across the grid etched into the blue screen. With every bounce, a trail smeared the screen like a tiny comet. Beyond the wires, a clear tube emerged from beneath her skin. She stared at the milky fluid pulsing its way toward her chest cavity in time with the sound—chirp, chirp, chirp. Panicking, she reached for the tube. Her arms were too heavy to lift. *I said no chemo! You can't do this to me. I do not consent.* Desperate to dislodge the tube before the fluid creeped up the line and into her body, she threw herself off the bed. Chirp, chirp.

"Fuck." Molly landed against the wall on the floor of her bedroom. The cheap carpet scraped her knee raw. Panting, she searched her body for the wires. Molly pushed herself against the wall, clasping her knees to her chest. She clenched every muscle in her body, but she could not hold back the tears. Caged between her thighs and arms, her belly lurched with each sob. She hated crying. It was painful to feel the words drowning in the salt and snot, her throat constricting in a last-ditch effort to prevent the truth from escaping. Had she been arrogant to think she could have it all, one last year in living color, putting Penelope and Scottie back together, and then fading out pain-free? It was clear she would not escape the pain. Unmerciful, the nightmares alternated between terror of the cure and terror of the inevitable.

Chirp. Chirp.

As her breath stilled, the sound creeped back in. Molly rocked forward and reached for her phone. Her tears blurred the screen. She lifted her T-shirt and wiped her eyes.

Penelope: You're probably not awake yet, but I wanted to let you know we're on our way. Hoping there will be no bloodshed between here and NV.

Molly: Bloodshed?!?

She reached for the box of tissues on her nightstand, knocking her alarm clock to the floor. The box was empty. She lifted the damp hem of her shirt to her nose and blew. The indignity of it angered her. This was only the beginning. With or without chemo, she would shrivel up. She would be forced to stare into eyes that once envied her battery power and watch the awe turn to pity. They would say it was a waste. Such a pretty girl and so talented. They would speculate on her regrets. No family of her own. Not even a lover here to hold her hand. They would offer her ice chips, mop her brow with a damp cloth, wipe her ass. She ripped the clock from the plug and hurled it across the room. *Chirp. Chirp.*

Penelope: That brute of hers is looking at Lucy like she's lunch.

Molly: She's right next to you!

Penelope: Settle down. She thinks I'm working.

Molly: You settle down. Burnie is sweet. He won't hurt Lucy. Scottie would never let that happen.

Molly hoisted herself up to the bed and dragged the T-shirt over her head. *I have bigger things to worry about, Penelope.* Wadding it into a ball, she tossed it into the trash. She had enough clothes to last the rest of her life, and she wasn't going to waste any of it doing laundry. *Chirp. Chirp.*

Penelope: Did you see the Dr?

Molly: We'll talk when you get here. I can't text all that.

Penelope: Call & tell me about it then.

Molly: You know all I know.

Penelope: I know nothing.

Molly: Same.

Penelope: Jeez-could you be serious?!?

Penelope: Molly?

Penelope: Molly, I'm sorry. I know you know this is serious. I hate this for you. I'm trying to help.

Dust motes danced in the slab of light, sneaking through the gap in the curtains. Molly reached out to touch them. A wave rippled through the tiny specks, but she felt nothing. Maybe death would be like that. Suspended like particles. Unable to make contact. No physical force.

Molly: I'll talk to you when you get here. Don't be mean to Scottie. Or Burnie.

Penelope: I'm never mean. See you in 13 hours 22 minutes-but who's counting?

Molly: Is there traffic already at 0500? Why 13:22?

Penelope: Because Sister Scarlett refused to take I-5.

Molly: How are you getting here?

Penelope: Through northern Canada.

Molly: Funny. Seriously tho?

Penelope: Tri-Cities then eastern OR.

Molly: Yikes. That's the long way.

Hope sparked. Molly had been counting on Scottie to win this battle. A lot had changed on that highway in twenty-five years, but she prayed a vestige of memory had survived the hurt and neglect.

Penelope: They're all the long way.

Penelope: Except flying.

Molly: Let it go. On the upside, you can work for the next 13 hours and 17 minutes and thus avoid all conversation with your sister.

Penelope: I wish. There won't be cell service for most of the trip.

Molly: Maybe Scottie planned it that way so you would have to talk to her.

Penelope: Hardly.

Molly: I've heard lawyers are good with words. You could start it off. So, Scottie, what've you been up to the last couple decades?

Penelope: Cute. I'm better known for negotiation and interrogation. I could try one of those.

Molly: Be nice.

Penelope: I'm never not nice.

Molly: Hmm . . . Try this. I am nice.

Penelope: I love you.

Molly: I love you too.

Molly turned the ringer off her phone and set it on her bedside table facedown. Pulling the hefty comforter over her head, she drew her knees to her chest. Her warm breath cooled before it passed her arms. She ran her hands over her legs. Bones she once only felt as they terminated at her joints were now sneaking out between the waning muscle and fat. Now the outcroppings formed a relief map of her history. Her fingers followed the curve of her kneecap, jumping the chasm to her tibia, searching for the dent. It had filled in over the last thirty-five years, and she had filled out. Even if no one else could see it, she could feel it like it was yesterday.

The snow fell like confetti that night. Penelope had predicted school would be canceled. Molly waited until she heard her mother turn off the TV and close her bedroom door before tiptoeing back to the living room. She climbed up on the sofa and lifted the rough curtains, tucking her head and shoulders beneath them. With the palm of her hand, she cleared the fog from the window so she could watch the flurries. Flakes meandered to the earth, covering the car across the street like coconut sprinkles on the cakes her grandma made. She fell asleep with her cheek on her forearms. Sometime in the night, her father lifted her into his arms and took her back to bed. He kissed her forehead.

"Get some sleep, Mollypop. There will still be snow tomorrow."

Molly jumped out of bed in the morning when she heard him walking around. She found him in the kitchen, dressed for work.

"Where are you going? I want to go sledding."

"I have to go to work." He unscrewed the lid from his thermos. "You play in the snow with Penny. We can sled when I get home tonight."

Molly nodded, but she knew they wouldn't. He would be tired. Mom would be tired from taking care of Scottie. He filled the metal cylinder with coffee, leaving some in the pot for her mother. "You have fun today, Mollypop. Someday you won't be able to play in the snow anytime you want. Someday, you'll have a job."

"I'm not going to have a job."

He chuckled and ruffled her hair. "Someday you will."

"Mom doesn't."

"Don't let her hear you say that. She sure does. Her job is to take care of all of us."

"I don't want to do that, either."

"Someday, you won't have a choice." He kissed her forehead. "For now, enjoy the snow."

They had both been right. She had a job. It didn't keep her from skiing when she wanted to. She didn't have a family of her own, though. If she had, he still wouldn't recognize it. Through the pall of her impending demise, it struck her that she'd blamed her father for that. But it hadn't been his definition that had robbed her of a family. What seemed monolithic in her youth was inconsequential now. She'd missed out on that joy, not because they wouldn't acknowledge it as a family, but because she couldn't do it without their acknowledgement.

Molly rubbed the dent in her shin. If she'd only waited for him, asked for his help, how many dents would she have avoided? She could still see her mother running out of the house in her bathrobe, gripping the collar to hide her nightgown. On her feet, a pair of galoshes flapped open as she hurried to the mailbox. Her mother left the sled upended on the post for her father to see. She deemed the leg nothing more than bruised and marched Molly to the house. Scottie cried in her mother's arms as she scolded Molly. Her mother called her irresponsible. Something terrible, even death, could have happened to the baby while she'd been out rescuing Molly. Selfish. A hot pool of shame bubbled in Molly's stomach. She pushed her mother over the edge again. Penelope was perfect. Scottie was too little to know better. But Molly was reckless.

She ran her finger over the dent and wondered if this trip would smooth over the dent that kept Penelope and Scottie apart. Or was she turning the dent into a break?

Chapter Eleven

Scottie

"Pull over. I have to get Lucy." Penelope hunted for the seat belt release like a downed fighter pilot searching for the ejector button.

Scottie adjusted the rearview mirror to check on the dogs. She had to crane her neck to find Lucy, who had burrowed her head into the long fur of Burnie's haunches. Burnie stared back at her with the wide-eyed gaze of a confirmed bachelor holding a crying baby. "They're fine, Penny."

"Lucy is not fine." The restraint released, and Penelope twisted until she was kneeling on the seat.

"No one's growling," said Scottie. "They're fine." *Two minutes. That's got to be a record. Thirteen and a half hours to go. Holy hell.*

"Yeah, she's fine now. But I can't help her from up here if something happens. Would you stop the car? Please. Scarlett."

Scottie stepped on the brake. Penelope used the momentum to lean over the seat and snatch Lucy from her nook. Holding her tightly to her chest, she latched her belt with her free hand. "OK. We're good, now. You can go."

Scottie looked over at her sister, petting the dog in long strokes. It reminded her of the time Meaghan ran off in a department store. Scottie called and called for her, more frantic with each moment. The salesclerk called for security. A man, whose shape reminded her of a wine barrel with a head, lumbered over. He could have walked faster had he not been grasping his utility belt at a point directly above each hip to prevent his pants from falling down under the weight of his enormous flashlight. Through wet gasps of air, he questioned Scottie. Though he faced her, his eyes searched the store as they spoke. An announcement came over the PA. Scottie's fear blistered into anger.

"What good is that? The kidnapper is not going to return my four-year-old because you made an announcement. Jesus. Call the police. The real police." She could see herself turning into that abusive woman everyone dismisses as irrational, but she could not stop herself. Terror wiped away the self-consciousness that otherwise kept her in line.

The security guard put a beefy hand on her shoulder. A bold move, Scottie thought, since she often said she would gnaw off her own arm to save her kids. She certainly wouldn't hesitate to chew off his.

"Sometimes, they're just a little lost. Let's give it a minute."

Something in his touch and the kindness of his voice made her pause. In that moment, Meaghan emerged from beneath a rack of long winter overcoats, looking more afraid of being found than being lost. Scottie scooped her up and held her so tight that not a molecule of air could pass between them. She rocked her, stroking her hair, and chanted, "You're OK." Regarding Penelope now, she knew she'd been wrong. She should have said, "I'm OK."

Scottie again focused on the road. "Burnie wouldn't hurt her."

"You don't know that. He's so much bigger than her. She has

no idea what annoys him. All it takes is one mistake. He could turn on her."

Scottie wondered if they were still talking about the dog.

※

By the time they hit the highway, Lucy was asleep on Penelope's lap. She cradled her phone while her thumbs slid across the screen and back. While she seemed to ground the dog, Penelope electrified Scottie. Just sitting so close to her for the first time in decades made her edgy. Stuck somewhere between wanting her older sister to pay attention to her and wishing she did not care about her at all, the only comment she could think to make, awkward and inane, came out with a zing.

"I can't believe anyone in the city is awake, let alone at work this early."

"Farmers aren't the only ones who get up early. Besides, I'm going to lose service when we hit the pass, so I need to send some emails now." Penelope never took her eyes off the screen.

"We're not farmers." Scottie shook her head. *Let it go.*

"You know what I mean." Penelope flicked her wrist as if to wipe away the censure. "Working with animals."

"Big difference between training dogs and milking cows." Scottie had nothing against dairy farmers, or any farmers for that matter, but Penelope brought out her need to be the champion of those who chose jeans and boots for their utility rather than the vagaries of fashion.

"I didn't mean anything by it."

That made it worse. Penelope doled out careless judgments like shuffled cards. Nothing intentional. Just statements of fact reinforcing Scottie's caste.

She plugged her phone into the stereo and selected her road trip playlist. The first song was an old one, and she knew every word. Her dad had taken her to hear the artist after he'd fallen from sellout crowds in stadiums to the state fair circuit. It was still Hank's favorite song. Scottie held the words to a whisper, but she couldn't help but sing along. She pictured the man in old jeans and dusty boots, skin lined with the evidence of a misspent youth, leaning into the mic. When he needed to hit a high note, he'd stop strumming to brush the shock of bangs from his brow, and then he would rock onto his toes as he squeezed out the note. With a touchdown-smile, he dropped back down, never missing a beat. Her father's foot kept time. High praise, indeed.

"I know this song." Penelope turned the music up. "Dad had the lyrics taped up on the mirror in his bathroom. What were those called? From the album?"

"Liner notes?" Scottie offered. "Man, I haven't seen those in years."

"That's it." Penelope's attention returned to her phone.

"I'm surprised you remember that."

"Why?" She looked over at Scottie with a tight smile. "I hated this song. Don't you remember things you hate?"

"Isn't hate kind of strong for a song? I mean, outside of bubblegum pop, which deserves nothing short of blind rage."

"No. I literally hate this song. If I went the rest of my life and never heard it again, I would be happy. It's like a tapeworm boring into my brain." Her smile snaked into a sneer as she spoke.

"OK, well, that's not where tapeworms live." Scottie skipped to the next song. Billy Joel proclaimed he didn't start the fire. *That's because you never took a road trip with Penelope Casey.*

"You get my point," Penelope said.

"Oh, I hear you loud and clear. I don't understand, but I hear. I will not play that song again on this trip. Would you like me to kill the tapeworm with a little mall rock? I think Meaghan downloaded something from a former Disney star that's guaranteed to burrow into your psyche and eat your brain worms."

"No need to go that far, but thanks for changing the song." Penelope flexed her cheeks, drawing her lips into a brief smile that Scottie found insincere.

"Why do you hate it so much? I love that song, maybe more than Dad does."

"I guess because it's like his freedom song." Penelope turned away to face the trees speeding by.

"What's that even mean?"

"You know. Freedom song. Like in high school when you find that song that says screw you to rules and your parents and tells you to go out and dance and smoke pot."

"How can you even equate that?"

"Because it's everything Mom wasn't. Country living, dirt roads, a hound dog on the porch. Not a cocktail party or string of pearls in the whole song."

"Seriously. Cocktail party?"

"You know what I mean. How did those two end up together, honestly? But that song said it all. That's what he wanted, and Mom was never going to be that. So, he left."

"I'm sure that's the story Mary told everyone. But it's not what he said. He told me she asked him to leave."

"Yeah? Did he tell you why Mom asked him to leave?" Penelope emphasized the word mom.

"No. He didn't tell me, and I didn't ask."

"Figures."

"Whatever happened, it goes both ways. It wasn't all his fault."

"Mostly, though." Penelope leaned over to dig out her laptop. Lucy let out a yelp when Penelope squished her in the hinge of her hip. "Stop. That didn't hurt." She slid toward the door and placed the dog on the seat between her hip and the console. As she opened the computer, Lucy tried to make a dash for the back seat, but she wasn't fast enough. Penelope grabbed her mid-stride and tucked her next to her thigh. As soon as she logged in, a series of chimes went off. Scottie assumed the device was announcing her many missed emails.

Conversation over, apparently. For the record, it wasn't all him. It wasn't even mostly him. She got rid of him like she got rid of me. But you don't want to hear that.

Scottie turned up the volume to drown out Penelope's nails, which were clicking across her keyboard like a halftime drum line trying to distract the crowd from a losing score. Lucy took advantage of her focus and edged her front paws toward the back seat. Scottie dug a piece of kibble from her pocket and placed it halfway between them. With a tentative paw, Lucy dragged the food toward her. She took one sniff and scarfed it down.

Penelope slipped the dog back in place beside her. "You stay put. Quit antagonizing Burnie."

"Busted," Scottie said.

"And you. If you keep that up, you're going to have to stop and pick up some upholstery cleaner. I'm not helping you scrub the seat, either." Without looking from her screen, Penelope said, "Busted."

Scottie stuck out her tongue.

~⚜~

Penelope must have given up trying to stay connected. When they skirted the canyon toward Yakima, she put away her laptop and leaned her seat back. Lucy took it as an invitation and crawled onto her lap. The two of them fell asleep in minutes.

Scottie turned down the music and glanced at the woman snoring in the passenger seat, the platinum mop wheezing in her lap. Her chestnut hair curled behind one ear to reveal the sharp right turn of her father's jaw and the gentle slope of her mother's nose. From this angle, an outsider would assume they were related, but it was an optical illusion, like the way the road ahead disappeared into nowhere.

The three of them shared just enough physical features to obscure Scottie's origins. Sharing the same brown hair and hazel eyes, genetics were more likely than coincidence when it came to Penelope and Scottie. While solidly built like Molly, Scottie's height made her a better candidate for a roof thatcher than an Amazon warrior. Molly, though lighter haired and blue eyed, was tall like Penelope. The three together would hold up to cursory inspection as likely sisters. But, of course, it was simply the luck of the draw when it came to her. Though, when they were little, the similarities were enough to make Scottie feel like a real sister. Since Mary insisted her adoption not be discussed outside the family, it was easy for Scottie to pretend along with her—until the day Mary stopped pretending.

Now the similarities taunted her. She would never be quite right, never fully in the sisterhood. She wondered if there had been a family where her belonging would never have been in question.

Since she hadn't met her biological parents, Scottie could only guess what they looked like. In her childhood musings, she pictured a short couple in all the scenarios. In the story where her father is a war hero shot down over Vietnam, still pining for her as he wastes away in a POW camp; her mother is slender and beautiful, a wisp of a woman heartsick from the loss of her husband. With no family of her own to help her and shunned by her in-laws, she gives her child up in hopes of a better life. Scottie is so loved that her mother makes the ultimate sacrifice.

Her mother is fat and hideous in the other story—the one she told herself when she was angry and alone. In that story, the mother is selfish. Upon hearing the news of her husband, she immediately believes the worst. Knowing there is no hope she will attract another man with a needy child on her hip, she puts the baby up for adoption and lives out her life alone. She rents a dingy apartment with avocado appliances and yellowing wallpaper. During the day, she waits tables in a diner by a bus station. At night, she fixes her hair, puts on her one nice dress, and drinks cheap whisky in a tavern down the street. No one loves her because they can sense what she has done.

In between, there were a hundred versions of the couple. In all of them, Scottie is short and stocky like her dad and has her mother's hazel eyes and chestnut hair. Lucky for her, when she stood next to Penelope and Molly, only they knew the truth. While the truth never seemed to make a difference to Molly, Penelope was another story.

❧

"Penny." Scottie gave her a gentle nudge. By the sound of her growl, Lucy took offense. "We're almost to Pasco. I'm going to pull off and fill up the tank. It might be a good time to let the dogs out."

Penelope looked at the passing scenery. "How long was I out?"

"Not too long. A couple hours. You must have been tired. You crashed."

"I need coffee." Penelope searched for her phone.

"I know a place with the best pan dulce. You'll love it. Trust me." Scottie slowed to follow the off-ramp as it curved around in front of the gas station. Assorted vehicles cluttered the street, from shiny new pickups to rust buckets, all carrying sleepy-eyed workers. Her SUV fit seamlessly in the middle, old but not decaying.

Penelope was pulling on her boots as Scottie rolled up to the pumps. She opened the door and judged the skill it would take to land outside the oily puddle on the ground. Stiff from driving,

Scottie didn't dare attempt anything even mildly acrobatic, so she slid to the running bar and pushed. Her feet straddled the soup. One heel landed too close, splashing on the hem of her jeans. She gave herself a seven for the fault on the landing.

As the tank filled, she stretched. When she took a long drive, her lower back seized up where the surgeries had been. She had to coax the scar tissue loose in stages until she could stand upright. With her arms outstretched above her head, gripping the roof of the vehicle, she pressed her shoulders forward until she felt her spine click just below her rib cage. Relief washed over her. In the hospital, they told her not to fear this, that her body would not let her hurt herself. Still, she held her breath every time. She knew what it felt like to separate the vertebrae and stretch the nerves taut. As fresh as the day it happened, she could feel the searing pain shooting down her legs as she lay pinned beneath the three-wheeler. She had no desire to feel it again.

For the next part, she leaned against the rail between the pumps. It was filthy, but it couldn't be helped. She spread her feet apart and locked her knees. The rail dug into her lower back and hips. Heaving her arms above her head, she reached backward. When she could move no farther, she took a deep breath and let it out, softening her muscles. *Click. Click. Click.* The vertebra slid back into place. She dropped her head and listened for the last pop. She swayed her hips from side to side to be sure they would hold. Nothing was quite as scary as helplessness. And nothing made her feel more helpless than when her legs crumpled, useless, beneath her.

Chapter Twelve

Penelope

Penelope tugged on her boots, which was a trick with her legs clamped tight to dam her bursting bladder. She took one look at the grimy door that announced, "KEYS INSIDE CUSTAMERS ONLY" and knew there was no way she was using the gas station toilet. There was not enough disinfectant in the world. Dubious spelling ability aside, she doubted the author's attention to detail in janitorial services would be any greater. Penelope crossed her legs and willed Scottie to hurry.

In the corner of her eye, she registered movement in the side-view mirror of the SUV. Scottie was attempting a backward bend over a railing that was covered, no doubt, in a layer of human filth. Rather than the graceful curve of a tender limb in a breeze, as her serene yoga teacher would describe the pose, she looked more like a plank on a seesaw. Her toes barely contacted the ground. A couple more millimeters and she would topple over on her head. Penelope made a note to tell her about the flexibility benefits of yoga and Pilates and the dangers of public microscopic flora and fauna.

Scottie opened the driver's door, letting in a rush of cool air. "I'm going to take Burnie out to pee. You might want to do the same."

"I'm not using that bathroom. I can just imagine what's growing in there."

"I meant your dog."

Penelope looked around at the minefield of oil stains and discarded junk food wrappers. "Can we go somewhere with grass?"

Scottie dropped her chin and lifted her eyes to Penelope. The look slammed her right back into the seventies when she'd caught Scottie crouched down, fingers intertwined, giving Molly a boost up in the garage so she could grab the tools their dad had purposely put out of reach. They wanted to do something adventurous, as defined by two little girls of single-digit age—like build a fort in the ravine where, according to the big kids, a criminal was hiding, having killed his whole family. Penelope was the voice of reason and talked Molly down before she toppled the shelf and crushed the two of them. Scottie gave her a look that said, *Come on. Don't be such a stick in the mud.*

"Look, Lucy's paws will soak up all the grease and dirt. It'll get all over your car. We can find a coffee shop. My treat. Go to the bathroom. Let the dogs out. What do you say?" How easily she slipped back into cajoling the headstrong baby of the family. "We can get that pastry thing."

"OK. I'll give into your big city sensibilities, but only because pastry has been promised."

"All I need is a skinny latte with an extra shot."

"Come on. You have to try the pan dulce. It's a sin to pass it up." Scottie spoke into the windshield as she checked for traffic and pulled onto the road.

"I don't believe in sin," Penelope said.

"You don't believe it exists? Or you don't believe in committing sin?"

"I don't believe in sin. At least, not the way you do."

"Oh, yeah?" She turned to Penelope. Her brow furrowed. "And how exactly do I believe in sin?"

"You know what I mean. Sin. Capital S. As determined by mummified priests and sexually repressed nuns who demand eight-year-olds confess theirs, great and small. I mean, honestly, the psychic damage caused by the confessional was way, way worse than any sin I committed at eight."

"Well, I guess we can add religion to the list of things we can't talk about on this trip. Sin and the song that shall not be named. The list grows."

"My beliefs are just as valid as yours."

"I'm not the one criticizing someone else's religion."

Penelope wasn't sure what she believed in, but she had a long list of things she didn't. Catholicism was at the top of that list. Though, to be fair, she had quit practicing four decades ago when her parents divorced. The vocal resentment of her marriage-predicated, coerced-convert mother drowned out everything she'd learned in Sunday school. Before the ink dried on their separation, Mary Casey stopped going to Mass. She didn't hesitate to share with Penelope the many ways she begrudged the Church. Her husband, so devout, had violated standards etched in granite and handed down for centuries. Hank just tossed them aside, and his priest expected Mary to join him in bestowing absolution as if his dalliance had not come with a lifetime consequence. Where was that priest when Mary needed grace?

Did Penelope really not believe in sin? What her father had done was sinful. What she did not believe in was repentance or absolution. Repentance was convenient and expeditious, but rarely heartfelt in her experience. Absolution was the get-out-of-jail card that allowed you to overlook the gaping scar your actions left behind on people you vowed to protect. Meanwhile, those you sinned against were left with a phantom pain that surfaced just often enough to remind them of the betrayal and how inconsequential their suffering was to the sinner.

"Do you still go to Mass?" Penelope asked.

"No." Scottie didn't offer an explanation.

"You don't believe in it anymore?"

"Catholicism? Most of it. I believe in God, and I trust Him. I don't believe in man, and I certainly don't trust all of them."

"So, you didn't raise Meaghan and Justin Catholic?" Penelope asked.

"I started to, but I pulled them out."

"I bet that was a fun conversation to have with Dad."

"It wasn't much of a conversation at all. I just told him. It's not like he was going to take them to Mass. That would require him going."

"He doesn't go to Mass anymore?"

"He hasn't gone since the divorce. It didn't stop him from making me go, though." Scottie pulled into a parking space. "We're here. Why don't you go to the bathroom, and I'll take the dogs out?"

Penelope cursed her bladder, which was currently winning the war over her curiosity. She had so many questions about her dad.

∽

When she returned from the coffee shop, Penelope found Scottie across the street in a small park. Burnie darted furiously from bush to tree, cataloging the aromas left by man and beast. Lucy bounced on her front paws in a fruitless attempt to break free. From the bench, Scottie's arm jutted out to give Lucy the best opportunity to catch him.

"I took a chance and got you a mocha." Penelope handed her the coffee and a pastry. "If you don't like it, I'll get you something else."

Scottie looked up, squinting into the sunrise behind her. "You were that way as a kid." She took a sip of her coffee. "Taking care of everyone." She turned back to the dogs, who were now nose to nose. "I saw it. Before they got divorced, and things were getting bad. You took care of me and Molly. I used to think it would be OK when they went after each other because I knew we would get to do something fun with you." She stood and handed Lucy's lead to Penelope. "Thanks for the coffee. It's perfect." She slipped the pastry into her coat pocket and walked away.

Lucy tugged on the leash, trying to catch up with the pair. The tiny dog could have lifted her from the bench. Penelope was stunned by the revelation. And she had. She had protected them and tried to give them carefree moments like the ones she'd had when she was their age, before transgression and recrimination became the daily fare.

She watched as Scottie crouched down and took Burnie's head in her hands. She ruffled his fur. When he nosed her jacket, Scottie lifted his head and gave him a kiss, but she didn't share her treat. As she headed for the truck, she called back to Penelope, "Time to go!"

Chapter Thirteen

Scottie

Scottie shook her head. Once again, she'd made Penelope uncomfortable—so much so that the woman who talked for a living had nothing to say. It was her curse. She either stared tongue-tied or vomited cringe-worthy platitudes. *Admitting you were happy they were fighting because then Penny had to entertain you. I bet she loved that glimpse into your psyche. Maybe I can put her to sleep with some classical music. Crank the heat up. Penny might think she dreamed the whole thing.* Just as she was about to test her theory, Penelope's phone rang. She turned to Scottie, silencing her with a finger across her lips.

"Penelope Casey speaking." She dug for her laptop. "Yes, Jackson. I am aware the contract was delivered. I have reviewed it, and it is on its way to Ashbridge." With the computer teetering on her knees, Penelope set her phone on the dashboard and put her earbuds in. Lucy took this opportunity to jump into the back seat. "I'm unclear as to why you are even checking on this. This is not your client." Though she spoke with confidence, her hands told the real story. Between her index and middle fingers, she twirled a pen back and forth. That Penelope did not retrieve her prized pup, who was making a nest on Burnie's tail, put an exclamation point on it.

She hammered the keyboard. "Jackson. I appreciate your advice. Truly, I do."

From the tone of her voice, Scottie doubted the veracity of that statement. The girl who had whisked them all away at the first sign of confrontation had become a woman standing tall.

"I'm sure it's being offered in a generous spirit with the intention of supporting a valued colleague. I cannot help but wonder, however, why you have time to worry about my client. Do you not have enough of your own? Perhaps you could ask the other associates, highlight your legal acumen, and your availability to assist them in their projects. No doubt you have thought of strategies to, what was it, oh yes, yield the best resolution for their clients. I am certain they will welcome your ideas. Just keep in mind, what goes around, comes around."

Scottie upgraded her estimation. She wasn't standing against it; she was inviting it.

Penelope fell silent. Her fingers froze above the keyboard. "Make no mistake, Jackson." The words came out cold and calm—not a hint of threat, just a foregone conclusion. "You will not like the outcome if you continue to interfere with my clients."

That, Scottie believed. Though she'd never met Jackson, she pitied his future as the focus of Penelope's rage. On the surface, she might be water like glass, but she was a fierce undertow beneath. Scottie knew all too well she would watch you drown.

Penelope disconnected the call and punched in another number. "Victoria." She paused. "Yes, he just called me." Her nails tattooed the keyboard. "I hope no one is close enough to hear you say that. True as it is." Scottie looked over. Files opened on the screen. "I have the documents saved on the server. Print them and courier them to the client this morning." Penelope let out a sigh of relief. "I should have known. I should have asked. I'm so sorry. You are the absolute best." Penelope searched her files. "Well, that's just going to make Jackson look like the weasel he is. OK. Keep me posted. We just crossed into Oregon and reception is going to be spotty. I'll check in as often as I can. Nine-one-one me if things go sideways." She hung up the phone.

"What was that all about?" Scottie asked.

"This colossal asshole thinks screwing with me will open up a partnership for him. He takes every chance to remind me my shelf life is running out. Dick." Penelope shoved her laptop into her bag.

Scottie laughed.

"It's not funny." She reached behind her and scooped up her sleeping dog.

"It's not. Sorry. It just didn't occur to me that you would have to put up with that crap at your level. You have an education. You're a successful lawyer. I guess I thought you'd be at this place where you belonged. You deserve to be there. Earned it. Does that make sense?"

"Yeah. It does. And no, I'm not. I'm not sure any woman is. I see how hard they all fight—the women, I mean. Proving themselves, their worth, every damn day." Penelope took out her earbuds. "It's exhausting." She tucked the dog next to her on the seat.

"I bet. It is for me, and my job is so much easier."

"How so?"

"Guys come in and assume Dad's in charge. It never occurs to them that I own an equal share of the kennel or that I have any education or experience to run it. They ask for him and treat me like I'm lucky I got a job walking their dogs." Her anger dampened by the shared injustice, the words, though resolute, came out fit for dinner guests.

"That's not what I mean," Penelope said.

Five small words and the anger thickened. *Of course not. Why would I think we're the same?* Scottie gripped the wheel. All the things she wanted to say flooded her clenched teeth. Penelope stopped her cold.

"How is your job easier than mine?" she asked.

"Easier? Come on, Penelope, you're a lawyer. You spent years in college. You do stuff that requires thinking and strategy. My job is not that tough compared to yours."

"Don't put yourself down," she scolded. After a pause, her words softened. "I see you too. You have a gift. You connect. Running a kennel, hell any business, takes a lot of knowledge. I might have more years in college, but you also have years of learning. I suspect you've been learning every day since you went to live with Dad at the kennel."

A single word wiped out the victory of her recognition. "Sent, you mean."

"What?" Penelope asked.

"Not went. Since I was sent to live with Dad at the kennel. You made it sound like I chose to go."

"You're reading too much into it."

Scottie had imagined the moment, when she finally mustered the courage to speak her truth, as a triumph. The idea that she was defective might wither. Yet, here was Penelope, dismissing it—dismissing her. As if the act that knocked her life off course had been a mere misunderstanding on her part.

Though her backbone weakened, she pressed on. "Mary sent me there, away from you and Molly."

"Mom wasn't trying to separate us."

Scottie's throat constricted. *What was the point of speaking the truth?* She turned on the radio, hoping a sad song would not come on to release the threatening tears. Scottie sensed Penelope silently looking at her, but she kept her eyes on the road. Surely she had been old enough to realize what was happening. She didn't blame her. Penelope was just a kid too, but she had to know the truth. Mary must have told her. Scottie hadn't chosen her dad.

She could still feel the cold cement of the carport through her jeans as she leaned against the boxes holding her clothes and the few toys deemed by her mother to be her own. She crammed her hands in the pockets of her down jacket and hugged her body. Drizzle fell. Quiet weather, she'd called it. She could have waited in the house, but she felt like a bug under glass there. No one spoke to her. Molly's eyes were red from crying, but she wouldn't look at her. Penelope had gone to her room as if nothing was happening.

She loved their dog more than any of them, but her mother said it belonged to the family. Scottie was no longer a part of that. So, she held Max tight to her belly and said goodbye. Her tears matted the Lhasa Apso's long fur. He licked them off her cheeks. Though fully grown, the dog was small enough to fit on Scottie's eight-year-old lap. She refused to wait in the house. She couldn't bear to look at her mother. Was Mary even her mother still? She had adopted her, but that was just a piece of paper. If you send your adopted daughter away, doesn't that mean you don't want her anymore?

The night before, she'd been hiding behind the kitchen wall beneath a bar stool. "I can't stand to look at her anymore! You need to come get this child." Scottie crumpled to the ground at the words and crawled past the door, back to her bedroom. She met her mother's eyes as she passed. For a moment, she stopped talking, and Scottie thought she would put the phone down, scoop her into her arms, and tell her she misunderstood. Instead, she turned her back and said, "Tomorrow morning, first thing, Hank. I mean it. Do not try to make this my fault."

The words echoed in her head all night. *I can't stand to look at her anymore. Do not try to make this my fault.* She'd hid beneath the covers, feigning sleep. Even through the pink chenille bedspread, she could hear her mother tiptoeing around the room, emptying her drawers. In the morning, boxes lined the carport. Her mother announced to the girls that Scottie was going to live with her dad. Penelope made breakfast, but no one ate. When the mush was cold and she was numb and empty inside, Scottie found a box and went to her room. She filled it with books.

Penelope hugged the casing of the door, hiding all but her face and hand. In a quiet voice, she said, "You can't take those. They belong to all of us."

"That means they belong to me too." Scottie stood, box in hand.

"You can use them when you visit."

"Why would I visit?" Scottie asked.

Molly slipped from behind Penelope. "To see us." She took the box from her arms and put it on the floor. Taking its place, she hugged Scottie and wiped away her tears.

Scottie left the half-filled box in front of the shelf and put on her coat to wait in the carport for her dad. She had some thinking to do. She had to figure out what she did wrong that made her mom hate her so much she had to get rid of her. She must not do whatever that was again or her dad would have to get rid of her too. And then where would she be? Even if she could find her real mom, she didn't want Scottie, either. In none of her dreams was her real mom looking for her. That was too much to even dream about.

I must be happy, and do my chores, and not contradict Dad. Scottie wasn't sure what that meant exactly, but she did it a lot, according to her parents. And it made them angry. *That's probably why Mom can't stand to look at me. And maybe, because I'm not pretty like Molly and Penelope, I'm hard to look at.* Scottie was short and chubby, and her hair was always full of leaves and dirt from playing in the yard. The ballet teacher said she was hopeless. Scottie couldn't be prettier, but she could be cleaner. *I must be careful not to get so dirty.* She wasn't even sure her dad knew how to wash clothes. Maybe she could learn.

She had nothing to lose now. Scottie turned down the radio. "I was listening the night she called Dad. I heard it all."

"Mom told me. Maybe you misunderstood what you heard."

"Well, enlighten me. How could I misunderstand 'Hank, I can't stand to look at this kid. Come get her.'?" Scottie glanced at Penelope who was staring out the window.

"It's not my story to tell."

Chapter Fourteen

Penelope

THE WORDS STEPPED off her tongue. She'd practiced them a million times, anticipating this moment. *It's not my story to tell.* They didn't blanket her in satisfaction, though, the way they had in her adolescent fantasies.

Of course, back then, she hadn't yet been skewered by the realization that her own secrets were the cautionary tales told in coffee shops and wine bars by people who could have reached out to help her. Penelope was on the delivery end of that stabbing pain now and she finally understood those friends.

Victoria's ringtone interrupted her thoughts. Much like Victoria, it was subtle, but impossible to ignore. "Hello." She woke up her computer.

"I confirmed receipt of the contract. I told them to call me directly if they had any questions or concerns and I would put them in contact with you immediately," Victoria said. "I'm currently praying that, when they call, you will not be passing through some mountain village with only rudimentary amenities but well-developed fears of cancer and governmental monitoring from cell towers. I need you to check in every time you come back into range."

"Will do. And thank you. Is Jackson still spinning?"

"He's certainly getting his steps in today. I'll poke around at lunch and see what he's up to. Are you sure you don't want me to notify someone you're out today?"

"No need. I'll be back by Monday. I can work on the road. It's a down and back trip. I should be home tomorrow night, and I can work all day Sunday while Molly settles in. Could you do me a huge favor?"

"You don't need to ask that. Of course I will," Victoria said.

"I hate to ask you to do personal things for me. It makes me feel like a misogynistic ad exec from the fifties. I'm in a bind, though. Would you order some groceries for delivery? Scratch that. I don't cook. Can you order a meal delivery service, but from a healthy company? I don't have a name, so you'll have to do some research. Go ahead and put me on a schedule for two people for dinner and one person for breakfast and lunch. You know what I don't eat. Molly will eat anything. Maybe avoid spicy stuff since she doesn't feel good. Only order for a week, though—you know, in case it's awful." *Uncertainty is the crack that lets hopelessness in. I will not be hopeless.* "I have no idea how these things work. I assume we can continue or cancel."

"Don't worry. I'll handle it. Healthy food, not spicy, cooking skills zero. Got it."

"Cute. But seriously, thanks for taking care of that for me," Penelope said.

"Do you need anything else? Do you even have a guest room?"

"Yes. It's all set up. Never been used, actually."

"We need to talk about that later."

"We do not."

"OK. Signing off. Try not to worry. I know you will, but I have it handled here."

Penelope made a mental note to increase Victoria's Christmas bonus. She always took care of her—no judgment of her competence or will. Though an uncomfortable experience at first, once she accepted it as genuine and not transactional, she leaned in. Still, like wearing a warm sweater that belonged to someone else, the threat that you would have to give it up, and be left colder than ever, loomed.

"You're kind of making an assumption there," Scottie said. "Why is Molly staying with you and not me?"

"Think about it. I'm in the city. The best hospitals are right there. I have the means to support her." *Could you drop the chip on your shoulder just one time and think of someone else?*

"You have the means? We're not exactly paupers, Penelope. We make a good living running the kennel. People drive long distances to leave their very expensive dogs with us."

"I'm not saying you're poor. I'm just saying it's closer to treatment. I have space. I have a car service. It makes sense she would stay with me."

"Hardly. I can be flexible in my work. I can take her into Seattle for treatment. Every day, if I have to. Besides, she shouldn't have to go through this alone. Are you going to pay some driver, a stranger, to sit with her during chemo? Take notes for her when she talks to doctors? Make appointments for her? You work twenty-four seven."

"I can work from home." Penelope said it with resolve, though she was not at all confident the partners would allow it.

"You can't even work from this vehicle."

It was a slap in the face which Penelope returned without hesitation.

"I think Molly would be more comfortable with me."

"What the hell does that mean? Molly is plenty comfortable with me."

"I don't mean you."

"Well, then. You don't know much. Just forget it. Molly is the one who should be deciding, anyway."

Arguing was pointless. Penelope put her earbuds in and slid her computer into the bag at her feet. Lucy scrambled onto her lap, and she cradled the pup in her arms. It was selfish, but she hoped Molly would see it her way. She missed being needed, being important to someone else. When Michael passed, she told herself she'd had her fill of serving everyone else's needs. It was her turn. She'd packed her calendar with her career. Now, she felt incomplete.

Molly didn't need her much anymore. Her mom was gone, which left a crater in the need department. Her need made Penelope feel special at first, but it acclimated to a dependency that distanced her from her sisters and her dad. It forced her to assume burdens not hers to own. When Mary needed validation, she would turn to Penelope and say, *It wasn't my fault. I tried to love her. I did. I'm a good mom.* Penelope would reassure her. She'd never told her mother she knew the truth about Scottie.

The day Scottie's mom came to the door to take her back, they were playing in the living room. When the pounding on the front door began, her mom quieted them. Penelope took her sisters' hands as her mother peeked through a slit in the drapes. Mary took a step back and froze.

"Mom?" Penelope asked.

Taking her shoulders in her hands, Mary leaned over until they were eye to eye.

"Take Molly and Scottie to my room and shut the door tight. Stay there until I come get you." Mary released Penelope, but grabbed her wrist as she turned to walk away. "What do you do in an emergency?"

"Call nine-one-one."

"Right. Go!" Mary pushed her away.

Penelope pulled the girls down the hall and put them on her mother's bed. They stared at her wide-eyed and pleading. She put their hands together.

"Stay here. It'll be OK." She slipped the door open and slid through. Holding her breath, she hugged the wall. When she heard the front door open, Penelope scurried to the end of the hall and peeked around the corner. A woman stood just outside the doorway yelling at her mother, who gripped the knob like she might slam it at any moment.

"Where is she?" the woman demanded.

"Who?"

"You know damn well who. Lily."

"Her name is Scarlett." Her mother's composure only seemed to fuel the woman's fury.

"Maybe now. But it won't be tomorrow."

"You're not taking my child." Her mother let go of the handle and slowly crossed her arms.

"She's my child. I consulted a lawyer, and he said I can get her back."

"Well, I hope you have a lot of money because I'll be getting a lawyer too. That lawyer will make sure my child is safe from you. The world will know you dumped your child on our doorstep and walked away."

"Try it. That's not the whole truth, is it? It would be pretty embarrassing for the world to know who Lily's father is. I bet he still hasn't claimed her."

"You wouldn't dare. Everyone will see you for what you are. Although I doubt the crowd of tramps you run with would disapprove. What is it you really want? Clearly, you don't want to raise your kid."

"What are you offering?"

"I see. OK." Her mother shut the door and went to the kitchen. She came back with her checkbook. Leaning against the door, she scribbled on the paper and ripped it from the pad. When she opened the door again, the woman was still there. Her mother held the check in front of her face. When the woman reached for it, she pulled it back.

"This is all you are going to get from us. Now or ever." Her mother pulled a piece of paper from her pocket and handed it to the woman with her pen. "Write that you give up all of your rights to Scarlett and sign and date it."

"Learned a few tricks from your daddy, huh?"

The woman held the paper against the door and scratched the words out. She tossed the paper at her mother.

"Pick it up," her mother said in a tone that sent shivers down Penelope's spine. She meant business.

A smile crossed the woman's face, and she said, "Pick it up yourself."

"Pick it up or I'll rip up the check. Try me."

Her mother's words wiped the smile right off the woman's face. She leaned over and snatched the page off the stoop. She shook it at her mother, who leaned back just a hair, cocked her hip, and crossed her arms. Penelope knew this move. Her mother'd had enough. The woman must have known that too. The shaking stopped. Her mom took the piece of paper and handed the woman a check in return.

"Don't come back. You'll be sorry if you do. I'm not going to let you hurt my husband or my child."

With that, her mother slammed the door. The force of it shook the plate-glass window. Penelope had never seen her so angry, but what came next was far scarier. Her mother sank to the floor and sobbed. She wanted to hug her and ask her what was happening. She had so many questions. Penelope took a step and bumped into the fireplace tools.

Her mother did not look up. "Go back to my room with your sisters. Do not say one word about this to anyone. Do you hear me, Penelope? No one. Not to your sisters. Not your father. No one."

Penelope ran to her bedroom and shut the door. Something aged in her, and she knew then she was not one of the little kids anymore. She'd never shared a secret with her mother. This secret, like a gigantic piece of birthday cake, made her feel special and sick all at the same time. She looked around the room at her dolls and stuffed animals. They seemed so childish now. She picked up Elizabeth in her pajamas and Teddy with his bow tie and took them to her mother's room.

"Where did you go?" Molly asked, wiping away her tears.

"I went to get you something to play with until Mom is done talking to her friend." She handed Molly the doll and Scarlett the teddy bear. With a look of suspicion, they took them in their arms. "You can have those. I mean it."

"Don't you want them anymore?" Molly asked.

"No." Penelope couldn't find a way to tell them what was happening inside her. They were too little to understand. Penelope was special now, and she didn't even have to be perfect to earn it.

Her mom burst through the door. She'd wiped the stream of mascara from her eyes and freshened her lipstick. "Hey, girls. What do you say we go see Grandma and Grandpa? I bet Grandpa has some special treats for you." She put an arm around Penelope's shoulder and pulled her in. "Grab your coats, girls."

Penelope heard her father's car. "Daddy's home!" She rounded up her sisters. They stopped on the way to hug their daddy and tell him where they were going.

She looked to her mother. "Can he come with us?"

Her mother reached down and stroked her hair. "Not tonight, Penelope. I'm sure he has work to do. Take your sisters to the car."

Penelope told him she understood he had to work. She didn't, really. But that was what adults said. I understand you have to. And she was getting older. She would have to learn to understand. Though her father looked confused, he did not answer.

As Penelope walked away, her mother said, "Well, she's the spitting image of her mother. I suppose I should say that's lucky for us. The truth is it's really only lucky for you."

As she buckled her sisters into their seat belts, Penelope looked at Scottie and wondered what luck had to do with any of it. She did know that somehow Scottie was the reason her father was standing on the stoop watching her mother walk away.

Maybe it was her story to tell.

Chapter Fifteen

Molly

Scottie: I'm saying this in the spirit of honesty to save our relationship. Do not ask me to do this again. I'm never getting in a car with Princess Penny again. Ever. NOT LOL. Never.

Molly: LOL

Scottie: Not LOL. We've run out of safe things to talk about. Thank God we're almost through Oregon.

Molly tapped the phone on her chin. *On the upside, they're talking.* She'd been picturing them in stony silence, staring straight ahead as miles of verdant forests faded unnoticed into rocky crags.

Molly: What have you covered?

Scottie: Religion music parents work money

Molly: OK, well, that's five things. You still have art, dance, sports, politics, every guy you've ever dated, TV shows, movies, the weather, astronomy, the rising cost of land.

Crime podcasts. Lots of stuff. Get creative. AND FYI you picked the five worst topics.

Scottie: Didn't pick them

Molly: She did?

Scottie: No. They just came up.

Molly: Religion just came up? Why would religion just come up? Like, hey Penelope, do you practice a religion? Or hey Scottie, are you still Catholic?

Scottie: No, we got to talking about sin.

Molly closed her eyes and prayed for a sliver of that stony silence to descend on them. Not thirteen hours of it but enough to make them forget sin was on the discussion table.

Molly: Sin. Really? Have. You. Lost. Your. Mind. You don't bring up sin. With anyone.

Scottie: Yeah, I get it. I'm weird and awkward. You don't have to say it.

Molly: No, you are not. But sin. Really?

Scottie: It's fine. Never mind. Are you OK?

Molly: I'm fine. Where are you?

Scottie: Stopped outside Lakeview so PP could get cell service and call the mothership. She is not happy with my trip planning.

Molly: Stop it. She has a big job. She needs to be connected.

Scottie: So I've been told. Repeatedly!

Molly: Cut her some slack. You take things too personally.

Scottie: Sure.

Molly: Sure as in I will or as in I'm mad at you for asking because I think you are taking her side?

Scottie: Yes.

Molly: I'm not taking sides.

Scottie: GTG

Molly lifted the covers off. Sometime during the day, her chills had turned to fever. The damp bedsheets leached what little body heat she had. Pulling the comforter from her bed, she wrapped herself in the pillows of down. The weight of the fabric across her shoulders, enveloping her body, transported her back to bath nights before stony silence had become the soundtrack of the trio.

Mary would hold out a towel three times Molly's size and catch her as she left the bath. She'd giggle as her mother twirled her around, cocooning her in the thick terry cloth. On the last pass, she would wrap her in a hug and kiss her forehead. Lifting her off the linoleum floor, she'd set her on the bathmat and repeated the exercise until all three girls stood shoulder to shoulder on the shaggy piece of carpet. By the time Mary wrapped up Scottie, Penelope and Molly would be laughing. Wiggle worms, Mary would call them as they hip-checked each other. She slipped matching flannel nightgowns over their upstretched arms and brushed their hair flat.

It occurred to Molly, now, that there was a time when they were all her mother's girls. She tried to remember when that had ended. When had their mother turned on Scottie? Molly had been old enough to remember, surely. But when she searched the flashes of her childhood and the echoes of Penelope's retelling, the runway was missing. Scottie was one of them one day and leaving them the next.

Molly padded to the bathroom and turned the shower on.

Her legs shook, though she'd only gone a few yards. So, she sat on the edge of the tub to wait. As steam filled the space, she tried to stand. In the end, she snaked a hand from beneath the warm cover and pressed it onto the cold tile. Her first attempt failed, not because she could not muster the energy to force her body upward, but because she didn't have the energy to hold back the wave of sadness for the loss of independence it promised. She sank back to the tub and let the tears flow. She needed to get every last one of them out before Scottie and Penelope arrived. It was a delicate balance—enough need and sorrow to motivate them to work together but not so much as to distract them from healing the brokenness between them. She would have to bear the bulk of her own pain to make space for them to share theirs.

As sobs turned to sniffles, she pushed off again. Inside the shower, she let the steam wrap around her body. The hot spray pelted her skin until she was numb. The humid air felt thick in her lungs. It reminded her of when she would take a hot shower after a day of skiing. Though her muscles were spent, and her bones were chilled, she always wanted one more run. Afterward, she would stand beneath the hot stream and let it seep into her pores and fill her up. Her skin tingled as her body temperature rose. When she was done, if she came home alone, she would fall on the bed and wrap herself in the covers.

If she met someone, she might spend the night with them. It never amounted to anything long term. It couldn't. They would eventually tire of sharing only half her life. Her mother made her views known, and they were the direct result of her grandfather's influence. His views on sexuality aligned with his fire-breathing pastor. She wasn't close enough to her own dad to talk to him about it. It was sex, after all, and he was Catholic. Molly wasn't entirely sure her sisters would not align with the parent who raised them. She didn't want to be different from the other girls, but she was. She wasn't ashamed. She just didn't have it in her to defend herself. Maybe defend was too strong a word. But Penelope and Scottie didn't have to explain their relationships. Why should she?

Her legs shook from the exertion of holding herself up. Though she would love to stay there all day absorbing the heat, she was afraid she might buckle. With her luck, she would land on the drain cover and her scrawny butt would seal it off. The water would rise, not enough to mercifully drown her, but enough to overflow the short lip of the cubicle. It would flow into her apartment and seep into the one below which was inhabited by one of those women who was always cheerful. So cheerful, in fact, that you knew it was a kind of armor—not the kind that protects the wearer from the penetration of emotional arrows but the kind that can withstand the mounting pressure of a whole lot of unprocessed rage and disappointment. A deluge of water coming through her ceiling might just crack that armor. Cheerful Cathy would turn into Homicidal Helen, march up the stairs in her unscuffed Manolos, and break the door down in a decidedly unladylike manner. Molly figured she would be discovered naked and barely conscious, precipitating a 911 call that would no doubt be answered by a gorgeous firefighter with whom she might have had a long and meaningful weekend had her hero not met Molly in a state of sopping decay.

She turned off the water and patted her skin dry with a gentleness she had once reserved for lovers. She'd always been in a hurry. Rub the water off, throw on some clothes, and dash out the door with one hand in her coat, the other searching her pockets for keys. She was careless with everyone and everything—well, nearly. With the exception of Angie and Mateo and her car, she treated the rest like recycling. The product inside was useful, and the packaging was enduring, but she passed it along to be repurposed.

It wasn't that she lacked appreciation. She just took it as

inevitable that people would move on, and things would eventually go out of style or break. So, while she enjoyed them, she never invested. Molly compacted the grief of loss with the weight of forced acceptance. Even Penelope and Scottie occupied a finite place in her life. It wasn't until her life actually became finite that she realized they occupied an infinite place in her heart, and they had no idea. She'd never been truly honest. Not about how she felt. Not about who she was. Not about what she needed. She'd never grieved the repeated loss of them.

Molly pulled on a pair of sweatpants and a long-sleeved T-shirt, hoping they were bulky enough to obscure the protrusions that were emerging as her flesh receded where her legs and arms met her torso. In the few hours she had left before Hurricane Penelope and Scottie Glacier arrived, she wanted to go back to bed. She could just see Penelope's face if she showed up to the door with bed head, no makeup, and wrinkled clothes. Penelope would transform into Sister Mary Francis Battle Axe and take charge of the situation.

Molly had always been powerless over that. She could not take any more powerlessness. The only way to combat Penelope's well-orchestrated campaign to heal Molly would be to fix her hair, put on some makeup, and bury her pain in the deepest pit of her being.

Scottie was a completely different problem. She was slow but relentless. She would sit back and let Penelope peck away at her resolve. All the while, Scottie would advance, wearing away at her rough edges, sweeping her up with the rest of the debris, until she could do nothing but agree to move forward. Lipstick would be a must. Lipstick says you have your shit together and you're not taking any crap from anyone. Finding the one tube of lipstick she owned might be a trick, though.

Molly had emptied the bathroom drawers, putting equal parts into the garbage and her travel kit. The makeup kit was just for show. That would be the kind of thing Scottie would notice. Penelope would write it off as Molly's lackluster attention to her appearance. Scottie would see it as defeat. Sweats, no makeup, ponytail. That was the trifecta, signaling an impending showerless weekend in her granny pajamas, curled up with Ben and Jerry, *Boys on the Side*, and a case of Kleenex. She dumped her cosmetic bag on the bed. The cap had come off her eyeliner, and it left a dark brown streak across the bed when she sorted through the various tubes and jars. She scooped them up and placed them in the sink. She had nothing to clean the sheet with. Though it hardly mattered, she started to cry.

"Fuck. Fuck. Fuck. Why are you crying about some goddamned sheet? Pull it together, Molly." She stormed into the kitchen where she'd set the garbage bag. Something about being terminal made her able to stomach things she never could before. Yanking the bag open, she shoved her hand into the mess and felt around. It was shocking how many of her completely essential belongings she had just tossed in the trash. No one would care about them but her. Half-used or dented, no one wanted hand-me-downs. That was what all of this was. They certainly weren't heirlooms. Her fingers slid over the cylinder, and she pulled it out. Half-used—but plenty for the short time she would have to wear it. Two days. They wouldn't be happy, but that was what she needed. Two days.

Chapter Sixteen

Scottie

SCOTTIE'S PRAYERS WERE answered when they passed a state trooper outside of Hermiston. It would be miles before they saw another one on a two-lane state highway. She rarely sped, but desperate times called for desperate measures. Penelope made her pull over in every town along the way so she could try to connect to a cell tower. In between, Scottie put the pedal down. By the time they rolled into John Day, Penelope was fit to be tied. Her laptop was still loading when her phone connected and began chirping like a flock of seagulls over the lunch crowd at Jim's Fish Basket.

Scottie pulled into the first diner she saw and took the dogs out to pee. Penelope had an uninviting look on her face, so she didn't bother asking for permission. Lucy was happy to tag along. A block down the street, cement turned to lawn. A guidepost announced the Kam Wah Chung State Heritage site.

"This is not a dog park. You can pee, but please do not embarrass me by pooping here. This place is old, and important stuff must have happened here." The dogs stood, staring up at her, tails wagging. "I get it. A dog's gotta do what a dog's gotta do." She checked her pocket to confirm she had bags.

"We have three more tours today. But we don't allow dogs in the building, I'm afraid."

Scottie looked up to find an older gentleman approaching. He held his hand out, palm down. After Burnie sniffed it, he bent to let Lucy do the same.

"Beautiful dogs. Such a difference in size, though. I have a small dog, like this one." He scratched behind Lucy's ears. "Do they play well together?"

"They just met, actually. The small one belongs to my sister."

"And they just met? Did she adopt?"

"No. She got Lucy as a puppy. We just don't see much of her."

The man frowned. His face was gentle, though, and the frown seemed born of his own regret rather than a commentary on her familial relationships. Still, Scottie felt a twinge of shame at the admission.

"We have tours starting every hour or so. Perhaps your sister could join you."

"I would love to take a tour. I have to check with her, though. We're in a bit of a hurry." Scottie surveyed the wooden structure capping the stone foundation. "I'd never heard of this place. It's hard to imagine eastern medicine in Oregon a hundred and fifty years ago." Scottie's hand went to her hip. She reached her fingers backward to knead the edge of her spine. The pressure felt good. Was there anything here that could take away her pain? She'd considered acupuncture. Penny would never understand it, but she would consult a Ouija board if there was a chance it would relieve her pain. As long as it wasn't a narcotic or opiate, she would try it.

The man smiled at her as though he knew what she was thinking. "Well, I hope to see you again later, then. In either case, safe travels."

Penelope was still on the phone when Scottie returned to the vehicle. She pressed her index finger across her lips to silence her. Five-year-old Scottie wanted to bite Penelope's finger. Forty-two-year-old Scottie knew it would be wrong. She dug for a piece of paper, settling for an old gas receipt, on which she wrote "Starving. Must eat. Meet you inside. Roll the windows down some and lock the doors when you come." Penelope nodded several times, though Scottie wasn't sure they were for her.

She reached over and took her wallet from the glove box.

"Try it," Penelope said. "You've left out some key facts. I'm sure you don't want that getting out."

Her words made Scottie's stomach drop. Though no one would know it, conflict made her nauseous. On the outside, her face went blank, and she centered her body ever so slightly on the balls of her feet. Ready to run. She had perfected looking straight ahead but seeing everything in her peripheral vision. Scottie knew where the exits were at all times. She cataloged danger by its position and speed.

She made her way to the restaurant. As the waitress passed with a tray of burgers and fries, she told Scottie to grab any table. She took a menu off the counter and sat at the first booth she came to. From her vantage point, she could see Penelope in the SUV still talking on the phone. She saw no evidence of flying fur or upholstery stuffing, so she thought it safe to relax for a moment.

The waitress stopped by the empty bench. "Are you waiting for someone?"

"Always, it seems." She took a sip of water. "I'm sorry. Yes, my sister. Maybe."

"I can come back."

"No. I'll probably order something to go for her." She scanned the menu. "How are the burgers?"

"Best burgers in a couple hundred miles."

"Aren't they the only burgers in a couple hundred miles?" The waitress gave Scottie a smile and a wink. "Sure are."

"Well, OK then. I'll have a bacon burger, well done, with fries. I'll text her and figure out what she wants. Thanks." She handed the woman her menu.

Scottie pulled her phone from her pocket and touched the screen to turn it on. Nothing happened. *Great, dead.* With her luck, her father and Meaghan were locked in a debate that probably started like *Face the Nation* but was devolving into the presidential primaries. They were so alike and couldn't see it. Scottie closed her eyes and shook her head. The possibilities were endless. It could be about boys who got gauges in their ears. Meaghan thought it a courageous expression of self-concept. More practical by nature, her dad thought it the pinnacle of foolishness which the bearer of the adornment would regret when his ears sagged and the extra skin, now too weak to hold the appliance, would have to be lopped off.

Or perhaps they were arguing about social justice. Her father believed in society's responsibility for vulnerable people. He believed in justice. He did not trust the term social justice, as he suspected it to be liberal code for something entirely different. The fact that he did not know what, though, did not deter him from arguing his position. Meaghan, in contrast, thought old white men resisted the term because it confronted their belief they got everything solely on merit instead of from the astronomical boost of privilege.

Meaghan wouldn't dare question his stance on women's rights. He had a spotless record on that count. *Hank Casey is raising a capable, independent woman.* She could still hear him proclaim it in the third person. There were days when Scottie would have liked a tiny morsel of the *women shouldn't be doing that* ethos, but only when it came to chopping wood, digging ditches, and roofing. In her younger days, she'd played right into his hand when she defiantly took up the ax and said she could damn well chop wood as well as any man, including him. To which he replied, *Prove it*. Meaghan was a smarter version of her mother and instead said she could damn well do it but had no desire and so would not be proving anything. He would have to take her word for it. She couldn't be prodded into hubris.

The dead phone was out of her control. *Accept the things you cannot change.* Her father had said the words a million times. In her head, they seemed right. She would nod in agreement every time. In her body, though, acceptance felt like defeat. Just a hint of powerlessness made her itch. Though she never made the argument to him, she wondered how you would know something couldn't be changed if you didn't first refuse to accept it. Acceptance had not braced her legs or forced them forward. Defiance did.

Still, she didn't bother to hit the ON button again. Dead batteries did not respond to will. She would need to wrestle the charger from Penelope when she got back to the car. She was surprised she hadn't killed the car battery by now. That would be the icing on the cake. Stuck in the middle of nowhere with Penelope jonesing for an email fix as they waited on the side of the road, praying the two guys who stopped in a rusted-out pickup truck weren't amassing middle-aged women in a remote cabin to reenact their pioneer times fantasies. Penelope's rapier tongue would be useless against men of that ilk. She made a mental note to unlock the gun compartment in the console before they headed out for the next unpopulated stretch. Scottie had no intention of growing her hair out, wearing potato sack dresses, and calling Clem and Earl "Father and Master."

Her food arrived, shaking her from the nightmares that were her imagination. Scottie glanced through the window. In the front seat of the Suburban, Penelope gesticulated wildly, which she took as evidence she was not wrapping up the call and coming for lunch anytime soon.

"Do you have some kind of salad I could get to go for my sister?" she asked the waitress.

"Sure. We have a Cobb salad and a Caesar with chicken."

"I bet she's a chicken Caesar person."

"You don't know?"

"Nope." Scottie gave her an unapologetic shrug, then picked up her fork.

"Huh. Well, chicken Caesar it is, then." The waitress seemed more curious than judgmental, though it wouldn't have mattered. Scottie didn't have the bandwidth to contemplate the judgment of waitresses. That was all taken up by Penelope and her father. Ironic that two such different people, who did not even like each other, would have the same stifling effect on her.

As only back-road diners can do, the burger was perfectly made. A thick patty snuck out just beyond the bun. The bread was substantial, but it didn't overshadow the other elements. Crisp lettuce, beefsteak tomato slices, dill pickle sliced longwise, and ribbons of red onion. The condiments were on the side, which Scottie appreciated, since the amount and combination were highly personal. She was a bit of a burger snob.

When she'd first moved in with her dad, it was the only thing he knew how to cook. Being in charge of the backyard grill in the summer, as her mother was afraid of cooking with fire, he'd taken his responsibility seriously. His domain mushroomed from the ten-square-foot corner of the patio, on which his Weber sat, to the kitchen where he mixed garlic, salt, pepper, onion powder, and paprika into the ground beef. Her mother had always complained about the size of the patties. He'd argued that the meat shrunk. In time, he took to buying it at the meat market on his way home from work on Fridays to solve the shrinkage issue.

When he found himself a single father, he asked for the Weber and, in a moment of uncharacteristic charity, her mother gave it to him. He expanded his repertoire to other meats and added vegetables when he realized that a steady diet of oatmeal, peanut butter and jelly sandwiches, and cheeseburgers might stunt Scottie's growth. She loved his burgers best, though. Her father knew it. When they couldn't talk about something easily, he would make them special for her. Burgers became the salve for broken hearts and disappointments and the celebratory entrée for birthdays and first-place ribbons. Scottie knew they weren't healthy connections, burgers and sadness or burgers and joy, but she didn't want to break the bond.

The salad came in a cardboard container. Two small cups of dressing sat on top.

"Thanks for putting the dressing on the side. I should have asked for it."

"I suspected." The waitress grinned through pursed lips like they were sharing a secret only younger sisters knew. "I put a plastic fork and a napkin in there too. I could throw in a roll if you like."

"Nah, I doubt she's eaten bread since she was ten." Scottie paid and took the bag to the truck. She tried to hand the food to Penelope, but she just pointed to the dashboard and kept talking. Scottie reached over the seat to put the food in back.

Penelope covered the phone with her palm. "What are you doing? The dogs will get into it."

"Mine won't."

Penelope rolled her eyes. She took the bag from her and set it on the floor at her feet.

"We need to get going," Scottie whispered.

Hold on, Penelope mouthed in response.

Scottie put the truck in drive, and Penelope slapped her arm. She stepped on the brake and Penelope lurched forward.

"What? I need to get gas."

Penelope twirled her finger as if to say, *Get on with it*. Scottie tensed. Turning her face to the side mirror to look for traffic, she said, "I don't need your permission." As she pulled onto the road, she glanced at Penelope and twirled her finger. "I need to charge my phone. You're gonna have to disconnect or operate on your battery."

"Look, Victoria, I need to go. We're leaving town soon. I'll be out of range for a while. From the looks of it, until we get to California."

◈

Scottie opened her door and headed for the gas cap. "Dammit!" she said.

"You're being ridiculous. I was trying to get some work done. So, you had to eat lunch alone. Big deal."

"What are you even talking about?" Scottie put her hands on her hips and tipped her head to the sky.

"Why are you cussing at me?" Penelope asked.

She pointed to the rear tire where a nail protruded. "We're about to have a flat tire."

"Great. Where are you going to get a tire in this Podunk town?"

"I'm not gonna get a tire. I'm going to change my tire and find a shop that can get this nail out and fix it. You really are a city girl." Imagining Penelope parked on the bumper googling *How do you change a tire,* she laughed.

"Don't laugh at me. I could change a tire if I had to. I just don't want to."

"Sure you can, Princess Penny."

"Don't call me that." Penelope's brows knitted together, and a scowl crossed her face. "Where do you get off calling me that? You don't know the first thing about me, and I sure as hell have not lived the life of a princess. Quit being a martyr. You might check your assumptions before you call people names."

With that, she opened the rear door and grabbed her dog. She carried Lucy in her arms until she reached a strip of grass, then she led her down the street. Scottie watched her brush off a bench and sit down. The dog jumped up and crawled into her lap. She held Lucy to her chest and buried her face in the dog's fur.

Scottie was ashamed. She'd done the same thing to Penelope that she'd accused her of. What did she really know about her? It had been years since they spent any time together, and never alone. Molly was always there, like a hinge between them—connected but never making contact. What did she even know? Penelope was a lawyer. She had been married once, but the man died young. Of what, Scottie never heard. Penelope was close to her mother but not to her father. She was a stylish dresser who had a nice car and a sweet pup. Other than that, she was a mystery.

Molly rarely talked about her. Scottie appreciated that because she hated the thought of Molly talking about her to Penelope. If she was honest, the stories she told herself about Penelope were fabricated from the threads of old wounds and incomplete memories. In them, she was always the antagonist. She looked down the street to the woman cradling her pup. She didn't look like much of a villain. Maybe it was time to admit they shared the role.

Unfortunately, the tire came first. Scottie went into the office and paid for her gas. The attendant, an older man in coveralls, sat half propped on a stool, one leg braced against the floor. She told him about the spike in her tire and asked where she could change it. Under the guise of limiting his liability and speeding up her exit from the pumps, he offered to help, but she declined. He insisted on loaning her his shop lift. Scottie got the impression he wasn't comfortable having a woman changing a tire while he stood by and watched. To smooth things over, she asked if he could patch the hole.

Scottie lifted the rear door and took out her utility blanket and the tire iron. She laid the blanket on the ground. Holding on to the bumper, she eased herself to her knees. She lowered the spare from beneath the frame. When it hit the ground, she grabbed hold of the tow hitch and lay on the pavement to disconnect the tire. She was grateful the serviceman had not seen her lever herself to standing like a ninety-year-old woman. She didn't need the pitying eyes of a man twice her age and four times as spry.

He arrived with his jack, and she removed the damaged tire in record time. While she attached the spare and put her gear away, he removed the nail and patched the tire. He refused her money at first, but she insisted.

"I would still be trying to lift that beast up with my tiny jack if you hadn't loaned me yours. Paying for the repair is the least I can do. Believe me, you deserve more."

He looked like he might blush at her thanks. In the end, he took the money and shook her hand.

"You're wrong, you know. I've been doing this a long time. You didn't need my help."

She did blush at his words. "All the same, I'm glad I had it." It was strange to accept help and feel undiminished.

※

Scottie stared at the figure still perched on the bench. Apologies were not her strong suit. In her defense, she hadn't received many. Saying I'm sorry was so easy. Making it right was so hard. Her dad was big on that. *Don't tell me you're sorry. Show me you are.* Only she was never sure what proof he needed. What the upper limit was. She could do penance for days and not know exactly when she'd been forgiven.

Scottie pulled up next to the bench and parked. She slid down from the cab.

"Come on, Burnie. Let's go make peace." He jumped into the

driver's seat and hopped to the ground. Oblivious to her mood, he enthusiastically headed for the nearest bush. Lucy followed suit, yanking Penelope from her seat.

"Damn dog."

"Yours or mine?" Scottie asked.

"Mine. Yours just had to pee. Mine did not want to be left behind."

"I can relate." Scottie called Burnie back to her. "Look. I'm sorry. I shouldn't call you princess. It's mean and unfair. I won't do it again."

"Thanks." Penelope reached down and took hold of Lucy's lead. "Sit. Stay." Lucy did neither.

"And you're right. I don't know what your life's been like. I've made assumptions. I shouldn't do that. But neither should you. You don't know what I've been through, either. And even though we were in the same house, you can't know what it was like for me to be the hand-me-down child."

"No. I can't. That's true. But just remember I was there. I was older. I saw things you didn't see. I heard things you didn't hear. You can believe me when I say Mom loved you. And before you remind me she sent you away, I just want to say it wasn't any easier on her."

Scottie was poised to refute her claim, but the faintest echo of truth followed the words. Though she wanted Penelope to understand her, she was just weary enough of the fight to hold on to the possibility her version wasn't the whole story.

Penelope stood. She put her hand out. "You've been driving a long time. You must be getting tired. Why don't you let me drive the rest of the way?"

"Don't you have to work?" Scottie asked.

"I can check in when we stop. The reception is terrible out here. Give me the keys."

Scottie realized how tired she was. Her neck and back were in knots. She handed Penelope the keys.

Chapter Seventeen

Penelope

Scottie kicked off her boots and leaned her seat back. She and Penelope were like a child running after a receding ocean wave, only to retreat as it returned to chase her back up the beach. She wasn't sure who was the child and who was the tide. They were always out of sync, one advancing, one withdrawing.

"You can put my bag in the back to give you more room," Penelope offered.

"It's fine."

She bent over, one hand on the wheel and one eye on the road. She grabbed the bag and set it on the floor behind Scottie's seat.

"Thanks." Scottie wedged her feet against the dash and pushed herself backward. She turned away from Penelope, rolled her jacket, and placed it between her knees. Burnie stood, taking up much of the rearview mirror. Penelope feared he might jump into the front seat. Lucy would have. Instead, he lumbered over to where Scottie's head lay on her hands and rested his chin on the edge of her seat.

Penelope could hear him sniffing her. The tenderness of the moment tugged at her belly. It reminded her of how Lucy seemed to sense her sadness before the first tear formed. She would attach herself to Penelope, following her around the house, as if she might edge out the sorrow.

Burnie reclined, staring at Scottie. After a time, she reached her hand back and scratched his head. "I'm OK, big guy. You can relax."

Penelope wrestled off her sweater and handed it to Scottie.

"For your neck."

Scottie lifted her head and angled it toward her. While only part of one eye and a corner of her mouth were visible, Penelope got the impression she was in pain.

"Thanks," Scottie said. She rolled it up and placed it under her neck. Before long, she fell asleep.

Penelope stopped for gas in Burns and checked the map for the cutoff to Highway 395. Scottie woke up briefly and offered to pay, but Penelope had taken care of it. By the time she remembered her salad, she figured it was a breeding ground for salmonella. She tossed it at the gas station and grabbed a bag of white cheddar popcorn. Not her usual fare; she felt decadent eating it.

Penelope had been a dancer into her twenties, and the list of approved snacks did not include popcorn covered in cheddar powder, no doubt created in a chemistry lab. Actually, there were no approved snacks. By middle school, she subsisted on a steady diet of black coffee and scrambled egg whites for breakfast, and a skinless chicken breast and steamed vegetables for dinner. On special occasions when money allowed, her mother made salmon.

Until high school, when Penelope eschewed even carrot sticks for their high carb count, her mother packed her lunch. Diet soda sustained her through the day. Her mother couldn't object since Penelope learned how to eat by watching her. Her mother had her weaknesses, though. She loved heavy cream on sugary breakfast cereal. Penelope knew when her mother was having a hard day because that was what she would eat for dinner while standing over the stove tending to the broccoli and cauliflower.

Penelope had her dalliances too. Oreos beckoned her. She still hid them behind the whole wheat pasta in the cupboard, though she was only hiding them from herself. Absence made the lie less painful.

She envied Scottie, who didn't seem to have any hang-ups about her body or what she ate. It made sense. She had been raised by a man, after all. Men didn't seem to worry about what they ate or looked like. Penelope'd seen plenty of rotund men with young, slender wives. Maybe Scottie just didn't know she was supposed to be self-conscious about every bite that passed her lips. Maybe she didn't know her ass would spread and her breasts would droop. Penelope bet she saved a fortune not chasing the latest anti-aging, anti-wrinkle, anti-expression cream.

Lost in her thoughts, she heard the siren before she saw the blue lights.

"Fuck."

She pulled over to the shoulder and searched for her license. When she opened the console to find the registration, a second lid dropped, revealing a firearm. She slammed it shut.

"Scottie," Penelope whispered, snaking a hand over the console to give her a covert nudge. She nearly knocked the truck back into gear when the officer knocked on the window. A female officer. *Crap. This should be fun.*

"License, registration, and insurance."

Penelope handed her the license. "It's my sister's car. I think the registration's in the glove box." She leaned over and pulled out a stack of papers.

"Is she OK?"

"Her? Yes. We left Snoqualmie before the sun came up and

she drove most of the way. She's just really tired." Penelope located the registration and insurance papers and handed them to the officer. "Why did you pull me over?"

"You were speeding. It's sixty on this road and you were going seventy."

"I'm sorry. I'm not used to this car. No excuse, of course."

"Where are you headed?"

"Reno."

"Girls' weekend? Doin' a little shooting?"

"Shooting? Why would you think that?" Penelope could feel a drop of sweat forming on her forehead and prayed it would not slip down in front of the officer.

"Shooting. Like shooting dice or shooting craps?" The officer furrowed her brow and glanced into the cab. "What do you have there?"

"What? Nothing."

"The animals, ma'am."

"The dogs? Just our dogs. We are taking them to see our sister in Reno." She prayed Scottie would not wake up in the middle of this awkward exchange.

"Sisters' weekend? Sounds like fun."

"I wish. No. Our other sister is sick. Cancer. We're bringing her home for treatment."

"I'm sorry. That's tough." The officer sighed. "I'll be right back, and we'll get you on your way."

Penelope took one finger and lifted the console high enough to confirm she had seen the gun. *What the hell, Scottie. Crossing state lines with a gun. I'm going to kick your ass.*

"Ma'am, here are your documents." The officer held them up. "Keep to the speed limit. I'm giving you a warning this time."

"Thank you."

"I hope your sister is OK." The officer gave her a sad smile and walked back to her car. It hit Penelope how pathetic it was that a perfect stranger could show sadness over the illness of someone she didn't even remotely know. Penelope hadn't yet shed a tear—until that moment. She wept silently on the shoulder of the highway.

Scottie rolled over. She reached out, eyes closed, and took hold of Penelope's hand. "It sucks, I know."

They sat there without talking until her tears died out. She squeezed Scottie's hand and pulled out onto the highway. Dusty evergreens and winter-burned scrub passed by her. Tears drying on her face, she looked over at Scottie next to her, asleep again. This road had been the beginning of the end of their family. She feared it would be the beginning of the end of Molly.

Chapter Eighteen

Molly

Scottie: Get ready. We're coming in hot.

Molly: Sounds ominous.

Scottie: I'm taking the dogs out. You can have a moment with Penelope alone.

Molly: Stop. Don't need a moment alone. Just come up you goof.

Scottie: She may need a moment alone. Either way, dogs have to pee. Be up soon.

Molly: K. Need help?

Scottie: Be serious. Penelope is self-sufficient and I travel light.

Molly: Can't wait to see you and Burnie.

Scottie: and Lucy

Molly: Her too.

Molly grasped the doorknob but thought better. She turned,

searching the apartment one last time for anything that would give her plan away. Satisfied, she took a step outside. Her chest tightened at the sight of Penelope rushing down the hallway toward her. Though she'd insisted they come, now that they were here, she felt like she was bracing for an invasion. Even from a distance, Molly could see her smile fading as she approached.

"Molly!"

She put a hand up to stave off the patented combination of disappointment and reproach that pulsed like a shock wave from Penelope's mouth.

"Don't say it."

"Say what?" She stopped in front of Molly. While her chin was directed at her face, Penelope's eyes were clearly roving her body. "Hello? I missed you? I am so happy to be here?"

"And."

Penelope let out the thinnest sigh. "You've lost too much weight. Your weekend pick-up-game sweats aren't hiding anything from me."

"There it is." Molly stepped back and twirled around. "Well, the cancer diet is brutal but effective."

"Don't make jokes." Penelope crossed her arms. "I hate it when you do that."

"I'm sorry. Just trying to keep it light." Molly wrapped her arms around her waist. Every week they seemed to stretch farther. She imagined being able to clasp them behind her back like a straitjacket soon. "Scottie has the dogs?"

"Yes. She'll be here in a minute. In the meantime, let's go inside. It's cold out here."

She stopped just inside the door, and Molly could feel the barometer shift in the room. Penelope scanned the space.

"This doesn't look like a trip home, Molly. It looks like you're moving out," she said.

"I am. For a while, at least. Treatment will take months,

maybe even a year or more. There's no reason to keep this place if I can't use it even for a visit."

"Is it the money? Because I'll pay for you to keep it. You love this place."

Molly hadn't planned for that. Not that Penelope wasn't generous, but this wasn't a new pair of skis. She opened her eyes wide to pull back the mist pooling in them at her generosity. Penelope might be a lawyer, but she was still working her way up the ladder. Rent for a year would put a dent in her savings. A window opened to one of those rare moments when the depth of love and gratitude could be expressed with no need for reciprocation. Though she wanted nothing but those moments until the day she died, Molly's naked profession of her feelings now would knock their fragile journey off course.

"Keep your money. That's not it. Anyway, it's time for me to move on. Reno's a kids' town. I'm not a kid anymore. I'm thinking Denver or Albuquerque. Maybe some place you and Scottie might actually visit." She hated to lie, but they couldn't be mad at a dead woman. Having the conversation now would be pointless. She needed to get them on the road.

"Where's all your stuff?"

"I rented a storage space. One of those container places. When I decide where I'm going to land, I can have it shipped."

"Don't you want to ship it to Seattle and store it there? That way you can get to your stuff if you need it. When you're feeling good enough to work, you might want the distraction."

"Penelope, I have it all under control. I can send it to Seattle later, if I decide to. Right now, it's fine where it is, and I have other things to think about."

"What about your car?"

"My friend Angie will keep an eye on it. When I'm ready, she'll send it to me, or maybe she'll bring it herself." That lie made her sad. She imagined Angie and Mateo driving to Seattle to see her. Tearful embrace. Spontaneous admissions of love. They'd find a cabin on an island populated by artists who were too busy creating to spend any effort on judging.

Energy filled the space, jarring her from the fantasy.

"Burnie, don't knock your aunt over!" Scottie said.

"Jeez, Scottie, put him on his leash!" Penelope grabbed for his collar as he pushed past her.

Molly dropped to her knees and took the big dog, full force, in her arms. His tail wagged so hard that his entire body shook. She soaked in the unbridled love. If only people could unlock the door and release their love as if it held no memory, no list of transgressions unhealed. On the periphery, she could hear Lucy yipping and jumping. Burnie wasn't giving up any acreage for the little dog, however.

"OK, that's enough. I have to love Lucy too." Molly's butt hit the floor, and she fell back laughing. Penelope gasped. Scottie grabbed Burnie. Lucy squirmed under him until she stood on top of Molly, licking her face. "You are a ferocious beast!" She rubbed the little dog's ears and then bench-pressed her into the air so she could see her sisters. "Are you hungry? I can order food." Scottie's eyebrows were knit together, and Molly could almost hear the words she wasn't saying. *When was the last time you ate anything?*

"Let me order pizza," Scottie offered.

Penelope groaned. "That's not very healthy."

"Don't get sanctimonious. I saw the cheddar popcorn bag. Empty, I might add."

"Well, I couldn't very well eat the salad with ptomaine dressing you bought me." Penelope dropped her purse on the table and dug out her phone.

"You should have eaten it when I got it for you."

"You'll remember, I had to drive."

"You didn't have to drive. You offered to drive. After I'd already driven through most of two states."

"Oh. My. God. Have you two been doing this all the way here?" Molly put Lucy on the floor and pushed herself up. "Scottie, order a pizza and a couple salads. Penelope, put the phone away. You're with humans now." She shook her head. "How will you survive without me?"

As soon as the words were out, the room chilled. Molly couldn't take it back, so she pretended she hadn't said it. To avoid their eyes, she busied herself scratching the dogs' bellies. "OK, Lucy, you fluffy pup, help your mom put her stuff in the guest room. Burnie, you can bunk with me. I don't think your mama's back can take an air mattress."

"I didn't know this was a camping situation," Penelope said.

"You can sleep with us if you want. I have a king."

"I'll brave the air mattress. I'm not sure a king can hold the three of us."

"Four," Scottie added.

Penelope rolled her suitcase into the guest room. Lucy followed, leaving Molly behind on the floor like a discarded bone. Scottie wedged her toes in front of Molly's and reached her hands out. Like they were kids on the playfield, she pulled her to standing. They stood nose to nose, hand in hand.

"How are you, really?" she asked. "I don't need to tell you what you look like."

"It's a wonder the diplomatic service did not scoop you up." Molly dropped Scottie's hands and went to the kitchen. "You have to use your cell to order pizza. I don't have a landline. Look up Paras Pizza."

"French pizza is highly suspect."

"It's Greek, smart-ass."

Penelope returned to the kitchen with a bottle of wine and an opener. Molly caught her before she began searching the cupboards for glasses. She pulled two from the dishwasher, where she'd set the last of her dishes. Molly figured it would be a bonus for the new tenants. *Service for two included, at no extra charge.* For Scottie, she pulled out a beer and placed it on the table. She didn't bother with a glass. Her sister liked it cold and straight from the bottle.

The pizza came quickly. The awkward sound of chewing replaced the awkward conversation. There was so much that Molly was trying not to say that only the most innocuous subjects were left. She asked about the trip in painful detail. When she'd squeezed that topic dry, she asked about Penelope's job, Scottie's kids and husband, and finally Hank. All elicited the sparsest response. In turn, they did not ask any questions, a tactic she knew well.

Her whole life, the two of them had an unfounded paranoia about each other. Each believed they had a deeper relationship with Molly than the other, that she doled out her secrets to only one of them. In fact, she didn't have many secrets and the big one she had not shared with either. Perhaps they should be more suspicious of her and less of each other. It made for the kind of uncomfortable meal that even beer and wine would not loosen up.

Scottie cleared the table and made her excuses. The earliest riser of the three, she hit the sheets soon after. She gave Molly a hug. After sharing decades of hugs, she could tell that Scottie was holding back. "Hugs have arms," Molly reminded her in the words of their father. Scottie snickered and draped her arms around her. With all the strength she could muster, Molly held her to her bony frame, memorizing the feel of her. Remembering all the hellos and goodbyes they'd shared in just this way.

"I'll see you in the morning," Scottie said.

More a directive than a statement of fact, Molly wondered who she was trying to convince with the words.

Scottie turned to Penelope. "Good night. And thanks for driving down with me." The words came out like they were pleasantries she'd been taught to say. Molly knew she meant it, but Scottie could never invest in the words. Always waiting to be let down by someone, she moderated her gratitude. She guarded her affection too. So, there were no hugs between Scottie and Penelope. Molly's heart clenched with the sadness of it. They had each other but were satisfied to be acquaintances.

"Penelope, come get your dog. She's confused," Scottie yelled from the bedroom.

"She likes you. You're right, that is confusing," Penelope mumbled.

"I heard that. Shoo, dog."

"Her name is Lucy."

"Shoo, Lucifer."

"Very funny. Lucy! Come away from the mean old lady."

"Who are you calling old?"

Chapter Nineteen

Penelope

DESPITE HER PROTESTS, Molly would not allow Penelope to wash the dinner dishes. Some habits die hard. Die. She mustn't even think that word. Words had power. How many times had she wished Michael would die? Look how that turned out.

Molly darted around the kitchen, doing everything in her power to avoid eye contact. Penelope recognized the strategy she'd used since middle school to avoid a come-to-Jesus conversation with their mom or her. How many times had she let her grades slip, missed curfew, or skipped school? Molly would remedy the situation with housework in an effort to either redeem herself or wear down the lecturer. Penelope would watch, amused, particularly if she attempted to draw it out, which meant starting in on Penelope's chores. Their mother's tenacity eroded after Scottie had left. By the time Molly hit her teens, Mary had lost all her staying power. Like a firecracker, she would light up and explode, painful but short-lived. Penelope, on the other hand, liked to talk about Molly's decisions and the consequences. She could wait forever.

Molly washed each dish by hand and set them in the strainer. With unnecessary ceremony, she pulled a spray bottle from beneath the sink and wiped down the counters.

"OK. That's enough. Sit down," Penelope said.

Molly leaned against the counter. "I'm beat. Can we talk in the morning?"

"You've been putting me off since you called me down here. It's time to come clean. What are we dealing with here?"

"Penelope, it's going to be fine. Let's get home and hear what the doctors have to say in Seattle."

"What are the doctors here saying?"

Molly folded the washrag and hung it from the faucet. She leaned over the sink and took a breath. Penelope was not going to let this go. She stared at Molly until she cracked.

"I have a mass in my abdomen. I might need chemo to shrink it before they can take it out. They might not even take it out. Look, I don't trust the doctors here. I just want to go home. Can you just do that for me without taking charge?"

"Why am I here, Molly?" She was so tired of being the one she called at the first sign of a problem and then the one she resented for overstepping her bounds. "I drove all the way down here just to drive you home? You aren't going to tell me what's really going on?"

"I did tell you." She plucked a towel from the oven door and dried her hands.

"You know more than you're telling me. I don't understand why you aren't giving me the whole story. If you don't want my help, say so."

"Penelope, I just want you to be with me. Can you understand that?"

"Tell me how bad it is."

"I honestly don't know."

"What is it? Exactly."

"Pancreatic cancer."

The words hit Penelope in the chest, and the air went out of her.

"How long have you known?"

Molly looked down at the towel in her hands and picked at the stray threads. "I called you as soon as I found out."

Penelope tipped her head down, as if repositioning her ear would make a lie easier to detect. "How's that possible, Molly? Look at yourself."

Molly stood. "I'm exhausted. I need to go to bed. We can talk more in the morning." She took a step, but Penelope stopped her.

"I'm sorry. Don't go. I need to know what we're facing."

"I love you. And I know you mean well." She leaned over and gave her a hug. "You're not the one facing this. Not really."

"I know." Penelope refused to let go. "Please, sit down and talk to me."

Molly lowered herself to the chair next to her. They had shared a lot in their lives. When their father left and Mary sank into depression, Penelope had to grow up. While her mother stared vacantly into the dawn from her nest in their father's armchair, Penelope kept the girls quiet, dressed them in clean clothes that didn't clash, filled their lunch boxes, and made breakfast. Too tired after working all day and making supper to deal with the petty drama of little girls, Mary withdrew. Penelope filled the gap. She developed a second sense with Molly and Scottie. Scottie's tummy ached when she did something wrong. Molly avoided eye contact and cleaned. When Penelope felt the chaos creeping in, she tried to put the world in order. She was doing that now.

Molly leaned over and rested her elbows on her knees. She stared at the floor. Penelope wanted to shake it out of her, but she was skittish, and one false move would have her running for cover. Talking to the floor, Molly said, "I tried to convince myself it was nothing. My friend, Angie, who doesn't pull any punches, let me tell you, she thought I was starving myself. I wasn't. She pushed me to go to the doctor. It's a blur. I just don't want to be here. I want to be with you and Scottie right now. Can you be here and give me space to figure this all out?"

"Of course, but you might need help. It's a lot to process."

"I'm sure I'll need help—from both of you. I need you to include her. Be nice to her."

"You know, it's not all me. Scottie doesn't want to be included."

"You don't know that. Maybe she's tired of trying."

"Did she say that?"

"No. And I'm not going to do this anymore. I don't have it in me."

"Do what?"

"Mediate. Talk to you. Talk to her. You two need to work your shit out. I can't be worrying about making both of you happy now." She stood and gave her another hug. "I love you. I love her. Can you try to love each other?" Molly held her eyes, no doubt waiting for words that Penelope could not say.

When Molly closed the door to her bedroom, Penelope slipped onto the balcony and looked out at the lights of the city. Careful not to make a sound, she started to cry. Penelope had perfected silent crying a long time ago. There was only room for one crying person in Mary Casey's house, and that was her. She had told Penelope little girls have simple lives where they are given everything they need. Unlike adults, they had nothing to cry about. Tears were the selfish act of needy children. Penelope preferred to endure her sadness rather than to incur her mother's anger. Unfortunately, refusing to cry had only added gasoline to her husband Michael's fire. Where her mother mistook disassociation for compliance, though, he mistook it for defiance and gave her something to cry about.

Now she wanted to cry with Molly, but she couldn't ask her

to bear her sadness. Molly needed her to be strong. The tears would pass. Action would hold them at bay. Molly was the feisty one. If she lost hope, all was really lost. Penelope couldn't let that happen. She had to provoke the headstrong kid who never took no for an answer.

In her head, she formulated a plan for as many eventualities as she could predict. It's nothing at all. A technical lab error. She discarded that possibility. Molly's emaciated body proved that. It's benign. It's cancerous. It's operable. It's inoperable. They caught it early. They caught it late. They caught it too late. Each thought became a branch on a tree she would be compelled to follow until she reached the farthest leaf. She would start with the worst possibility and then reward herself with a benign operable tumor with no residual effect as the prize for maintaining her optimism—a quality in short supply in Penelope.

She went to the kitchen table and pulled out her laptop to research the treatment options. Her mailbox notifications sounded like machine gun fire. How had she missed so many emails? She grabbed her phone. Damn, she'd silenced it while Scottie slept in the car. Her text app announced fourteen missed texts. She scrolled through the increasingly urgent texts from Victoria, asking her to call the office.

Opening her email, she pieced together the mystery. Jackson, weaseling prick that he was, had not heeded her warning. Under the guise of fulfilling his vision for what he called five-star treatment for five-star clients, he took it upon himself to contact Ashbridge and ascertain his level of satisfaction with Penelope's contract preparation. Without any background on the project, he answered the client's questions. She'd spent months working on the project, and he unraveled it in one afternoon. He did not have the first idea what the client needed. The client didn't even know what he needed. It was going to take days to get him back on track, if she could at all. When the contract failed to deliver, the client would leave the firm.

She should never have allowed herself to be pressured into bringing him in on any of her projects. Her track record would never be enough to combat the seeds of doubt he could plant in between holes at the country club. She could see him buying a couple rounds in the men's bar. The oldest of them reminiscing about the good old days when *Gentlemen Only, Ladies Forbidden* was an edict. Now it was part of a secret handshake to suss out lesser men who sympathized with the struggles of women and to ensure your progeny were not shackled to some closet feminist who thought it beneath her to throw a cocktail party.

Penelope looked at her watch. Responding now would look desperate. She needed some of that zen she was always reading about to calm her lizard brain, which was morphing at that moment into a dragon that could roast a village in one breath. When she talked to Jackson, she had to be calm. Scary calm. The kind of calm that stopped charging dogs in their tracks and sent them running for the hills with their tail between their legs. She'd spent decades repairing the damage Michael had done to her confidence. *I am not going back there, not at work, not at home.*

Chapter Twenty

Scottie

THE WALLS WERE thin, and the bedroom door was open just enough to hear Molly and Penelope.

"OK. That's enough. Sit down."

"I'm beat. Can we talk in the morning?"

Burnie took up residence in the crook behind her knees, pinning Scottie on her side. Like all dogs, he had the ability to increase gravity while sleeping. Scottie couldn't have moved him if she'd wanted to. She didn't want to. Scottie hated sleeping alone. She welcomed the heat of the big dog seeping into her stiff legs. Burnie was solid. She needed something solid next to her when the lights went out.

In the hospital, her father had waited until she was asleep before he'd leave. When the nightmares woke her, she would look for him through the blue haze of the monitors, disoriented and defenseless. Screwed into the frame, being alone scared her more than anything else. It wasn't so much that she couldn't take care of herself, though that was true. Terror unfurled from the possibility that she'd broken that final straw in a lifetime of being too much trouble and her father might not come back. He had, of course. Constant as the tide. The ghosts of those fears stung her in unpredictable moments, unabated by his reliability.

Burnie grounded her, but he was no replacement for her husband. For twenty-three years, she'd slept next to Jason nearly every night—steadfast and solid. Scottie missed him now, though she had done her best to push him away in the beginning. As a result of their teachers' uninspired tendency toward alphabetical seating arrangements, they'd been casual friends at the time of her accident, but only just. Yet, Jason visited her in the hospital daily, which made him suspect in Scottie's eyes. What kind of guy wanted to be with a girl who was broken in so many places? Every day after school, he brought her homework, nonetheless.

Sometimes her frustration would leak out on him. It was unfair to Jason, but she couldn't pile that pain on her father, whose guilt pulsed as regularly as the beat of his heart. Besides, her anger would surely hasten his leaving, and then she could concentrate on healing all her wounds at once. There would be no screwing back together a broken heart. But Jason didn't break her heart, and he didn't walk away. He gave her space for her feelings without demanding she explain those she had no words for.

"You've been putting me off since you called me down here. It's time to come clean. What are we dealing with here?"

Frustration colored the leading edge of Penelope's words as they bled into the bedroom. Lucy hopped up on the bed and spun around in circles until she pressed into Scottie's belly. From the intensity of the conversation happening just beyond the door, she guessed no one had noticed Lucy's departure. Scottie didn't want to miss hearing the truth she knew Molly would not share with her, so she pulled the dog close and stroked her to sleep.

"I have a mass in my abdomen. I might need chemo to shrink it before they can take it out. They might not even take it out . . . Pancreatic cancer."

Cancer. Scottie panicked at the word. She hated this for Molly. Better than anyone, she knew the horror of listening to doctors, with their incomprehensible words, objectively describing your prognosis as if they were hunters contemplating the best way to dress out an elk. Scottie could take it, but Molly was sensitive and kind. It would scar her hope so deeply that it might not heal.

"No. And I'm not going to do this anymore. I don't have it in me."

"Do what?"

"Mediate. Talk to you. Talk to her. You two need to work your shit out. I can't be worrying about making both of you happy now."

Scottie's stomach clenched. As Molly spoke, she could feel the burden she'd dumped on her sister. *Selfish little girl.* Mary's voice whispered in Scottie's head. Is this why Molly kept the apartment in Reno? Did she need a break from the tension of choosing between them all the time?

She was being selfish. Leaving all the decisions up to her still meant she had to pick between the two of them. That wasn't supportive. It was a way to side with Molly and disagree with Penelope. The only two sides right now were for her or against her. Scottie was on the wrong one.

Penelope was right. She had greater means. Molly would be more comfortable in her high-rise apartment. Besides, Scottie could drive in and see her anytime. Maybe Penelope would let her go to the doctor's appointments. She would hold Molly's hand through them.

Her heart clinched. Molly's hand in hers. She was the fun one. The popular girl. She had always reached out to Scottie. *Come play. Don't be afraid.* Scottie would take Molly's hand and feel the courage grow inside her. Her big sister. Well, one of them. Standing up for her. *You're OK. It's just a scratch.* Drying her tears. Brushing off her scuffed knees. Lying to her when she needed it most. *You're going to be good as new when these screws come out.* Molly had taken Scottie's hand in hers and sat silently through the endless hours of knitting ligaments and regrowing dead men's bones to fuse her spine. It was her turn to take Molly's hand and soak up her fear. Tell her the lies she needed to hear. The lies that would seal Molly's hope in armor.

~⑤~

Scottie woke before dawn. She hadn't heard Molly come to bed or Lucy leave. Captive in the valley between her legs and Molly's, Burnie lifted his head to look at her when she moved. His lack of motion, beyond that, was evidence he knew it would take some time before she was standing clothed to take him out. Scottie tried not to groan as she straightened her legs and let them drop to the floor. She used the momentum and a shove of her right hand against the mattress to propel herself upright.

By the time Burnie hopped off the bed, Lucy was waiting at the apartment door for them. A walk would loosen Scottie up and give her time to think. Out of habit, she pushed in the lock button and shut the door behind her. At the click, she realized her mistake.

"Shit." Scottie tipped forward until her forehead rested against the peephole. *Great. Now I'll have to wake them up to get back in.* She pushed off the door and turned to scan the hallway.

Ten feet away, a woman crouched, placing the boy in her arms on the floor. He clung to her neck. She kept Scottie in her sights as she tried to disengage the boy.

"Are you OK?" she asked.

"I'm so sorry for swearing. I didn't realize the little guy was behind me."

"It's fine. You must be Molly's sister. I can see the resemblance. I'm a friend of hers." The little boy let go of his mother. She stood, straightened her jacket, and put out her hand. "Angie."

She didn't say the two things she found most interesting—that Molly had not shared Scottie was adopted, and that she had a friend she'd never mentioned.

"Nice to meet you." Scottie took her hand. "Despite my language. I'm OK. I just locked myself out, but I can knock when I get back." The woman radiated an openness that she found disconcerting. "Could you point me toward the nearest coffee shop?"

The little boy sidled up to Burnie. Scottie considered stopping him, but Angie was watching and looked relaxed.

"Are you the friend who's taking care of Molly's vehicle?" Scottie swiped Lucy from the pavement as she launched herself toward the little boy. He was already teetering against the weight of Burnie's joy. Lucy might just tip the scales. Besides, Scottie wasn't entirely sure Lucy was bringing joy.

"Yes, I am." Angie took hold of the little boy's hand.

"Well, let me know if you need help. That's quite a generous thing you're doing."

"Oh, my. Molly is the generous one. We cannot thank her enough, though I hate the circumstances." She picked up the boy. "I have to go, but if you have problems getting back into the apartment, knock on my door. I have a key."

"Thanks so much. I'll probably see you in Seattle."

Angie gave her a wistful smile. "I doubt it. But I guess, never say never."

Before Scottie could ask why, Burnie and Lucy pulled her away.

༺

Scottie ambled along behind the two dogs, who'd formed a relationship that vacillated between tolerance and friendship. A bit like sisters. Their long hair bounced with each step, though

Lucy's was lighter and professionally groomed. Her hair floated like a blond model jogging on a beach. Burnie, in contrast, looked more like a lumberjack in need of a haircut. It jumped and flopped as he plodded along.

Every few yards, Burnie stopped to smell the grass or a parking sign. Lucy continued on until the tether pulled her to a stop. She looked back, and Scottie could swear she was tapping a paw in annoyance. For her part, Lucy bounded along, zigzagging in front and behind Burnie. He slowed his pace and kept a watchful eye on her. With measured steps, he seemed afraid one would land on her. Scottie let them be. An imperfect pair. Temporarily connected. Moving forward, though not in a straight line.

The coffee shop was an outdoor affair with a walk-up window. Two octagonal picnic tables adorned a postage stamp lawn in front. Scottie silently thanked Angie for not sending her to one of those places where people embed themselves in overstuffed chairs and sip skinny triple half-caff sugar-free caramel lattes for hours while waxing poetic on weighty topics they got a PhD in from TikTok U. Not a place for the odd couple, she mused. Burnie could be trusted tied to a bike rack, but Lucy was a wildcard. Scottie had a sneaking suspicion she would lose her mind if she were left alone in a strange city tied to a pole. She pictured Lucy yipping until some passerby stopped to comfort her while simultaneously recording a rant on irresponsible dog owners for her Instagram reel. That would not have ended well.

Her dad was not a fan of coffee shops. Hank was a no-frills kind of guy. He preferred his coffee as black as a cloudy winter night in a ceramic mug. She took after him, eschewing the fruity syrups, but she liked cream. She ordered the biggest coffee they had and some muffins. The barista gave her a couple of treats for the dogs. Scottie sat at a picnic table and drank her coffee as the dogs scarfed down their treats.

The town was slowly waking up. From her vantage point,

she watched the mix of people heading to work or home from a workout as they refueled for the day ahead. It had a good feel. She regretted never having visited, and now she might never come again. Scottie wished she'd met Angie and the little boy—or even knew they existed—before today. For her, regret never seemed to follow an action, rather what she didn't do plagued her. She didn't visit Molly in Reno. She didn't ask Mary what she'd done to get kicked out of the house, or Penelope why she didn't like her. She didn't ask who her mother and father were.

Before she had time to think herself out of it, she took out her phone and called her husband.

"Hey. How's it going?" Jason asked.

"Good. We got in late last night or I would have called."

"How's your sister?"

"She looks terrible. We need to get her home. Have you heard anything from my dad or Meaghan?" She traced the outline of a coffee cup someone had carved into the wooden table.

"No. And I'm taking that as a good sign. Unless they killed each other."

"Not funny." A chuckle escaped. Scottie pictured them. She marveled at her daughter fearlessly arguing with Hank like she knew he would love her no matter what.

"Sorry." He paused. "Are you OK?"

"Yes." *Then why did you call. God, just say it.* "I'm just missing you." She took a breath. "You know I love you, right?"

"Of course I do. What brought this on?"

"I don't know." Tears filled her eyes. She sniffled. "Life's short. Maybe shorter than I thought." She forced herself forward, her words stilted. "I know I am not an emotional person. I just wanted to be sure, you know. You're my best friend. I've loved you forever."

"I know. I love you more."

"No. You don't," she whispered.

"Do you want me to come down there?"

"No. I need to deal with this on my own. It's hard. Molly doesn't look good. I think I'm going to lose her. That will be the end." Her tears bubbled over. She tipped her head skyward and closed her eyes. Cool morning air, with a hint of warmth from the sun, fell on her face. She wiped her tears.

"Scottie. You have a family. It would be awful to lose her, but you have me and the kids and your dad. If you're worried about Penny, don't. How can you miss someone you never even see?"

"I can't explain it." Scottie picked at the rough edge of the table. "I know it's stupid, but I just want her to like me. I'm stupid. I shouldn't care what she thinks."

"You're not stupid."

"I know." She was embarrassed, not for the thought but for saying it out loud. "Thanks. Listen, I should get back. I love you. I'll be home soon."

"Call me later and let me know when you get on the road."

Jason disconnected, leaving her adrift for a moment. Burnie put his head in her lap and raised his eyes to her. She wiped her tears with the back of her jacket sleeve. Someday Jason would leave her too. She felt the jagged tearing of her heart at the thought of it. She'd tried so hard not to love him completely. Like, if she reserved a sliver, then it wouldn't hurt so bad when he left. But he wasn't going to leave on his own two feet. He'd proven that time and again when her crazy leaked out in irrational worry or raging anger. No, if he was going to walk out, he'd had more than enough reason to do so already. He'd leave in a box. She knew she'd not loved him the way he deserved to be loved. He knew how to love her. That was regret.

Chapter Twenty-One

Molly

MOLLY AWOKE TO a cold bed. Scottie had been asleep by the time she'd left Penelope. Hoping not to wake her or the dogs snoring next to her, she'd slid under the covers, melting into the heat of the three bodies. Burnie lay on his side at the foot of the bed. Once Molly settled, he rested his head on her legs. As she drifted off, she heard Penelope call for Lucy. Scottie groaned. Molly smiled.

Now she was alone and chilled by the emptiness. Scottie had always been an early riser. Molly remembered waking one morning to the sound of her mother screaming. She and Penelope ran to find her staring at the half-open sliding glass door that led to the backyard. Penelope hugged her mom, who was frozen in place.

"Where's Scarlett?" her mother asked Penelope as she broke from the embrace and headed for the bedroom.

Molly slid the door open and stepped out. Though the concrete patio looked smooth, the frigid surface scraped her bare feet with each step. She walked out slowly, unsure why her mother was so scared. As she neared the corner of the house, she could hear Scottie humming.

"Molly, no! Come back here." Her mother threw the door open.

She looked back but kept walking. In the grass, Scottie sat against the wall at the side of their house. Their dog Max rested in her lap. She rocked from side to side as she stroked the dog's silky hair. Molly couldn't place the tune, but she knew it was a song they'd heard on her mom's record player.

"You scared me to death, Scottie!" Her mother arrived like a tornado. She leaned over and plucked her off the ground, dumping the dog unceremoniously on the lawn. "I should paddle you with a wooden spoon. You never, never leave the house without telling me. You could get stolen or hurt." Her mom stormed back to the house with a stunned Scottie on her hip. Though they were all wide awake from the excitement, her mother put them back in bed.

Molly leaned over the top bunk. "What were you doing?"

"Max wanted to go out. I didn't want him to be alone."

"Wake me up next time."

"Why?"

"I don't want you to be alone, either."

The front door lock clicked, scattering the memory. Molly heard Scottie thank Angie for letting her in. By the time she got dressed and made it to the kitchen, Scottie had set out muffins and napkins. Though her body faced the cupboards, her head was tipped downward. She stood motionless.

"Everything OK?" Molly asked.

Scottie turned around and held out her hand. In her outstretched palm, she held six joints. Molly snatched them, red-faced.

"Is there something you want to tell me?"

"No, *Dad*. There is not." She turned and headed for the deck. Scottie followed her.

"Do you think smoking weed is a good idea, as sick as you are?"

"For your information, it's medicinal."

"Right."

"It is. It gives me an appetite. You might have noticed, I've lost a little weight. Anyway, it's not illegal. I don't need your permission."

"What don't you need her permission for?" Penelope walked out on the patio, compounding her embarrassment.

"Molly has taken up smoking pot," Scottie said.

"Nice. Do you have some?" Penelope asked.

Molly leaned on the rail and looked over the city. She lit up the joint and took a toke. Penelope reached out and took it from her. She took a drag and offered it to Scottie.

"No. I don't want that."

"Oh, loosen up. It's no big deal. Besides, Molly needs the munchies bad. And that's the worst thing that can happen to you."

"No. Addiction is."

"Jeez, Scottie. Addiction is the least of my problems," Molly said, taking another puff and passing it back to Penelope. "Tell me you never got high before."

"I haven't."

Molly and Penelope stared at her for a moment and then burst out laughing. When Scottie did not join in, Molly said, "Oh, God. You're not lying. You really haven't ever smoked pot. How is that even possible? Did Dad send you to a convent for high school?"

"No." Scottie leaned against the corner wall of the deck, as far from them as she could get. "Dad would have killed me, and I am not exaggerating."

"Did you get drunk in high school?" Penelope asked.

"No. Do we have to talk about this?" She pushed off the wall and headed into the apartment. They followed her.

"We're sorry, Scottie," Molly offered. "Mom always said she'd kill us too if she caught us. Like that was ever going to happen. She'd have to be paying attention to catch us. I guess I didn't realize Dad was so strict."

"He was a hard ass. He still is."

"That must have sucked." Penelope sat down. Her eyes widened. "Oh, my God. I just realized he had to take you shopping for your first bra."

"How did that even work?" Molly looked at Scottie and stifled a laugh. Scottie's face went blank. "Sorry, weed makes me giggle. It's not you."

"Much as I would love to discuss my introduction to bras, I think I'll pass."

"Come on." Penelope pressed her hands together in mock prayer. "I'm curious, and not about your breasts. How did you handle all that? It had to be awkward, to say the least. And your period. Oh, lord. Did Mom help you with that one?"

"Mom didn't help me with anything." Scottie reached down and untied the laces on her boots. When she stood back up, they were staring at her. "I think he called her, though, about bras. He took me to the mall. To Bon Marche," Scottie said. "He turned five shades of red. A lady who worked there took mercy on him and suggested he come back in a half an hour. She was really nice. I think she felt sorry for me."

"Hell, I feel sorry for you," Penelope said.

"Well, you don't have to. I did just fine." She kicked her boots off.

Molly could hear the shame beneath the anger rising in her voice. "I know you did. I'm just saying that it had to be hard, Scottie. I'm not saying you're pitiful. It was hard enough talking to Mom about that stuff. I can't imagine going to Dad and saying, 'so I just started my period'."

"Dad is the king of avoiding awkwardness. If he doesn't want to talk about something, you aren't talking about it. It's no big deal. He went to the store and bought one of every type of feminine product and put them under my sink. I read the directions on the boxes. When I figured out what I wanted to use, I left the box out and he bought more. We never really talked about it. I think he must have spoken to my doctor, though, because she talked to me. Of course, small town. Everyone knew I was the girl without a mom. So maybe she just put two and two together. Who knows?"

Molly wanted to cry, but she knew it would make Scottie feel bad. She bit her lip.

"Oh, jeez. Don't start crying. I survived. I am not scarred by being raised by Dad. Well, I'm probably scarred, but no more than any other human being."

"But what about makeup, boys, prom dresses? You missed all of that. And sex. What about sex?" Molly couldn't remember Scottie ever calling her about those things. She hated herself for not asking back then.

Penelope didn't say a word.

"OK, this conversation is over. I am writing it off as the dope. I grew up fine. I figured everything out. I have two kids, so I know how to have sex. I'm fine. And now I'm going to take a shower and get dressed so we can get on the road before dinner." Scottie called her dog and marched into the bedroom.

Penelope put her hands on her hips. "Well, that was tactful."

"I blame the weed."

"You've never been tactful. It's not the weed."

"You have to be nice to me. I have cancer."

"That's not something to joke about." Penelope stood, Lucy in her arms, and marched to her bedroom.

Molly sat in the living room, staring at the two closed doors. Penelope was wrong. She'd held in so many things over the years in an effort not to alienate either of them. Or worse, further alienate them from each other. Maybe she lacked tact, but she didn't lack restraint. She would have to cut back on smoking pot when they were all together. None of them had much tolerance for a reality outside of the one each clung to.

What were you doing?
Max wanted to go out. I didn't want him to be alone.
Wake me up next time.
Why?
I don't want you to be alone.

But Scottie had been alone. Too afraid to be sent away herself, Molly hadn't taken a stand. She should have visited her more or begged her mother to bring her back.

Chapter Twenty-Two

Penelope

Penelope dropped Lucy on the bed and dug out her laptop. She began reading from the top, a lesson she learned from her mother, whose communication followed the same path and cadence as a roller coaster. A *never* that hurled your body to the right followed every *always* that lurched you to the left. Each building tirade ended at a precipice of regret. Penelope learned early on to wait until Mary came to a full stop to determine what she really wanted. Even then, she knew the ride could leave again any minute.

And so it was with emails. The first, from the managing partner who wanted to review the Ashbridge case with her, was short, which was never good coming from a lawyer. She checked her calendar and found he'd added a meeting at 3:00 p.m. Click, click, click. Up they climbed. She needed to get back to Seattle. She couldn't risk being in some backwater town without Wi-Fi for the meeting. They would have to wait here until after the meeting to leave for home.

She opened the second email and felt the rapid descent. This one was from Ashbridge himself. He'd copied the managing partner and, Penelope was sure, blind-copied that weasel, Jackson. It too was painfully short.

We appreciate your efforts on our behalf . . . *blah, blah, blah. My efforts? Are you kidding me? I have done nothing but work on your case for the last eighteen months.* It has come to our attention that an alternate path might be better aligned with our goals and expeditious in achieving them . . . *Translated, Jackson thinks he knows better after two days of snooping through my files. You bastard. This is going to cost the firm. When he's done fucking this up, Ashbridge will leave, and he'll find a way to spin it so it was my fault.*

Penelope didn't read any further. She opened a browser and started looking for the first flight to Seattle. If she could make the 10:00 a.m. flight, she could be in the office in time to prepare for the meeting. That gave her one hour to get to the airport. She dialed Victoria.

"Call a car service and get it here as fast as you can."

"Good morning, Penelope. What happened? Why do you need a car service?" She spoke in that same calm tone Penelope used with her mother, and she did not appreciate it.

"Did you not see the three o'clock on my calendar?"

"I did. I assumed you would do it by Zoom."

"Victoria, are you serious? I'm not taking that meeting by Zoom. I should never have come down here."

"Penelope, slow down. You need to be there. You can do that meeting from Reno."

"Just order the car, Victoria." *Christ, I'm about to get fired. Stop arguing and do it! I do not need your mothering. I didn't need mothering forty years ago. I sure as hell do not need yours now.* "I just booked the 10:00 a.m., and I cannot miss that flight. Make that clear when you call."

"Yes, ma'am. It will be waiting for you. Is there anything else you need?" Victoria's voice had lost all emotion.

Penelope did not have the time to worry about her feelings. Her world was crumbling. If Molly died, her job would be all she had left. She could not risk losing it too. There wasn't anything she could do for Molly here right now. Once she got to Seattle, she would make sure she was available to help her. She would hire a nurse, even. Once she sorted this mess out, she would make time for Molly.

Penelope scooped up the pile of dirty clothes she'd discarded next to the bed the night before. Too exhausted to roll them neatly and place them in the dirty clothes bag she'd packed, she shoved them into the front of her suitcase and began searching her brain for all the things she'd carelessly left around the apartment. Her makeup bag and brush were in the bathroom. She could hear the shower turn on and looked at her watch. The car service would arrive any minute.

As she reached for the doorknob, it swung open, and she stumbled back, narrowly avoiding a broken nose.

"Hey. Be careful. Try knocking first." Penelope brushed past Molly and headed for the bathroom.

"Slow down, I want to talk to you." She followed her down the hall. "What are you doing? Don't go in there."

"I just need to grab my makeup. We're all girls. It's fine." Penelope opened the door and reached for the makeup bag that lay by the sink. Just above, in the mirror, stood Scottie. Penelope saw the scar riddled with puckered flesh that ran from her shoulder blades to her tailbone. Though it followed the line of her spine, it meandered as if the surgeon intended to stop, but then thought better of it. At each end, the deep pink faded, and an angry purple splotch bloomed.

Scottie backed into the corner, clutching a towel to her chest. She looked Penelope in the eye. Defiance warred with shame.

"Get out." She wrapped the towel around her.

"My God, Scottie." Penelope's mouth hung open in horror.

"Well, what did you think it would look like?"

"What are you talking about?"

"Give me a break." Scottie took a step forward and leaned in. "Everyone imagines it. Just get out."

"Stop. What happened to you?" Penelope blocked the door.

"Molly, if you do not get her out of my way, I will move her out of the way." Angry tears dripped down Scottie's cheeks as she tightened the towel and reached for the door.

She took Penelope's arm. "Penelope, let's let Scottie get dressed and then we can talk."

Penelope shook her off. "No, somebody tell me what happened. You two always leave me out."

"Penelope, you know what happened. Mom said she called you when Scottie rolled her three-wheeler. Your last year in college. Don't you remember?"

Penelope snatched the makeup case from the counter and rushed back to her room. She sat down on the bed and sobbed. All the anger that had built up in her chest over the years flowed like a river. She'd been the one to take care of Mary. She'd been the one who sacrificed her adolescence to take care of her sister, keep the house clean, even pay some bills. Her mother had lied to her.

The phone call rushed back to her now. At the end of their weekly rambling review of the ups and downs of Mary's existence, her mother mentioned the accident. It was no big deal. Certainly not important enough to distract Penelope from studying for final exams, she insisted. Why had Mary kept them apart?

She closed her eyes and saw the craggy flesh. Scottie must have been in the hospital for weeks, maybe months. The thought of her pain made Penelope shudder. She must have been so angry at her for never calling or visiting her in the hospital. Had she gone to rehab? Did she have to learn to walk again?

Molly dragged Scottie through the door. "You two are going to be the death of me."

In chorus, they responded, "Not funny!"

"Well, now that I have your attention. I swear to God you two are a couple of billy goats. Stop knocking heads and talk to each other."

Penelope stared at the floor. So many emotions boiled inside her. Anger collided with shame. Sadness knotted around fear. If she could just hold on to one of them long enough to make sense of it.

"I didn't know. Not really." She looked Scottie in the eye. "Mom said you had an accident, but she made it seem like it was nothing. I asked if I should come home, but she said no. It was finals week. She thought it would be a distraction. I swear, Scottie, if I had known, I would have come home. I am so sorry you went through that alone."

"I didn't." Scottie backed against the wall and crossed her arms over her chest. "I had Dad, and Molly, and Jason."

"I know you weren't alone. That's not what I meant. For so long, I took care of you. Both of you. And then you were just gone. You didn't need me anymore. You didn't visit or talk to me. One day, you needed me and then the next day I didn't exist. I know it's because I didn't protect you, but it hurt all the same."

Scottie sat down next to her. Taking Penelope's hand in hers, she started to cry.

The chime of Penelope's phone severed the moment. She stood, slipping her hand from Scottie's, and tucked a piece of Scottie's hair behind her ear.

"That's my car. I have to go. I'm so sorry."

Chapter Twenty-Three

Scottie

SCOTTIE LOOKED DOWN at her empty hands. Penelope's hadn't stayed in hers long enough to warm them. She swiped her forearm beneath her nose, catching the ugly tears and the snot that came with them. Penelope couldn't be trusted with those drops. Scottie knew that, but like a fool, she gave them to her, anyway.

She watched as Penelope slipped her makeup bag into the outer pocket of her suitcase, grabbed the handle, and headed for the door. Lucy followed her.

"Penelope, what the hell? Where are you going?" Molly chased after her.

"Dammit." Penelope turned to Scottie. "Can you bring Lucy back to Seattle for me?"

"This is just like you. Shit gets real, and you cut and run. You just drop everything and everybody. Nothing's more important than your almighty job." Scottie picked up Lucy and hugged the dog to her chest. "You wouldn't have come to the hospital even if you'd known how bad it was. Nothing and no one distracts Penelope from her plans."

"You don't know what you're talking about. I'm not running from anything, and I'm sure as hell not dropping my dog. And how dare you disparage my job? I worked my ass off to get there. Nobody helped me. My dad didn't hand me half of his business to ease his guilty conscience. I paid my way."

Scottie took the blow standing. She wanted to fight back, but there was no point in fighting the truth. Shame bloomed on her neck.

Penelope left her standing frozen and turned to Molly. "I'm asking you to bring Lucy home for me. I have to be in the office by three, and I won't have time to take her home."

"Penelope, what's going on? You can't just leave."

"I don't have a choice, and I don't have time to explain. I'll call you later. Please, take care of my dog." With that, she hoisted her bag over her shoulder and walked out.

Molly crumpled onto the edge of the couch. Scottie sat down beside her. The pup squirmed out of her grasp and onto Molly's lap. Dogs were intuitive beings, and this one confirmed what she already knew—her pain was inconsequential in comparison to anyone else's.

Scottie packed up Penelope's words and stored them away where she couldn't see them. They would fade quicker if she focused on all the things she needed to do for Molly—not disappear, though. There would always be a ghost of them. Someday, the ghosts of all the words Penelope had said to her would rise up. For now, they had to be silenced for Molly's sake.

"Oh, Molly." Scottie gave her a hug. "You always did give people too much credit. Your heart is too big." She patted her on the leg and stood, a motion her father had done a hundred times to signal it was time to dust yourself off and move on. "We need to get on the road too."

Molly looked up at her, eyes red-rimmed. "There's not much I don't like about you. But I hate your cynical streak."

"I'm not cynical. I'm realistic."

"You're not realistic. You're defeatist. You're pessimistic. You're fatalistic. I might give people too much credit. But you don't give us enough." Molly handed her the dog. "I've been packed for a while. We can leave anytime."

Molly stomped into her bedroom and slammed the door. When she left the room, she took all the air with her. Scottie held her breath so she'd have something to focus on, other than the brutal truth that she could drive even Molly away.

Lucy licked her face. She glanced at her. "You don't count. You're a dog. A dog could make the devil himself feel redeemable."

She packed her bag and circled the apartment several times to make sure she hadn't forgotten anything. On the fourth pass through the bathroom, she turned to find Molly in the hallway shaking her head.

"I'm going to give the keys to Angie. I'll meet you at the car. Do you want me to take one of the dogs?"

"No. I've got them." An apology was in order. How do you apologize for being yourself? She stared, wordless, until Molly nodded and walked away.

A feeling of loss enveloped Scottie as she stood alone scanning the apartment. How could she miss something she'd known only one day? She wondered what the apartment had looked like when Molly was living in it, before she'd scoured away every remnant of her personality, all the evidence of who she was. Another regret to add to the pile growing large enough to fuel a bonfire.

It took some effort to get the dogs and her bag out the door. The dogs had formed an alliance. As soon as Scottie coaxed Lucy to stand next to Burnie, he shuffled behind her. Giving up all hope of getting them to stay on the same side, she high-stepped out of the tangle of leashes threatening to send her sprawling to the floor.

As she checked the door, Burnie nearly knocked her off her feet when he let out a mighty woof and started down the hall. Molly and Angie stood in the center, hugging. The sound of Angie crying bounced off the walls. Yet again, Scottie felt like an intruder. Surely if Molly had wanted to share that part of her life, she would have. But why didn't she want to? That troubled Scottie. Had she been too self-involved? Too disinterested? Too close-minded? She had to be better, for however long they had left together. Penelope was never going to be her friend. She was barely a sister. Scottie had to make this count. She was running out of time to figure it out.

Walking across the parking lot, the midmorning sun warmed her face. If she overlooked the cement and all the people, she could see the appeal of living there. Scottie hefted her bag on the hood of the truck and walked the dogs to a patch of crab-grass. They stared at her as if they expected a four-star potty spot. Scottie stared at the entrance to the apartment building, unmoved by their protest.

It took a moment for the chirping to register in her head.

"Hi, Dad, is everything OK?"

"I'm never going to get used to caller ID. Yeah, everything's great. Meaghan's been a trouper. How are you doing, kiddo?"

Without warning, her eyes teared up. She covered the mouthpiece so she could take a breath. After a moment, she recovered her voice. "Good. It's all good. We're heading back this morning."

"Quick trip. Is everything OK? How's your back?"

He was always protective of her with the other girls. His eyes dipped with a sadness, only she would notice, when he said their names, though. Hank never talked about it, but she could tell regret weighed him down. When she became a mom, she understood. The love she felt for her babies ran so deep, if stretched, it would go on forever. Even at that farthest point, she could feel it, like it was fresh and new and right in front of her. Still, the threat of loss was like the tip of a sharp knife piercing her chest. It never left that spot and it promised to plunge into her heart someday. His heart had felt that pain of separation.

When Meaghan came along, she realized love wasn't a pie. She didn't have half her love for Justin and half for Meaghan. She had all of it, for both of them, at the same moment. It was magical. It made it harder to understand Mary, but then she wasn't really her mom. Maybe she wasn't even a slice of that pie for her. Of course, Hank wasn't her dad, and she knew he had that kind of love for her. When she saw the regret in his eyes for her sisters, there was still an echo inside her that wondered why she hadn't been enough. Why did he have to miss Penelope and Molly so much?

"My back's fine. Everything is good. Molly just decided she wants to come home early," Scottie said.

"Great. Maybe we could all have dinner together before they head back to the city."

"It'll just be me and Molly. Penelope had some legal crisis no one else could handle and bailed on us."

"Go easy on her, pal. She has a big job."

"Man, I am so sick of everyone excusing her behavior because she thinks she's some kind of important lawyer." She kicked at a tuft of weeds.

"She really yanked your chain. Well, pal, you might want to put a lid on your resentment."

That's right. My resentment is the problem here. "I don't know why you defend her. She ghosts you constantly."

"I don't know what that means, but I know she has her reasons. Maybe someday, she'll tell me what they are. Meanwhile, she's still my daughter. I know you get that, or Justin would've been exiled to a military academy by sixth grade."

"Funny. OK, we'll see you tonight. I'll call you when we hit the pass."

"Drive safe. Take lots of breaks. I love you."

"I love you too, Dad." It was a small circle, her dad, her husband, her kids, and Molly. It was going to get smaller.

Chapter Twenty-Four

Molly

MOLLY KNEW THEY'D passed the awkward phase of the hug ninety seconds ago, but she wished she could stay there until she took her last breath, holding Angie. She felt like one of those scrawny pine poles they propped beneath a branch, fat with ripening apples. Like a fruit tree, Angie rested in her embrace.

Burnie's bark drifted through the breezeway, bringing her back to the present.

"They must be getting restless to leave." She gave Angie a squeeze.

"I don't care." Angie looked up at her. "I wish you wouldn't leave. It's not going to change anything."

"Sure it will. Change is inevitable. It's not always what we want, but it's gonna happen either way."

Angie took a step back and gave her a half-hearted punch on the shoulder.

"Hey. You're going to have to go to confession for hitting a dying woman." Molly rubbed her arm.

"Not funny." She hit her again. "You have to stop saying that. You're going to manifest yourself right into the grave."

"It won't be from manifesting." Molly put her hand up in mock protest of the next punch. "Besides, if manifesting worked, I would be tall, blond, rich, and married to a supermodel."

"Bullshit. You don't want any of that, except maybe the supermodel part." A chuckle escaped with her sniffles. "You wouldn't last a day with a high maintenance woman, though. None of that matters anyway. You're perfect the way God made you."

"I love you for believing that. I'm not sure the rest of the sighted world would agree." Molly glanced down the hall. Scottie had slipped away. "It could only be like ninety-nine percent true at most, since He gave me some defective organs." She reached up and wiped a tear from Angie's cheek. "I have to go. I'm sure Scottie is tapping her boot with the engine running."

"Whatever it is you have to do, can't you do it from here? You could Zoom or FaceTime them every day." Angie pulled back and looked down at her hands clutched to her chest. "Look, I don't know what you do when you're in Seattle. Maybe the three of you do stuff together. I do know they've never been here. If you're trying to reconcile with them or something like that, I don't know if it's gonna work out like you want it to."

"I'm not the one they need to reconcile with." Molly put her hands in the pockets of her jeans. In the stillness of the hallway, looking into Angie's pleading eyes, her heartbeat quickened. "There are some things you can't do in two dimensions. You have to be sitting right there. Holding hands. I wish I could deal with it from here. Tears are much less painful over the phone." She wiped a drop from her cheek with the back of her hand. "But then laughter is much less joyful too. I can't leave them this way."

Angie was silent.

Molly said, "I don't want Mateo, or you, to remember me

like I'm going to be, either. I want you to remember me like I was. Mateo will be fine."

"What about me?"

Molly's smile lifted toward the sadness in her eyes. "My ego wants you to pine away for years regretting what might have been, settle on some square-jawed guy half your age who made it big on Starbucks stock and has to give you half of everything, when you realize he could never love you as much as I could." She chuckled. Angie glowered. "But the truth is I hope you will find someone who thinks loving you is winning the goddamn lottery, 'cause it is."

Molly collected her in a hug and pressed her to her body like the feel of it could be imprinted onto her skin. She tried to let go, but Angie held on, crying. Molly didn't fight it.

Without a word, Angie turned away. The loss of her was like diving into the lake in late spring. The heat of the sun replaced by the shocking cold. Her door slammed. Molly reached for the handle but left her hand resting there. Taking no action was action. She knew that more than ever now. This was just the beginning of the goodbyes, and going after Angie would only leave a deeper scar.

Chapter Twenty-Five

Penelope

Penelope stepped into the elevator and hit the button for the first floor. Before it began to move, she punched the third floor. The door opened to a hallway indistinguishable from Molly's floor. She froze. All the energy in her body vibrated in her chest. Her jaw locked tight. She wished she could step out of the box and stand on the landing until the electric tug of war between her heart and mind dissipated. She wished she could embody both at once—the sister fully present with Molly and the lawyer winning cases and validating her life with accolades and promotions. Penelope was only masquerading as each. Her best bet for coming out whole was to do what she had always done. Lock it down. Focus on the immediate problem. Deal with the fallout later. Save her job. Then, save Molly. If there was anything left, deal with Scottie.

She pressed the button to close the doors and descended. Blocking the echoes, Penelope put on her game face and stepped onto the asphalt.

The driver was waiting for Penelope next to the open trunk of a spotless black sedan. She glanced at Victoria's text to confirm the vehicle. Ignoring his outstretched hand, she collapsed the handle of her rolling bag and hoisted it into the immaculate compartment.

Without looking at him, she said, "How long will it take to get to the airport?"

He jogged around her, reaching for the handle of the rear passenger door before she did.

"Good morning. Yes, um, our trip will be about a quarter of an hour." He opened the door with the flourish of Vanna White uncovering a vowel.

She tossed her laptop bag and purse on the seat and then slid in next to them. "I have a ten o'clock flight. Is that enough time to get through security?"

He held the top of the door. "Oh. Yes, I think so. More than enough. Usually, it is about fifteen minutes to get through security."

She reached for the door to pull it closed, but he was unmoved. A tiny red flag popped up in the front of her brain. She focused on the man for the first time. *Penelope Casey was last seen getting into a late model black sedan. Shit. Pay attention or you're going to end up in a trailer in the desert handcuffed to a rusty gurney with one less kidney.*

From her vantage point in the back seat, he looked taller than he was. She put him at five foot eleven, based on the fact she'd had to look down at him with her boots on. He was clean-cut and shaven. Medium build, brown eyes, brown hair. White, though he spoke with an eastern European accent. He was wearing jeans and a leather jacket. Ridiculously long and slightly pointed leather shoes slid him closer to the nefarious-intent category in

Penelope's mind. She hated those shoes, on older men especially. Adopting trendy footwear was sign number one of an impending midlife crisis that could only result in the acquisition of a newer model with fewer miles and more horsepower—wife and car.

Penelope completed her inventory of the driver for the potential police report and found him smiling down at her without the slightest hint of sleaze. She wondered if he was waiting for a tip. Surely Victoria had taken care of that when she booked the car.

"Well, thank you. We should be going then. I have to make this flight."

Still, he was unmoved. He glanced at her hand, which was clutching the door handle. She moved it to her lap. He smiled and nodded before closing the door.

A gentleman. That's unexpected. Ted Bundy was all manners too, though.

He hurried around the car and settled in, methodically checking all his mirrors before pulling out.

"My name is Alex. Please let me know if you are uncomfortable."

I'm always uncomfortable, Alex. "I'm fine. Thank you." She opened her phone, hoping he would not fill the drive with the inane, polite chatter of two strangers pretending there was a chance they would exchange numbers and become friends on a ten-mile ride. She opened her map app to confirm they were in route to the airport. Then Penelope texted Victoria.

Penelope: On my way to the airport. Remind me to get a tracking app for you.

Victoria: That bad?

Penelope: No. He's fine. Old-fashioned.

Victoria: Did he try to open the door for you?

Penelope: And put my luggage in the trunk.

Victoria: Gasp.

Penelope: I'll text you when I land. Do you have a car on the other end? I just remembered mine is at the kennel.

Victoria: Yes. You should have time to drop Lucy off too.

Penelope: Don't have her.

Victoria: What happened to Lucy?

Penelope: Nothing. Molly and Scottie are bringing her back.

Victoria: You just left her there?

Penelope: Yes. Moving on. What's the temperature there?

Victoria: Jackson has a spring in his step.

Penelope: I bet.

Victoria: You know he can't hold a candle to you.

Penelope: Let's hope the partners agree. I'm not so sure they will. We're here. I'll see you in a couple of hours.

Victoria: Safe travels. Try not to worry.

Too late. She was quite sure, though, that no one would be able to tell. Her mother had cured her of that.

❧

Penelope took one look at the crowd at the gate and was grateful she was flying first class. She stepped over the outstretched feet of weary travelers and squeezed between the bags littering the aisle to claim the last open seat in the waiting area. Scanning the sea of faces, Penelope wondered what brought them to this place. Were they going home or leaving it? Did they have business, or were they on vacation? Did they want to be here or were they, like her, serving the demands of their ingrained fear of failure and concomitant imposter syndrome?

At the next gate over, a plane was boarding for Austin. A client once said her favorite vacation had been a week in Austin, sitting by the hotel pool all day and listening to live music every night. Penelope wished she had Molly's moxie. She would see this as fate and waltz right up to the desk. The gate attendants would laugh at her request because they also had noticed the airlines made typos on their ticket destinations periodically. They too meant to go to Austin or Hawaii or anywhere but Seattle in monsoon season. Molly might even convince them to let her buy a new ticket. Penelope's moxie did not extend past the doors of the conference room. Could she even call it moxie then? There was no risk. She knew the law and had the sharp mind to make it work in her client's favor. She was outwardly confident—maybe even bold. But that was it.

Across from Penelope, a somber girl sat, staring at the planes. Her long chestnut hair was pulled back in a braid, so there was nothing to hide her sadness. Next to her, a woman, who shared the girl's eyes and nose, sat holding her hand.

"I don't want to go." Though tears welled in her eyes, the girl's words held no emotion.

The woman put an arm around her and pulled her closer. "We've been through this."

"I'll miss them. They'll forget about me." She buried her head in the woman's chest.

"Sweetie, it's two weeks. And your dad misses you too. Of course you'll miss them, and they'll miss you, but you'll all be together soon. No one will forget about you."

The girl tipped her face upward. "What about you?"

"Yes, me too. I'm your mama. I will always be with you, even when I'm not. No matter what happens." She scooped the crying girl onto her lap, unconcerned that she had grown too large for that.

I will always be with you, even when I'm not. Mary had said that so many times to Penelope. It was true. She was always with her, not in the comforting way a child needs, but in the echoes of her fears.

That wasn't the echo stirring at the sight of the girl and her mother, though. It was the memory of the day her mother sent Scottie away. Penelope had stood on her bed and pulled the drapes aside just a sliver. Scottie was sitting at the edge of the carport, staring at the road. No one comforted her. She still felt the burning shame of her silence as she had watched her mother pretend Scottie was already gone. Had she missed them? Worried about being forgotten? She never came back. Not for one visit.

They didn't talk about it after that first Christmas when Mary had collected all of her presents and left them in that same carport for Hank to pick up. Penelope had been angry at Scottie for making her mother cry. If she were honest with herself, she hadn't been angry because Mary's feelings were hurt. She'd been angry because Scottie knew it would take weeks of sunshine to clear out the storm clouds that bore Mary's tears. She knew Penelope would have to take care of Molly. And who would take care of her? No one. So, she had dug in her heels and let the resentment seep in until it fused with her bones.

Too much time had passed, and pride kept her from reaching out and admitting she'd been wrong. Mary had done nothing to disabuse her of the notion. Looking back, maybe she even encouraged it. Had Penelope known how badly Scottie had been injured? She wanted her memory to absolve her of the sin of spite. Still, she remembered it didn't take much convincing on Mary's part to keep Penelope away from the hospital.

So lost in the past, she hadn't noticed the pair leave. The line was dwindling, and a last call for boarding was made. Penelope stood and stared at the boarding pass on her phone.

Chapter Twenty-Six

Scottie

THE SUSPENSION CREAKED when Molly stepped into the SUV. Eyes, already watering, were now swollen and red. She hugged the door and lifted her chin toward the upper floors of the building. "You can go now."

Men were so much easier. They might recap the litany of your deficiencies using their outdoor fed-up voices, showing no concern for the drops of angry spit that accompanied their words, but you always knew where you stood. That was all she wanted. Clarity on her mistakes and character defects so she could correct or hide them. She was so tired of trying to figure out what her sisters meant by their carefully edited comments.

"I didn't mean to sound cynical back there." Scottie glanced at her sister, hoping the words would turn Molly back to her, as they had a thousand times before. "I like to think of it as a dysfunctional commitment to reality." Self-deprecation brought the fight out in Molly. This time it only dropped the temperature in the cab. "Whatever. It's just me, and I'm sorry about that, but it is. I wish I had your optimism." She glanced at Molly, who was unmoved. "You can't give me the silent treatment for the next thirteen hours."

"It's fine." She remained transfixed on the building.

"If it was fine, you would not be adding to the nose prints Burnie left on that window the last time I loaned Dad my truck."

Molly sniffled. She pulled her T-shirt up and buffed the window.

"Molly, I'm kidding. Stop." Scottie reached out to grab her wrist, but she pulled it away.

Molly laid her seat back and curled toward the window. Beneath her T-shirt, the fins of her spine poked out in an arch. Scottie reached down and tugged on the fabric. Molly slapped her hand away.

"You don't have to remind me. I'm hideous now, I know."

Scottie reached behind her seat for her jacket and laid it on Molly's hip. "I was worried you were cold."

Molly pulled her knees in. A wrinkled sleeve of the coat wrapped beneath her chin, leaving the impression of an aging turtle dressed for winter.

"And you're not hideous. You're beautiful. You've always been," Scottie said.

"You're full of shit. When did that start?"

She navigated the city streets in silence. Lucy took advantage of her concentration to sneak over the console and burrow into the cavern between Molly's knees and chest. Molly swept her beneath the makeshift blanket.

"I look like Mom," she said.

"And she was pretty."

"You didn't see her at the end. The chemo took care of that."

They hadn't talked about Mary much. Her anger over being cast away was like the calcium in her bones. Though integral to the structure of her being, she gave it little thought. Still, she fed it every day to prevent her from becoming brittle and broken.

"I've always regretted that," Scottie said.

"Not seeing her when she was sick?"

"No. I don't feel bad about that. She didn't visit me in the hospital. Why would I visit her?" *And what would be the point? Redemption was as likely as rebuke.* "I meant not being there for you when she was dying. I just couldn't do it. I wish I had."

"You're wrong about that."

"Regret? I doubt it. I'm rarely wrong about regret." Scottie chuckled.

"You're wrong about Mom." Molly rolled to face Scottie, upending Lucy, who scampered to the back seat. "She did visit you. In the hospital. At least every day that I did. She waited until you were asleep. Once Jason left and Dad went home to sleep, I would trade places with her in the waiting room. She stayed for hours."

A breaker popped in Scottie's mind, and all the power went out. She couldn't picture it—Mary sitting in the dark next to her hospital bed. Had she held her hand? Cried? Prayed to the God Scottie credited with all of this?

"Did Dad know?"

"Yes. They always talked before he left."

A tornado began to spin in her chest. Scottie searched her memory for some hint that Mary had asked Hank about the letter. She couldn't conjure the slightest image of his disappointment, let alone disgust, at her treachery. Surely, if he'd known about it, Hank would have confronted her. Maybe Mary assumed no answer was the answer. She would never beg. No, she wouldn't call attention to her need once his rejection was served. She would put on some lipstick, straighten her shoulders, look straight ahead, and pretend she'd never asked him to come back.

"Why didn't you tell me she came to the hospital?" They all knew. Hank. Jason. Molly. Not one word from any of them.

"You were so angry. We didn't want to make it worse."

We? Had they discussed it? All of them knew how she felt about Mary. Why did they let her in? They had to have known she wouldn't want that. Lying there helpless. Choiceless. And Mary was there alone for hours, no doubt asking for absolution. Making amends without permission.

"Well, I'm angry now," Scottie said.

"Oh, my God. I shouldn't have told you." Molly rolled to the other side, catching the jacket beneath her. "Fuck. Now I'm angry." She wrestled with the coat.

"Let me help you."

"Don't do that." Molly slapped her hand away. "I get to be angry sometimes. You always do that."

Scottie pulled off the highway and slammed the truck into park. "I do what all the time?"

"You manage me. You try to make everything OK. It's not OK. I'm not beautiful. I'm dried up. I'm wasting away. Fuck, I'm dying, Scottie."

"Molly, you aren't going to die. We'll get you to Seattle. The best doctors are there."

Molly raised the back of her seat and turned to Scottie. She reached for her hand. "Scottie . . ."

"No. Do not say it." Scottie pulled her hand away with much more force than was necessary to escape the bony grasp. She hit the turn signal and pulled back onto the highway. "Do not say another word." She dragged the back of her hand beneath her eyes and sniffed sharply.

Molly's face softened. "I don't want to hurt your feelings. But there are things I need to say. You can't keep going through life hiding from the hard stuff."

"Hiding? Are you kidding me? I've been facing the hard stuff my whole life."

"I love you, Scottie. But that's bullshit. You've been dusting yourself off and moving on. That's not facing it. That's avoiding it. You're not a little kid anymore. You can handle this. You have to, because I'm going to need you. Penelope is going to need you."

"What if I can't?" The words sunk to the floor.

"You're going to have to. I did." Molly paused. "But you're not going to be able to bear my feelings if you can't even acknowledge your own. I don't have the energy to hold anything back."

Scottie looked away. Molly was receding. She didn't know if she had the courage to let the storm of her emotions out.

Chapter Twenty-Seven

Penelope

PENELOPE RAN HER fingertips over the ebony leather of the town car. The familiar feel had been a thrill at first, but soon she'd come to demand it. She earned it. A tactile reminder that she'd survived her cracked-Naugahyde life and the man she thought would save her.

"Come on. You'll love it. It's the most famous wedding chapel in Vegas. Maybe the world." Michael looked out the front windshield as if he could see the event playing out on the big screen. Her silence turned him, arm over her shoulders, hand on one knee. A captive audience. Captive. "You don't want some stuffy church. Besides, we'd have to put it off at least a year for Scottie's wedding to blow over. Your mom would make us. A lot can happen in a year. You don't want to wait. Let's go buy you a dress. Anything you want. This is about us. You don't want all that drama, babe. We can have a party when we get back. I know you'll like that. Plus, with the money we save, we could get a house. That's what you want, right? A house full of kids? You're always saying that. Let's do it. Right now." His face had edged closer and closer until the last few words slapped her with

puffs of hot, sticky air. Facing him was respect lesson one. "But only if you really love me."
"Of course I really love you," she said. "If this is what you want." Half-truths bartered for more than she'd wanted in the end.
"Not what I want. What you want. I need to hear you say it."
"This is what I really want." *And just like that, she changed in all the stories told at parties. Penelope so fiercely wanted him, he'd say, insisting they sneak off to Vegas for a midnight wedding. He should have known, he'd joke, since elope was in her name. She would laugh less and less at each retelling until she believed the tale and blamed herself for everything that came after.*

In that ten-year-old Buick Grand National, picking at the crusty fake leather, she flushed her childhood dreams of blush rosebud showers and buttercream frosting. She swept away the entourage of tulle-ensconced sorority sisters. Molly, standing by her side at the altar, holding the cascade of virginal gardenias as Penelope said "I do"—faded to black. Her mom gushing over Michael. *Such a catch, so smart. And older. Older is always better where men are concerned.* Vanished. Her dad walking her down the aisle after a touching apology for his absence in her life and a heartfelt promise to be a better grandfather. Dissolved. All replaced by a fast-talking man with a dream she didn't know she had—an Elvis impersonator ordained by the Church of Rockabilly Redemption. Paid performers witnessing their solemn vows. The basic Viva Las Vegas package because *you don't want to waste money on confetti when you can buy champagne* . . . or a seat at the craps table.

"Ma'am? We're here."

She looked up at the monolith of cement and steel and glass and wondered if she'd just bought a classier version of the same lie. Had she let another fast-talking man convince her that his dream was hers? Like any skilled attorney, she looked for the evidence. Clients had been happy, based on their repeat business.

Contracts were airtight. Disputes were successfully litigated with an unapologetic ferocity. And yet, fifteen years later, she still had not made partner. None of her hard work mattered now. They hadn't just permitted Jackson to throw her under the bus. They got on board and put it in reverse so he could roll over her again.

She wanted the Deluxe Package. She had damn well earned it. She'd put in her time at the cost of nearly everyone else in her life. When was the last time she'd made space in her schedule for dinner with a friend? She couldn't picture that last man she'd dated, although she vividly remembered him calling for the check the second time her phone rang during dinner. Even her relationship with Molly had been compacted into superficial thirty-minute phone calls every other day—her trying to connect while Penelope listened with one ear, both eyes and all ten fingers on her laptop. What had she missed?

She looked at the building she'd once dreamed of being good enough to work in and shivered. Without turning back to the driver, she said, "I believe my assistant made arrangements to take me to pick up my car after this meeting."

"She did."

"Don't go far. This isn't going to take long."

⁂

Mercifully, Victoria was not at her desk. There were a million logical reasons to halt this campaign, not the least of which were the number of casualties—one. Victoria. Her desk was a monument to what she treasured. A photo of her children and their families in a silver frame that was so shiny from care that the metal had turned to pearl. One smooth stone her husband of thirty-five years gave her on the vacation they took to the coast just weeks before he passed. A nameplate that cleverly displayed the words *Just Breathe* on the back. Everything else was tucked away neatly in trays, sized exactly for her particular office supplies. Penelope lingered. There was the faintest whisper of her perfume—Victoria's one rebellion.

She slipped through the door of her office. The lights came on automatically. They'd told everyone it was a conservation measure. More likely, they were all too busy and important to turn on lights when they stalked into a room. Her office looked like every other one held by a lawyer of her rank. Just enough luxury to make you think you were special, but uniform, as a subtle reminder that you could be easily replaced.

Her office was decorated to communicate warmth, counteracting the prevailing belief that women in power were hardened and bitchy. Succulents in spa-toned pots were scattered on the bookshelf amidst ancient legal tomes no one referred to anymore. She hadn't earned a table for meetings yet, so two chairs were set opposite her at the desk. She scanned the office for evidence of her existence. No photos. No curios. Everything was staged. She brought only herself to work, and only the self that was acceptable. She left behind the self that could smoke a joint while giggling with her sisters on a balcony in plain sight of the neighbors.

Penelope woke the computer on her desk, located her notes on the Ashbridge contract, and hit print.

"It's you. I was worried Jackson had tripped and fallen into your office by mistake," Victoria said.

Penelope chuckled. *That would be just like him.*

"What on earth are you wearing? I thought you were going home first."

"I changed my mind." Penelope grabbed the pages from the printer, carefully hidden from view in the credenza. For just a moment, her feet were rooted to this spot. So many times, they had stood like this, papers between them, instructions passing in bulleted phrases. Had she ever asked Victoria about her weekend?

She must have. She knew about the stone. Perhaps she overheard it in the elevator or standing in line for a single selfish latte. "I hope you know I think you're amazing."

"You've been generous in my performance reviews and raises." Victoria smiled.

"I'm not talking about money or words on a form. You are smarter and more capable than most of the people working here. The luckiest day of my career was the day I hired you."

"You're starting to worry me. Are you alright?" Victoria reached out and touched Penelope's sleeve. She pulled back just before her fingers reached her arm.

"I've never been better. I know I've not always been easy to work for. I want you to know how much I appreciate you. I'm grateful for the way you've taken care of me all these years. All the little things you didn't have to do did not go unnoticed. If I didn't thank you at the time, please know I was and am so grateful for everything." She held Victoria's eyes.

"It has been my pleasure."

Penelope reached out and squeezed her hand. In fifteen years, she had not touched the woman. Her skin was warm and firm. Penelope coveted it. Victoria had given nothing up. Her face heated at the patronizing thoughts she'd had over the years about Victoria's wasted talent. Penelope had diminished her, and it was no less painful for being unexpressed.

"And mine," she said.

≼

Penelope stunned the administrative assistant guarding the managing partner's office by saying hello and using her first name. The woman, confused no doubt by the combination, sat mouth agape long enough for her to breeze into the office.

An experienced litigator, not so much as a muscle twitched

when she burst through the door. "Ms. Casey. We aren't meeting for another hour."

Though not much older than she, the years driven by billable hours had taken a toll. The tone of his skin implied weekends on the lake, but only just so, lest the clients doubt his dedication to the job. The faintest graying said experience with vigor and screamed dye job. She guessed he'd have work done soon around his eyes that drooped from the years of carrying the bags.

"I thought I might save you some time and deliver my files on the Ashbridge contract to you."

"Not necessary. We'll review them with Jackson as we scheduled." So inconsequential was she that he returned to his work without waiting for her reply. When she did not move, he looked up.

"It is my understanding that Jackson has reviewed them, at least well enough to advise my former client on a better course of action."

He laid his pen down and leaned back in his chair. In a split second, she became the errant child. "I can see your feelings are hurt."

Penelope let the words slap her back into her body. "I'm curious. When one of the male associates comes in here angry about a case, do you do that?"

"Do what?"

She smirked at the feigned ignorance. "Tell him his feelings are hurt."

"I understand your sister is ill. Maybe this is not the best time to have this conversation." He turned back to the papers on his desk.

"Don't do that."

Raising his head slowly, his practiced eyebrows reached for each other in the center of his forehead. A warning Penelope knew he'd wielded effectively. But not today.

"Don't diminish my argument by implying it's motivated by an emotional response brought on by my personal life."

He raised his voice, clearly tiring of her. "Alright. I can see you're angry that Jackson interfered with your client. I have spoken with him about that. The fact remains that his assessment of the situation and plans for the client are sound. This is the normal course of business. You're going to need thicker skin to make it here."

"With all due respect, it's not the normal course of business to interfere with someone else's clients. It's barring on unethical. And as for thick skin, give me a goddamn break." He startled, another demonstration of his double standard. His reaction only fueled her. "The women in this organization have thick skin. Frankly, you couldn't pierce mine with a crossbow. Do you know why? Because we slap on a smile after every thinly veiled, misogynistic joke. Because we work harder every time we see you reach out your hand to hoist some substandard fraternity brother over us on the ladder. Because we have to waste precious evenings off on team-building dinners, where we are subjected to endless inane chatter about football games you played a quarter century ago and your predictions on the Mariners' season. And we cannot drift off because we must nod and smile at all the right moments to bolster your sense of importance."

"Ms. Casey, you would be wise to remember who you are speaking to," he growled. "I suggest you take a day off. We can resume this conversation when you're not quite so emotional."

"And there it is. My argument is emotional. Hence, there's no validity in it. No need to examine your policies, or practices, for the truth in my words." She paused to give him one last chance. Even the slightest self-reflection might have kept her there working seventy-hour weeks to finance his kids' Ivy League educations. He sat behind the glossy mahogany desk, his hands interlaced in front of him, his face devoid of emotion.

Following the advice of her blissful yoga instructor, she took a deep breath and let it roll past her lungs and belly until it reached her toes. As it traveled up and out of her, she felt herself let go. She was a balloon, light and lofty, covered with strips of papier mâché. If she could just peel them off, she could be who she was meant to be.

"I am tendering my resignation. I appreciate all I have learned in my time here. I recommend you review Jackson's work because he has made a mistake that will take this firm years to recover from."

"What do you want, Ms. Casey? A partnership? Fine. I'll take it to the committee. Recommend you, even."

"If you believed I was partnership material, I would already be one." Penelope turned toward the door.

Words collided in her stomach and breached her throat. She had been holding back so many words. A lifetime of protecting men from her truth. But this was not the acrid taste of words soaked in stomach acid swelling in her belly. The gift of her words would be wasted on him. He thought in dollar signs and he didn't have enough of them to buy back what she'd given away.

When she'd been freed by the failure of Michael's liver to survive his daily assaults, she never imagined being less again. She'd happily endured the caffeine-filled nights etching obscure legal precedents into her memory. Liberation was the prize, ironically paid for by the death of the man who tried to cage her dreams. That was what she was tasting now. Bold and sweet. Liberation.

"You're making a mistake that will haunt your career."

Penelope paused long enough for him to taste victory sweeping over his tongue. And then, with a backhanded wave of her fingers, she kept on walking.

Chapter Twenty-Eight

Scottie

IN THE DISTANCE, the sheet pan highway stretched to a point. The white lines, marking the edge between the space where you were expected to move forward and the space where you were permitted to rest, converged into a black dot. A four-inch yellow barrier, intended to prevent you from slamming into someone else's forward motion, ran down the center. The farther out Scottie looked, the less space she had to avoid a collision. It didn't stop her from staying in her lane.

She wondered how it came to be that everyone just followed these rules. Here she was, practically alone. There was nothing to prevent her from driving right down the center line. But she didn't—couldn't. As sure as the sun would rise tomorrow, she knew something bad would happen if she crossed that line. A cop, who hadn't had enough time for her morning coffee because she'd had it out with her boyfriend about not washing his own damn dishes, would be hiding in the scrub brush. A nail would be waiting in the middle of the road to puncture her tire and send the vehicle into a ditch. Molly would not wake up from her nap. Ever.

Breaking rules sent ripples through the universe. She wasn't sure what her father had done wrong, but she knew he was the fault line that sent tremors through their lives.

"Hallelujah!" Molly snapped up in the seat, knocking Lucy onto the floorboards.

"What the hell?"

"Hallelujah! Hallelujah!" Molly pointed to the side of the road. "Stop!"

Scottie veered onto the shoulder, stopping in front of the only thing green for miles—a road sign as big as her truck, announcing Hallelujah Junction.

Molly jumped out, leaving the door open behind her.

"Take my picture. It's a sign." She reached up and slapped the mottled bottom edge.

"I can see it's a sign." Scottie reached for the passenger door. "Shut the door or the dogs will . . . dammit." Burnie and Lucy had the same idea, apparently. "Grab the dogs!"

"They want to be in the picture. Leave them alone. Hurry up." Molly stood beneath the sign in the space between the two words and pointed. Her arms completed the wide V that started in the middle of her smile and reached to her fingertips. Just like everything else in Molly's life, the two dogs came right to her and sat like bookends adoring her.

Afraid her movements might disturb the scene, Scottie took the first pictures through the bug-encrusted windshield. Stifling a groan, she eased herself down from the truck and leaned on the hood. She zoomed in until only the tiniest margin of dirt and rocks framed the picture, and then she hit the button, over and over again, until Molly's smile was burned into her mind. Her chest filled with sadness, pulling at her breath. *So unfair. Why did it have to be her?*

"It's a sign!"

"Yes, Molly, it's a sign, you goof." Scottie whistled for the dogs, who were piddling on the posts.

"You don't remember, do you? The trip to California. Dad said that on the way down and on the way back. He thought he was so damn funny. 'Hallelujah Junction, it's a sign!' I thought Mom was going to jump out of the car and walk home." Molly sat back onto the bumper, bracing her hands on her knees, and chuckled. "He kept it up. She finally told him, 'Say it again and it'll be a sign that you're getting a divorce.' That shut him up." Molly pushed off the truck and scooped Lucy out of the dirt. "Ironic. They got divorced after that trip." Brushing the debris from the dog's paws, she said, "Let's take a pic together and send it to him. He'll crack up. Come on. Get Burnie."

Scottie stood beside her as she maneuvered the phone to capture their heads and the sign. It wasn't the most attractive angle and the only part of the dogs showing was a triangular swath of Lucy's right ear.

"How could you forget that trip?" Molly shook her head. "It was the last one we ever took as a family."

"Because I'm the youngest. And it sounds like it was traumatic, so I probably blocked it out."

As they loaded the dogs, the trip played in Scottie's mind. Sitting on the rockery, she had watched them load the Wagoneer. Even at seven years old, she could feel the animosity like a force field around her parents. Mary carried suitcases and stacked them in the rear compartment. The luggage rack on the top of the Jeep lay empty, a monument to the battles fought over the trip. The first round had gone to Mary.

"If a suitcase falls off that truck and our underwear is strewn all over the highway for complete strangers to see, I will have a fit."

"You're having a fit now."

Mary served up the winning blow. "This is nothing, Hank Casey."

Scottie didn't know what that meant, but it scared her. Collecting every pair of underwear she had, one pair of socks, and a T-shirt, she filled her suitcase. Before she could latch it, Mary took the case from her and dumped the contents on her bed.

"You're too little to pack. You'll forget something."

I sure will. I'll forget to pack that ugly jumper. She flicked a mosquito from her overalls. She would have squished it, but they were her favorite pants—bright red with lots of pockets for pretty rocks. Besides, she didn't need to give her mom any excuses to make Scottie change her clothes. Bug guts on her pant leg would do it for sure. Partly because her dad would carry her like a suitcase from the back strap of the overalls and partly because her mother hated her "boy" clothes, Scottie vowed to wear them every day on vacation.

She ran into the house and grabbed her crayons and coloring book. Before she reached the Jeep, she was plucked up and set back on the rockery. Being small stank. She always had to ride in the middle, hold someone's hand crossing the street, and go to bed early. She was so small, sometimes they forgot she was even there. When the yelling started, she flattened herself against the flowered wallpaper and pretended it was a jungle she could back into until silence returned.

Like the burnt-orange carpet that blanketed the house, there was a layer of anger everywhere. Over time, the shag matted and only on the farthest edges, where no one ever walked, was there the soft plush that tickled her feet. Scottie was sure, if you collected all that anger and followed it back to its source, somehow it led to her. Penelope was beautiful and a dancer. Molly was funny and athletic. Scottie was nothing special. She was the add-on kid her mom regretted.

Penelope slid her hand over her notebook, which was resting next to Scottie's thigh.

"Ow! You pinched me!" said Scottie.

"I barely touched you. Don't be such a baby."

"I'm not a baby. Don't put your stuff on my side."

"Mom, Scottie is sitting on my books."

As Penelope complained, Scottie let her feet slide to either side of the hump on the floor, spreading her thighs so they touched the edges of her third of the bench seat. A whisper of her skin touched each sister. Molly kicked her.

"Scottie. Move over. Those are important. Penelope has an assignment for school." Mary reached over the seat and slapped at her knee. "Honestly. We're not even out of the neighborhood and you're starting." She pulled down the visor and searched her bag. Leaning forward, open-mouthed, she punctuated her speech with a swipe of raspberry lipstick. "We are going to have a nice vacation. Do you hear me?"

"Scottie. Are you there?" Molly asked now.

"What? Sorry."

"You remembered, didn't you?"

"A little." She looked over her shoulder and pulled onto the highway.

"I don't remember it all, either."

"Who wants to remember all that fighting?"

"They weren't always that way," Molly said.

"Maybe before I came along."

"No. I mean, the whole time they were married. They fought off and on, but they didn't start arguing because of you."

"It felt like it. I could never do anything right. All day long, she just got more and more irritated with me and then he would come home, and she would let him have it over the stupidest shit." The admission soured in Scottie's stomach. The stress of trying so hard not to annoy her mother, but never knowing exactly what she'd done to set her off, simmered afresh in her belly.

"She was irritated with all of us," Molly said.

"Not like me."

"Lucky we had Penelope then."

"Why was that lucky?" Scottie laughed. She turned to Molly, expecting her to be doing the same. Instead, she found only confusion.

"Because she took care of us. Shielded us from it, or at least tried to."

"What are you talking about? We weren't shielded by her or anyone else." Ancient resentment broke to the surface.

"That's bullshit. On that trip, every little thing that went wrong turned into a fight. Holy hell. If a public bathroom had scratchy toilet paper, Mom would bitch for a hundred miles like it was his fault. When we weren't in the car, Penelope would take us away so we could get a break from it. I remember how excited she was for the trip because we were going to see all these historical sites so she could write about it for school. She brought her school notebook, and Mom got her new colored pencils. I think we only saw one thing that whole trip—Chimney Rock. Penelope spent the whole time there walking us around and reading the plaques. I don't know if she even did the assignment. Penelope was so hurt. I could tell, because she gave me the pencils. Like it didn't matter."

As she spoke, the trip took form, though not through Penelope's eyes as Molly had told the story.

"I remember that," Scottie said. "Well, part of it. I brought a coloring book and crayons, but I wanted her colored pencils. I tried to get her to trade with me. Sounds stupid to say it now. I thought she would do it because I had one of those big boxes and it was brand-new. She just had like ten pencils. But she wouldn't do it. Then she gave them to you. For nothing. I was so mad." Her dispassionate tone hid a hurt as solid as it had been when she was six years old. *How petty am I to still be pissed about colored pencils after forty years?*

"I want to see that place. We have to stop," Molly said.

"No."

"Why not? Come on."

"We need to get home. Why do you want to relive that?"

"I don't know. I just want to see it. You can't deny a dying woman."

"Jeez, Molly. Stop saying that." Scottie backhanded her on the shoulder.

"Ow. Lighten up. We're all dying. I'm just ahead of you, as usual. We're stopping."

Scottie didn't see much use in arguing. She was driving after all, and Molly would probably be asleep by the time they passed it.

They drove by a sign for Likely, California two hours later. *I bet Dad had a heyday with that one. Not Likely. City? Likely story.* Scottie snorted. Molly groaned and rolled toward her.

"You can't be groaning at me. That was all in my head." Her smile flattened at the emaciated figure next to her. Molly's eyes were closed. The next groan faded to a whimper. Scottie brushed the hair from her face and laid a hand on her cheek. An alarm went off in her head. Molly's skin was hot, but she was shivering.

"You have to pull over." Molly pushed herself up. "Now." She unhooked her belt and had the door half open before Scottie jerked to a stop. Molly lurched forward and her body heaved. What little she'd eaten that morning lay in a puddle on the blacktop.

Scottie set the brake and grabbed her water bottle. By the time she'd come around the truck, Molly was lying back, panting. Burnie and Lucy were on alert in the back seat, staring at her. She reached her hand back and let them lick her.

"Jeez, I know my driving is bad, but this is a little dramatic, don't you think?" She joked half-heartedly, tucking Molly's hair behind her ears.

"I can't drink that."

"I thought you might want to rinse out your mouth." Scottie found some napkins tucked in the door pocket and soaked them in water.

"You're not cleaning my face with your dog-slobber rags, are you?"

"What? It's the latest," Scottie joked. "All the big makeup companies are coming out with a line of dog-slobber moisturizers this year. The research shows owning a dog makes you live longer. The truth is, it's the slobber. It covers everything, even wrinkles. That's why rich people have to get Botox. They pick tiny dogs that don't slobber." She dabbed Molly's face. Scottie's humor hadn't eased the grimace there. "Alturas is not far. I think we should stop at the hospital and get you checked out."

"No. I have nausea medicine in my suitcase. Can you grab it?"

"Maybe I should call Penny. She could get you on a flight. I'm sure Alturas has planes. You know, what with all the historical sites."

"Funny." Molly waved her away with a force that wouldn't have moved a butterfly. "But no. Just get the pills, will you?"

Scottie called for Lucy, who happily jumped into the front seat and snuggled next to Molly. As Scottie scrambled to the back of the vehicle, she pulled her phone out.

"I mean it. Do not call Penelope. I don't want her here if she doesn't want to be. She'd only be coming out of obligation. I don't want to be an obligation."

Scottie quietly slipped her phone back into her pocket. For as long as she could remember, she'd longed to hear Molly choose her over Penelope. The victory was drowned out by the terror of doing this alone. Penelope would know what to do. She wouldn't hesitate or second-guess herself.

"Scottie, did you hear me?" Molly shouted from the front seat.

Steeling herself, she opened the cargo door. The luggage and dog supplies were neatly stacked. She pulled the suitcase out and tugged at the zipper.

"Am I going to find anything embarrassing in here?"

"Yes, I packed all my S and M gear. For crying out loud. Get the pills or I'm barfing on your seat. I swear you got Dad's sense of humor. You're not as funny as you think you are, either."

"I'm hilarious. The fact that you don't see that is evidence we do need to stop at a hospital soon." Any joking in her voice was lost in her growing panic.

"Pills!" Molly ordered.

Scottie rummaged through the clothes until she felt something hard wrapped in a towel. She didn't have to unwrap it to know what she had. "What. The. Actual. Fuck. Molly."

"Oh crap. I should have warned you. I see you met Morrigan."

Scottie quickly shoved the gun into her belt and pulled her shirt over it. It took all her strength to entomb the onslaught of fear and sadness. *Oh, Molly. A gun, really?* All the losses got in line like an army of grief marching in her chest. The loss of the mom she never knew. The loss of the mom who sent her away. The loss of the chance to be a part of the sisterhood that Molly and Penny shared.

Even though she should be grateful for Hank and Jason, there was a place they could not touch inside her. She didn't know how to heal that. She just knew that Molly was her only connection to it. Once she was gone, there would be no finding it. She didn't need her speeding up her departure.

She wiped her face on one of Molly's T-shirts and grabbed the pills from the bottom of the case. "Why do you have a gun in your bag?"

"Why do you keep a gun in your truck?" Molly stuck out her hand.

"Answer the question." They stared at each other. "Are you planning to hurt yourself?"

"Hurt? Kill, don't you mean?"

"Whatever. Quit dancing around."

"No. Absolutely not. Do you honestly think I would ask you to bring me home and then shoot myself on the way?"

"Why, then?" Scottie crouched down beside the truck and waited.

"I didn't want to leave it behind. It's important to me. I don't have many things that are. When I do die, I want some people to have things that were special to me, so they won't forget me."

"You're not going to die anytime soon." While Scottie had to force those words to sound convincing, the ones that followed required no effort. "No one who loves you is going to forget you. Ever."

"That's the thing. Some people are special to me. But I don't think they know it. I can't leave wondering." She spoke slowly, catching her breath with each word. "And I want to know I was special to them. Otherwise, what was the point in being alive at all?"

Scottie's tears fought their way out. When she spoke, her voice cracked. "Who is the gun for, Molly?"

"Dad."

"I don't understand. Why would a gun be special to him? He has a bunch of guns."

"It's not special to him. It's special to me. He gave me that gun when I got the place in Reno." Molly paused and tossed the pills in her mouth. With a swig from her water bottle, she tipped her head back and gulped. She took two panting breaths before continuing. "We never spent much time together, really. Honestly, I thought I wasn't that important to him, at least not like you are. But he called me before I left that first time and asked if I would come out. I don't know where you were, but you weren't around. We had a long talk."

She bent over her knees and held her face in her hands.

Scottie handed her a napkin, but she waved it away. "He took me to the range and showed me how to shoot. He said he was worried and wanted me to be safe since he couldn't be there. I remember I was so angry at first. I said some terrible things. He hadn't been there for me growing up. How did he know I was safe back then? He said he was sorry I felt that way. He also said that part of loving someone is giving them space and not making them uncomfortable. That's what he'd done, and he hoped that someday we could have a relationship." Molly rinsed her mouth out and spit the water onto the asphalt. "We never talked about it again. I tried to see him more, though. He wasn't as judgy as Mom about my life choices. I never came right out and said the words. I don't know. Giving him the gun back feels like telling him I know he kept me safe."

"It's not the same, though. You need to tell him. He's never come right out and said it, but I know he has a deep sadness over you two. I tried to fill it, but I can't. I get that now, but so much time has passed, and things have changed."

"That's what I mean. It's too late."

"It's not," said Scottie.

"You don't know that."

Chapter Twenty-Nine

Molly

"Hey. There's a wildlife viewing spot in a couple of miles. Do you want me to stop?" Scottie glanced at Molly with a hopeful smile.

She had been adamant about the hospital. Though the constant rumble of the old highway against the tires was making her carsick, she resisted Scottie's repeated offers to stop. With Penelope gone, a thousand miles of pointless discomfort lay ahead. Not that it would have been comfortable had she not dropped them for a business meeting, but the awkwardness and animosity had at least a chance of turning into something beautiful. Instead, she would have to endure two days of Scottie trying to make up for Penelope's rejection and distracting them both from the inevitable.

"Scottie. No. There's no point. We've been driving through wildlife country since we left Reno. I haven't seen a damn thing, with the notable exception of the gas station attendant who smelled like he was related to a wild boar."

"That's true. Hmm," Scottie said. "I mean, why even have a

viewpoint here? Do the elk and bears all take their lunch breaks here? Clearly not, since the elk is lunch. Maybe they bait the area to encourage animals to congregate. I wonder how you'd market that. Best Grass in California. That's OK for the elk, but then you'd need Best Elk in Two States for the bears—they have a larger range, right? Then what? You'd need an appeal for the smaller animals. Weasels are mean, so maybe Come for the Carnage, Stay for the Carrion. Mountain Beavers are herbivores and, if they're anything like vegetarians, a gentler breed. So, bears eating elk would not appeal to them. You'd need something like Burrow into the Softest Dirt in Cali."

"OK. Stop it." Molly slapped her arm. "What do you really want to talk about?"

"What? I'm just making conversation. You haven't really held up your part of the bargain on this trip so far. Nary a song has been belted." She turned to Molly and flashed a toothy grin. "The most noise you've made was gakking on the side of the road."

"You're not making conversation. You're rambling, and inanely at that, which you do whenever you did something wrong and don't know how to confess, or you have a question you don't want to ask. So, which is it?" Molly wedged herself upward in the seat and rolled her body toward Scottie.

"I have a bunch of questions, but they're all about your problem and you've made it clear you don't want to talk about it."

"Say it," she said.

"What are you talking about?"

Molly could see by the dramatic way Scottie raised her shoulders that the question was fake.

"Scottie, it's not 'a problem.' It's cancer. Say it." Her shoulders relaxed, but she continued to stare straight ahead. Molly refused to look away. The building anger came out in her voice. "Say it."

"Why are you doing this?"

"What am I doing, exactly, Scottie?" The words were sharp. Molly was not going to let her off the hook. They had danced around too many things. Protecting each other from the hurt that comes with honesty had only widened the divide between them all. It wasn't a bridge that kept the path open for a future when they were ready to meet in the middle. It was a tattered rope swing, knotted loosely to a dying branch that they would never have the courage to jump on because they could never allow themselves to believe someone on the other side would hold their hand out and catch them.

"Fine. Did you not notice you were getting sick? This didn't happen overnight. I'm not stupid. You've been sick for a while, but you didn't call me until now. Are you even seeing a doctor? Or is there just no point? Fuck, Molly."

"Well done. Spontaneous use of the F-word."

Scottie hit the steering wheel. "I'm not joking here, Molly. Do you want to die? Because if you did, why did you call me to bring you home?"

"Nobody wants to die. I just don't want to be half alive."

"So, what? You're just going to avoid treatment until it kills you? Does Penny know? Is that why she left with zero regard for us?"

"No. Penelope does not know."

"I bet."

"Don't call me a liar. Penelope does not know. She would have taken the whole thing over and smothered me. And she didn't leave with zero regard. She has a stressful job. She works her ass off."

"And I don't?"

"Jeez, Scottie. It's not a competition. I wasn't saying anything about you. I was talking about Penelope. I wouldn't have to defend her if you gave her even one inch of grace. You always see the bad in her. She took care of us. And she's still trying to. God, you're a mule. Pull over."

"I'm not pulling over. We need to have this conversation."

"Pull over or we'll be having this conversation in a puke-filled truck."

Scottie jerked the wheel to the shoulder. Molly unclipped her belt and stumbled out, bracing her hand on the door as she heaved. The small amount of fluid that was left in her stomach breached her throat. She tried to spit it out, but her mouth was dry. As if the snotty, bile-dripping mess were not enough, she crumpled to her knees, crying.

Scottie rushed around the truck. Molly fell back, gravel digging through her jeans. She slapped away Scottie's hands. "Don't touch me." Scottie groaned as she eased herself to the ground, but she didn't have the strength to share any of her pain. She couldn't bear their grief for them.

All the energy she'd stored up for this trip was gone already. Now, Penelope wasn't even there. She'd imagined them laughing with her as they recalled the good parts of that last trip and their childhood, the parts they'd shared before it all crumbled. And then they would grieve her loss together. The ultimate epiphany would hit them—that they loved each other like only sisters can and none of the bullshit from the last four decades mattered at all.

She needed more time, one more chance. She'd waited too long, banking on this one sure shot. That pain stabbed her hot and sharp in her gut.

"I'm sorry." Scottie patted Molly's hand.

"Not good enough." She swiped her sleeve across her open mouth, jutting her tongue out to clear away the bile.

"OK. I'm sorry I upset you. I'm sorry I'm being hard on Penny. But mostly, I'm sorry you're sick." Scottie leaned forward and hugged her knees. "So sorry, I can't breathe when I think about it. I feel powerless, and you won't tell me what's going on so I can do something about it."

Molly sat, staring at the scrub brush. She searched her mind to satisfy the growing hunger to say something that would put them back on track, but her head went numb. The world slipped out of focus. Words drifted through her head, but the order was all wrong. The once-sharp rocks she sat on now dulled against her skin. Without warning, her left leg detached from her brain, jerking her body flat on the ground, and everything went dark.

Chapter Thirty

Penelope

THE LAST TIME Penelope had sat in the back seat for the drive from Seattle to Snoqualmie, she'd been thirteen years old. Forced to visit her father every other weekend by a man in a black robe who spoke over her head, like she wasn't already old enough to take the bus down Aurora on her own to pick out clothes she paid for with her babysitting money. The judge could make her go, something she only conceded after finding the tear-soaked lawyer's bill crinkled next to her mother's cold coffee. He could not make her participate, though. Her defiance began the moment she buckled in and turned her head so the only thing her father could see in the rearview window was a sheet of shiny hair covering her profile.

Looking at the graffiti-lined streets now, she tried to conjure up a memory of these streets from her youth. There was a faint echo of Molly prattling on about her dolls or her teacher or the dog, but she could not remember her father's voice. Surely, he had said something.

Every other week, on the Sunday night drive home, she

tamped all that anger and sadness down and sewed it up tight. If even a single thread was loose, it could catch on the smallest thing—Scottie coloring in one of her books, Molly wearing her favorite T-shirt—and all the stuffing would come out in big tufts of hateful words.

Worse than the hurt it inflicted on her sisters was the way it fed Mary, who never even tried to contain her anger and sadness. Her mother was like one of Molly's toy sponges, as tiny as a pill until she dropped it in the water. As it absorbed, it grew bigger and bigger until it took up the whole container and morphed into a multi-colored monster. No matter how much the dam of feelings inside her swelled, Penelope held in every drop to prevent setting that in motion.

Every other Friday night as they drove toward his house, though, she would tug on the seam until it unraveled. Opening the dam, her anger and sadness flowed up and out until it filled every part of her body and mind. The days of containment had trained her, though. She wanted to spit it all out at her father, but the feelings congealed in her throat. Silence was the only punishment she could mete out.

"Ma'am? Are you alright?" the driver asked.

Penelope placed one hand on her belly and one on her chest and closed her eyes. This move, done hundreds of times in the last decade, had always been followed with "OK, what now?" or "Am I supposed to be feeling something?" or "I have got to quit wasting my time and money on this hippie yoga shit." Pressing her hands, she searched for the bees that were always swarming inside her, but she could not feel the tiniest vibration. She slid her hand beneath her shirt. Her belly was soft and warm. Her eyes closed, and damned if that yoga instructor hadn't been right all along. Inner peace was real.

She took another deep breath and sank into the seat with

her exhale. A smile floated toward the corners of her eyes. "I'm doing fine. Thank you."

"We'll be out of this traffic soon."

"It's fine. Don't worry on my account."

She opened her eyes and looked around. They stood still in a long queue of cars waiting their turn on the on-ramp. Where the interstate crossed over them, a homeless encampment had wedged itself between the dusty ground and the cement stanchions. When Michael was alive, he threatened her with this. *You'll be out on the streets without me. You can't even support yourself.* Fear should have filled her now. For the first time since she was fourteen years old, she was without a job. Still, she was unafraid.

Movement in the periphery of her vision caught her attention. Ill-fitting clothes hung from rendered bodies. She was ashamed of the opulence that had her worrying daily about every fraction of a pound she gained. The pilings announced "Angelz" and "Trez" in fat letters, painted by artists of burgeoning talent, proclaiming their need for belonging and safety. Though she'd passed this spot a thousand times, she'd never taken notice. The paintings had been a passing annoyance for which she'd done no more than bemoan the demise of Seattle and switch her voter registration. Looking at the scene just outside the window, with her hands on her heart and belly, she felt no animosity, no fear. She wondered who all these people had been before they were forced to rummage through garbage cans to survive. She wondered what secrets kept them from their families.

⁓

Penelope hadn't warned Hank she was coming. Worse, she hadn't warned herself he could be there. His truck shielded her car from the driveway. The sight of it warmed her. Penelope brushed the sensation aside. She was reading too much into the gesture. Taking the farthest spot from the door was probably nothing more than consideration for his clients, certainly not an attempt to protect her or her vehicle.

The driver transferred her bag from his trunk to hers and, though she knew Victoria would have tipped him well, she slipped him another twenty—a small reparation for her general lack of gratitude in the last decade. He left her standing there. His job done. Just another stranger in her life who completed their duties and moved on.

When had that happened? B.M., as she liked to refer to the years before Michael demanded her undivided attention, she'd had girlfriends. Though she'd met him while she was in college, he hadn't started isolating her right away. That was what her therapist had called it when she blamed herself for giving up her friends and allowing him to make her small and dependent. The distance of years made the picture so much clearer now.

The first year they were together, he doted on her. *I will take care of you.* Though seductive, she clutched her distrust like an iron shield. Hadn't Mary said that as well, after all? And yet, she'd been parenting herself and Molly for more than a dozen years by then. The manic displays of affection—roses, champagne, jewelry—eroded her resolve. She'd bought them with the only currency he would accept. Complete devotion. *She's jealous you have someone who loves you and she has no one. She wants me, can't you see that?* he would say as he picked off each of her friends until there were none left. For her part, she hadn't just walked into the cell willingly. She pulled the door shut and locked it for him. Penelope shed her friends, one by one, to prove her loyalty. Some slipped away like a river. Others clung, trying to warn her. Some released their venom about him. They left all the same.

Now, what did she have? She had Molly. She'd never thought about that as a finite thing. She didn't have Scottie. It wasn't the same thing, anyway. They hadn't shared a childhood like she and Molly had. Worse, there was a lie between them, and she'd been complicit all these years in keeping it. Though not a comforting thought, she could have had Hank in her circle. He had reached out through the years. If she were honest, she'd been the one building a wall, not him.

The lights switched off at the end of the kennel, and Penelope knew her father would be coming down the hall to lock up for the night. There was time to speed away, but something kept her rooted in her spot.

"Hey, Aunt Penny!" Meaghan crossed the parking lot to her. "Is my mom back?"

"Hey, you." Penelope couldn't help but smile at the sight of her niece. "No, she should be here tomorrow with Molly. I had to come back for a meeting." She wondered if Scottie knew how Molly had engineered chance meetings for her and Meaghan over the years.

"That's a bummer. I bet it wasn't as fun as a road trip with Molly and my mom. Those two think they're hilarious." Meaghan held the back of her hand next to her mouth as if she were spilling a state secret. "They kind of are, but I don't encourage it." She giggled, and Penelope wondered, not for the first time, how Scottie had produced such a carefree child. "Hey, Grandpa's in the office still. I bet he'd love to see you."

Penelope was trapped. She couldn't just drive away now. To the rest of the world, it might appear she had her life well in hand. The truth was, her bravado was late blooming and forced. There was a river of doubt running just beneath the surface.

Meaghan was the real deal. She knew who she was and what she would accept. Molly told her once that, much to her father's chagrin, she took advantage of a neighbor's lemonade stand on a hot summer day, in a town with a proud history of clear-cut logging, to march around with a sign boldly proclaiming, "Polr bars need ise to!" She didn't let her inability to spell deter her. She never backed down or played small for anyone. Penelope couldn't say the same.

"Absolutely. I wasn't sure if he was here," she said.

Stifling a grin, Meaghan glanced at his behemoth truck parked ten feet from them.

"Or busy," Penelope added, rolling her eyes.

Meaghan smiled. "You should come out here more. I'll take you to lunch at my favorite burger joint—if your fancy palate can handle that."

"I'd love it. I promise." She reached out, an awkward attempt at connection. Without warning, Meaghan hugged her. It took a second to get over the surprise, but Penelope leaned into it. She'd forgotten the joy of a big hug.

"Sorry, but I can't help it. We're a hugging family."

"You must get that from your dad."

Meaghan pulled her chin in and chuckled. "Hardly. That's all Mom."

Penelope turned her attention to the door. She drew in her breath and let it out, molecules at a time.

"It's unlocked. All you have to do is open the door."

She didn't answer. For Meaghan, it probably was just that easy.

߷

Penelope barely had a foot in the door when a Great Dane, the colors of a tuxedo, let out a mighty woof. Penelope stumbled backward until she came to rest on the pen across the aisle. When she heard the low rumble behind her, she pictured a pit bull ready to pounce at the slightest movement. To her surprise, a fat basset hound lay on the floor. The only thing moving was its tail in a lackadaisical thump. When she straightened up, the dog groaned and rolled onto its back. She wanted to go in and scratch its belly, but she remembered the safety rules from childhood.

The kennel had been updated since she'd been there last. Scottie was right to be proud of it. They clearly worked hard to keep it clean and modern. A few dogs sat up when she passed. Most appeared to be taking a post-dinner nap. Her dad was sitting at his desk, copying notes from the computer screen. She knocked gently on the doorjamb.

"Hi, Dad."

He pushed his chair back and turned toward her. "Well, hello, Penny. I didn't expect to see you." A chorus of barks erupted. He leaned over to look around her, down the hall.

"It's just me."

He furrowed his brow.

This was a mistake. She scanned the room for something to talk about. *So, still in the dog game, are you?* "Molly and Scottie are still on the road. I got called back for an emergency meeting at work," Penelope said.

"I was sorry to hear that."

"Really? Why?" *And what? You're sorry it's just me? You're sorry I had a meeting? You're sorry they aren't here?*

"Why? Because I bet you were having fun. I think it's the first time the three of you have done anything together in years. When you were kids, oh my, you were hilarious when the three of you were up to something together." He closed the folder on his desk and slipped it into the drawer. "They had you running in circles. But you loved it. Molly was always up to some mischief. Scottie would be tagging along, clueless. And you would chase after them, laughing." He leaned back in his chair and let out a hoot toward the ceiling.

"I don't remember."

His smile faded and separated from his eyes. "That's too bad because you all were so sweet together." He pushed himself up from the chair. "Say, I was just heading out. Do you have time for dinner?"

"I should get back to the city."

"You have to eat. You can put Lucy in here. I have an open kennel. Deluxe. Just like her."

The offer put her off guard. "Molly and Scottie have Lucy. It's just me tonight." She glanced at the clock and back to his face, which had softened with hope. "Oh, what the hell. I could eat."

Penelope followed him into town, skirting the interstate. The two-lane road hadn't changed much since she was a kid. Closer to town, farms had been converted to dense forests of two-story, single-family homes, complete with communal swing sets and carved rock monuments announcing what was lost—Windstrom's Pastures.

Hank didn't have to say where they were going. Until she was old enough to get a weekend job and eschew her court-ordered visits, she'd eaten there every other Friday night.

"I hope you don't mind. I know this place is old, but I hate to see it go out of business with all the new places popping up." He grabbed two menus off the counter and waved them at the waiter. Like a hawk, he claimed the booth in the center.

Penelope smiled at the busboy, who placed a basket of tortilla chips and salsa on the table between them. For years, she'd avoided eating Mexican food, saying it upset her stomach. Sitting there, she realized it hadn't been the food. Even now, childish fears bubbled in her belly.

"So. What was your meeting about? Must have been important." He scooped up some salsa. "It's OK if you can't say."

"No. It's fine." She picked up a chip and snapped it in half. "While I was at Molly's, one of my colleagues stole one of my clients. He accused me of not handling the case correctly." She took a sip of water to cool the shame spreading across her cheeks. "I didn't. Handle it incorrectly, that is."

"So, what'd you do about that?" Tiny worry lines formed at the outside corner of his eyes and fanned out.

"I quit, actually." She forced herself to hold his eyes.

"That seems extreme." The lines deepened on his forehead.

The vibration in her belly returned. This time, she did not want to quell the bees with grounding exercises or deep breathing. She wanted to let the hornet's nest loose on his judgment. Penelope had done it all on her own. Not even in the desolate moments had she asked for his help. She wasn't wasting a future he toiled to give her. She owned it and she could throw it away if she wanted to. Sure as hell, she wouldn't be asking for his help now, no matter what happened when the dust settled.

She studied his face. As her jaw tightened for the fight, his eyebrows knit together above worried eyes. Her hand slid to her belly. It was not his judgment the bees were after. They were searching for the residual voice of doubt and fear darting between her gut and mind.

"Not really," she said, leaving a space for him to push back. He leaned in instead, so she continued. "It was time to fish or cut bait. Isn't that what you always used to say? I've worked hard to get here. I do good work. But after Jackson's stunt, no matter how that turns out, my career there will be terminal." She flinched at her casual use of the word. "I'm not making partner anytime soon, and definitely not at McArthur Kane. There's a good chance I'll be blacklisted after today, at least from the major firms. I might have to go it alone. But I'll be fine."

"You've always been the brave one." He straightened.

"Hardly. That's Molly."

"Molly is the daredevil. There's a big difference. And Scottie works hard, but she's cautious. Well, anyway, I'm proud of you for following your gut." He raised his mug to her.

She'd waited a lifetime to hear him say those words to her. *I'm proud of you.* She thought she'd be filled with joy. But any joy she was feeling was shrouded by the rot of her resentment. She pushed his words away. "You might not be if I end up homeless."

"You're never going to be homeless. You have family."

Do I? Who? You? Scottie? My family is likely dying. From the youngest corner of her heart, she wanted to push back and say all those things she'd held inside. *We were a family until you screwed it up. Where was my family when Michael was abusing me?* But sitting there, across the table, she remembered the father he was before the divorce. The man who picked her up and twirled her around after dance recitals. The one who snuck a bit of icing when her mom wasn't looking and put it on the tip of her nose. Anger and joy and grief all swirled inside her. She wanted to hug him and slap him. As she was trying to figure out how to physically pull that off, the waiter stole her chance with two plates of enchiladas.

They ate without speaking. After the waiter took their plates away, Hank cleared his throat.

"Penny, I know this is not an ideal place to say this, but I haven't seen you in so long and I'm never sure when I will see you again. And there are things that need to be said. I'm getting old." He took a sip of his coffee. Staring at the cup, he took a deep breath. "I'm so sorry for all of the hurt you felt from the divorce."

Penelope looked to the door. "You mean the hurt you caused."

"Your mom and I had our problems."

"Stop." The seam unraveled, one stitch at a time. It broke open and all the angry stuffing billowed out. "I know about the affair."

Hank dropped his mug on the table. Wide-eyed and mouth agape, it took a beat before he spoke. "Did your mother tell you that?"

"Are you denying it? You can't just say you're sorry for the hurt and not take responsibility for causing it. You had an affair. Mom tried to stay with you. It was your fault."

"You're right. I was unhappy. That doesn't make it OK. I

should have tried to work on our marriage." He picked up his coffee and looked out the window. "Does Molly know?"

"No. Does Scottie know?" Penelope countered.

"No, she does not know. Unless you told her. She didn't hear it from me."

"Not about the affair. About the fact she's your daughter. Or are you still lying about that?"

Hank caught the waiter's eye and signaled for more coffee. Penelope grabbed her purse off the seat and scooted to the edge of the bench.

"Please, don't go. We need to finish this," he said.

Penelope stopped. "You have to be honest, or I'm leaving."

"How did you find this out? Did your mother tell you?"

"No. I was there when Scottie's mom showed up at the door, trying to take her away." Penelope saw the confusion on his face. "Didn't she tell you? She paid that horrible woman off to save Scottie. Maybe she needs to know that. She was horrible to Mom. All Mom ever did was try to save her."

"You're right. She does need to know. I will tell her."

"You haven't and you won't. You've had decades. You're always protecting her."

"I'm protecting you. You shouldn't have to tell her. I'm so sorry you've had to carry this secret around all these years. You should never have known. It wasn't your burden to bear."

"Why didn't you tell Scottie?"

"I was waiting until she was older and could understand more. None of this was her fault. I know you're still angry with her. Put yourself in her shoes. Her birth mother gave her up and her adopted mother sent her away. All she had was me. She'll hate me for this. But I was all she had back then."

"You were protecting yourself. You've had plenty of years to tell her."

"Not really. By the time she was old enough to know, she had the accident. It was years of healing. She wasn't in a good place. I couldn't drop that on her. And then it was too late." He picked his coffee cup up and stared into it like wisdom was going to float to the surface. "She didn't do anything to deserve this. I know I have to be honest with myself. I'm going to pay the price for that. You have to be honest too, though. You blame her for the divorce. It wasn't her fault. I'm to blame. I loved your mother. And I understand why she couldn't keep loving me."

"Is that why you didn't answer her letter?"

"What letter?"

"Dad, I saw it on her nightstand. She wanted to get back together. If you really loved her, why didn't you answer her?"

"I didn't get the letter." Hank turned away from her, and she knew he was lying.

"I don't believe you." Penelope's phone buzzed in her purse. Scottie's name flashed on the screen, and she declined the call. "I don't think you wanted to get back together with Mom or be a family."

"I'm not sure your mom did, either. I know you think I'm the only villain in this, but I'm not."

Penelope's phone buzzed again, and a text popped up from Scottie.

Scottie: 911 where are you? Call me ASAP.

"Your mom made me promise no one would ever know I was Scottie's dad. You're old enough to understand why."

"Because it was humiliating to raise your bastard child? Why would you even make her do that? You should have let someone else adopt her. It was cruel."

"Maybe you can't understand because you aren't a parent."

"Don't give me that."

"She was a baby, and we both loved her. Your mom did. Scottie looks like her birth mother. That's what your mom couldn't take. The sight of her was a slap in the face. She felt horrible about it, and she blamed me for that too. And she was right. It was all me. If you want to hate someone, hate me. But don't hate Scottie for something she didn't do and can't control."

Her phone buzzed again.

Scottie: Molly had a seizure. They took her to the hospital in Alturas. Please call me!

"I have to go."

"We aren't done." Hank reached out, but Penelope scooted out of the booth.

"We're done, Dad." She dropped two twenties on the table and walked out.

Chapter Thirty-One

Scottie

SCOTTIE GRIPPED THE wheel and leaned into the windshield. Every muscle tensed as if she could thrust the truck and aid car forward. A horn blared on the outskirts of her consciousness, but her foot remained glued to the gas pedal. The rearview mirror was a mass of fur and tongue.

"Down! I can't see." The dog didn't budge from the console. "Burnie, down." She reached her hand back to grab his leg, but he leaped past it to land on the front seat. "Get back, Burnie." The dog ignored her command and took up his post, standing guard on the front seat. Lucy waited a couple of breaths and followed, burrowing between him and the console until only a few tufts of white hair poked up. Scottie took that as a sign to surrender. "Fine, but don't think this is a thing. If I wasn't following an ambulance, I would stop and toss you in the back. This isn't happening again." She shot the dog a glare that he missed, intent on the road ahead.

With one hand on the wheel, she reached for her phone that she'd tossed on the passenger seat as she raced to follow the emergency vehicle. Her fingers danced across the upholstery finding nothing but leather and fur. Burnie made no attempt to accommodate her.

"Seriously, do not make me pull this car over or I swear I will leave you and the cotton ball on the side of the road. I am not kidding. Do not test me."

Burnie, whose unwavering attention had been on the blur of swirling red lights ahead, turned to look at Scottie. Holding her eyes, he lifted a paw, and she swept the phone out from under him. He resumed his vigil on the aid car.

Scottie knew the excruciating consequences of not paying attention while operating a moving vehicle at high speeds. Still, she would trade the use of her legs in a heartbeat for Molly's survival. Searching her memories of the hours she'd spent on her knees at morning Mass, she couldn't think of more than the first five words of any prayer. She hadn't prayed much since the day Mary had kicked her out of the house, not even when she lay skewered and drawn in the hospital bed. She prayed now. She prayed, and she promised. *God, I know I have not earned the right to ask for anything. But please don't make Molly die. Please. Please. She does not deserve this. She's the good one. I can't do this alone. You wouldn't have given me her if You didn't know that. So don't take her away.*

She thought about calling her dad. This would kill him, though. She hadn't told him the whole truth about the trip. He'd be angry about that. Worse, if Molly didn't make it, this would be the second time she'd lied and robbed him of the people he loved.

Though he didn't know about Mary's letter, Scottie knew. It was all unraveling. He'd taken care of her and loved her when everyone else abandoned her. He'd had no reason to. The only thing that bound them was an adoption paper, and Mary had shown her how easily that could be undone. She was a throwaway kid. If he found out she'd hidden the letter, if he knew she'd lied about why she was bringing Molly home, it would give him a reason to end his obligation to her. She couldn't risk that.

She searched her contacts, clicked on the picture, and said another prayer. *Please let this be the right thing.* The phone rang twice, and the call disconnected. They were still a few miles outside of Alturas. With her right thumb, she tapped out a text and hit send.

Scottie: 911 where are you? Call me ASAP.

In her head, she started mapping out all the possibilities, a skill she'd perfected on the bottom bunk of her childhood home as she listened to her parents bicker through the walls. As always, she started with the worst case: Molly is already dead. She would work her way back from dead to this is all a big misdiagnosis. But first, she had to make a list of what she had to do to survive and make it better for everyone else. Then, one by one, she would tick off the possibilities. Molly will rally, giving everyone false hope, and then suddenly die. Molly will rally and live in pain for some time, slowly wasting away. Molly will go into remission and live for years. This is all a big misdiagnosis and something completely curable and benign will be discovered. Strategizing for every eventuality would fill her time until she knew for sure. Then she would be ready. Whatever happened, she would have a plan. If she faced the worst possible scenario first, it surely would not happen.

The aid car slowed. On the right, a building too small to be a real hospital popped out of the desiccated earth. Though, in the dimming light, Scottie could not judge its footprint, she could tell it was a single story. Her stomach tightened at the sight of it. She put her foot on the brake and watched the ambulance roll toward the emergency room. Floodlights illuminated the driveway in front of the entrance. Hugging the steering wheel, she could see the medic jog to the back and slide the gurney out.

She prayed Molly was unconscious for this part. The aid

crew and medical personnel would shout things over her body. Dispassionate, objectifying words meant for efficiency and success that scared the living shit out of Scottie. *Sixteen-year-old female, five foot six, one hundred fifty pounds, three-wheel ATV accident, father reports vehicle flipped and landed on patient, wearing helmet, helmet intact, airway clear, patient unable to move legs and reports no sensation in legs, arms fully mobile, patient conscious and responsive, BP one thirty over eighty, pulse eighty, lacerations and bruises on arms and face, ETA fifteen.*

Scottie tightened all the muscles in her face and willed back the tears. The air disappeared from the cab, and she panted to collect it. The pounding of her heartbeat reverberated in her neck. She pulled off the road as the panic attack flooded through her.

You are not dying. You are not dying. You are not dying. You are safe.

She closed her eyes and reached for Burnie. She felt his tongue against her hand and the weight of his head on her thigh. Burying her hand in his fur, she focused on the wisps of hair coating it, the gentle give of the undercoat beneath her fingers.

Breathe in, two, three, four, five. Hold, two, three, four, five. Release, two, three, four, five.

Two tiny paws bore down on her shoulder. A cold, pointy nose touched her cheek. Scottie turned to face the cotton ball tickling her ear. Their eyes locked. Where she expected to see compassion, she saw defiance. Without warning, Lucy's tiny, wet tongue darted out and licked Scottie's nose. The dam cracked wide open. Old, ugly tears flowed first. New, frightened ones followed soon after.

Jesus, I'm losing it and I haven't even made it into the parking lot. What if she doesn't make it? I can't do this. Dammit, Penelope, you should be here.

She slapped the steering wheel and Lucy jumped over Burnie. She landed on the floor, cowering. "Shit. I'm sorry. Come here,

Lucy. It's OK." The dog leaped up on the seat but kept her distance. She wedged herself between Burnie's flank and the seat, keeping a watchful eye on Scottie. "You're OK. We're OK."

※

Despite the size and location, the medical center had that same serious feel Scottie was all too familiar with. The air was a stew of urgency, intention, and antiseptic cleaning products. The admitting clerk had been trained to get, rather than give, information. Scottie knew the drill. She didn't know enough about Molly's condition, medical or financial, to warrant any special consideration from the woman. They wouldn't let her see her, never a good sign in a hospital.

She texted Penelope again.

Scottie: Molly had a seizure. They took her to the hospital in Alturas. Please call me!

She scanned the waiting room. A man half her age sat in a rudimentary wheelchair, foot propped outward. Clearly, the pain phase had waned, and the humor of his situation was rising to the top. Scottie got the impression the man had eschewed the advice of his cautious friend and, in a moment that was one part courage and two parts complete idiocy, his ankle popped. Despite the warning, both men seemed surprised by the outcome. Scottie fought the urge to tell them to shut the hell up. She willed a nurse to call them back to the treatment area, not because she had any compassion for the consequences of their stupidity, but because it would be evidence that Molly did not require the whole medical team.

There was less revelry in the corner where a woman cradled her daughter. Dressed in cranberry plaid pajamas that reminded Scottie of Christmas mornings before their family broke apart, the girl was too tall to fit compactly on her mother's lap. Though her legs sprawled onto the adjacent chair, neither seemed bothered by the effort it took to cling to each other. Scottie's chest and arms burned with the memory of holding Justin, long past the age of wanting to sit in her lap, weak from coughing and fever as they waited at urgent care. Before the usual resentment for what she'd been denied could fully form in her head, she felt the echo of a warm hand rubbing her back and Mary whispering in her ear, "You're going to be alright, sweetie. The doctor will make it better." Scottie didn't have the emotional capacity in that moment to embrace or fight the idea Mary had cared at some point.

She found a seat equidistant from the others but strategically aligned to make eye contact as often as possible with the admitting clerk. The woman was impervious to Scottie's will and oblivious to her stare. Fifty-six minutes passed before they called her back. She checked her phone one last time and was admonished to turn it off inside the ER.

Molly lay on the bed, dwarfed by the pads covering the rails that surrounded her. Standing at the foot of the bed, Scottie watched her chest rise and fall. Her head was encased in a cap from which wires grew in every direction. It reminded Scottie of a perverse version of the cap her mother wore to get her hair frosted when they were kids. Her gut clenched at the thought of the needles of electricity zapping Molly's head.

"We're going to have to leave that on for now. I know it looks awful, but it doesn't hurt." Scottie hadn't noticed the nurse standing in the corner at her mobile desk. "We'll be taking her upstairs soon. The doctor will speak with you in a bit. Would you like a chair?" She didn't wait for an answer. The clang of the metal chair as she snapped it open startled Scottie.

"Is she in a coma?" She reached out for Molly's hand, but her confidence ebbed as she got closer. Only her index finger made contact. Her skin was warm and soft. Soon the other fingers followed, and Scottie sank to the edge of the chair, holding Molly's hand against her face. She wondered if this was a strategy the woman had learned in nursing school. *If the patient's family wants to know what's really wrong, distract them with a chair or coffee. While they're considering the tenuous grasp they have on life, say something innocuous that hints at hope but doesn't promise it.*

"She's sleeping. A seizure can take a lot out of you. Molly can hear you, though. Be mindful of what you say in front of her."

I always am. She waited until the nurse rolled her cart from the room before speaking.

"Molly, you are the toughest girl I've ever known. You can beat this. Come on, you have to fight." She had said the very same words to her three decades ago when Scottie's breaks were fresh and her bruises still angry and purple. She hadn't believed those words back then. Now, she vanquished the doubt from her mind. Molly deserved the same conviction of hope she had given Scottie.

Motionless, save for her shallow breath, Molly's dilapidated frame poked out from beneath the thin cotton gown where her arms met her shoulders. A sharp reminder of the obvious, she wondered how she could have been so wrong about the two of them. How could she think they were so close when Molly had been harboring a condition that led to all this? They'd talked so many times in the last year, and she hadn't said a word about it. What had she done that Molly couldn't trust her with this? Had Scottie been self-involved? Disinterested? Selfish? Scottie shuddered at the fear and loneliness Molly must have faced alone. *I will do better.*

Lost in her contrition, she did not hear the doctor come in. He went straight to Molly as if Scottie did not exist. She attributed his lack of introduction to arrogance and social ineptitude, then she promptly apologized to God for the uncharitable evaluation of the person He sent to treat Molly.

"I'm her sister, Scottie Dunn. Is she going to be OK?" She

looked away as the doctor placed his thumb on Molly's eyelid and lifted it open. He wore a white coat over his scrubs and a pair of clogs that appeared to be made of racing tires. Scottie hoped the gray hair signaled experience and not extreme stress of being exiled here from some prestigious hospital just in front of losing his license for some egregious error.

"We're going to admit her overnight."

"You didn't answer my question. Is she going to be alright? What's wrong with her?" Scottie's stomach dropped to the floor. She stayed rooted to the chair, gripping Molly's hand. The doctor waited, face softening.

"Let's talk somewhere else." He lifted his chin in Molly's direction. Scottie squeezed Molly's hand and pushed herself to standing. An ache was growing in her hips. Though he was much older, he had to wait for Scottie to hobble down the hallway. He directed her to a small waiting room and shut the door. In her experience, this was a move made to limit the number of witnesses to one's meltdown over horrific news. *Shit.* Her pulse picked up speed. *She is dying. Abort mission.* She forced her face to stone but could not stop her eyes from darting between the doctor and the door. *Let me the hell out of this room.*

The doctor waited for her to sit. She wasn't falling for that. They stood in the center of the room, no larger than a walk-in closet, and Scottie crossed her arms over her chest. He exhaled. His words flowed like an avalanche in one of those adventure movies. Snow, white and fluffy, sliding off in sheets, then tumbling. Deceptive. From afar, it was light and fresh. Up close, the heft of it slammed into everything in its path, leaving splinters where beams once stood.

"Molly regained consciousness in the emergency room. We spoke, and she is aware of her condition. She expressed her wishes. Your sister has given me permission to share with you and"—he pulled a notepad from his pocket—"Penelope Casey only that she had a seizure and will recover from that. I can also tell you I'm going to keep her tonight, and she will likely be released tomorrow afternoon as soon as she is safe to travel."

Scottie felt the wall of ice and snow hit her in the gut.

"Are you kidding? I'm her sister." Scottie fought the urge to grab his shoulders and shake him. She had never felt more powerless—never, not even in the dead of night, clamped into that medieval device, waiting for her bones to fill in the gaps and cement her back together.

"I'm sorry, but that's all I can tell you. I prefer being able to engage the family in a patient's care. Unfortunately, that is not my decision. It's up to the patient. Your sister is competent to make her own medical decisions." He placed his hands in the pockets of his jacket. When she didn't speak, he turned toward the door.

"I already know she has cancer," Scottie blurted to stop him leaving. "She told us that. Is that what caused this?" She stared at the man, mouth half-open, wishing she could form a coherent argument. *Damnit, Penelope. Why aren't you here? You could make him talk.*

"I'm sorry, but I cannot say more. You're welcome to stay here if you would like some time alone. It will be a couple of hours getting her settled in her room. I recommend you get some sleep. Leave your phone number at the desk, and they'll call you when she wants visitors." He reached out his hand. When Scottie made no move to shake it, he gave her a half-hearted smile and said, "Well. I have some other patients to attend to."

He left the door open behind him. As soon as he disappeared from sight, his words returned. *When she wants visitors. When? What the hell, Molly. You dragged me all the way to Reno to pick your ass up, and now you are just going to cut me out of it. I dropped everything. I spent hours sick to my stomach wondering what could be wrong with you, and you aren't going to tell me. Yeah, well, maybe*

I won't be here when you're ready to have visitors. Maybe you can wait until Penelope figures her shit out and comes to get you. Or call one of your ski bum friends. Kiss my ass, Molly.

Scottie's boots reverberated from the linoleum floor and bounced off the sheetrock walls as she pounded down the hall. The automatic door slowed her down. The men's revelry paused when she stormed into the room, and she could feel their eyes on her. She hoped it was fear and not pity that chilled them. Scottie had dropped everything to come to Molly's rescue once again. She needed her, but only on her terms. Scottie had long paid off her debt to Molly. A wave of cold air hit her as the door opened. She zipped up her vest, shoved her hands in the pockets, and stalked to the truck.

Burnie leaped from the seat the minute his leash was on. Scottie didn't have time to put Lucy's on before the big dog dug his paws in and dragged her across the parking lot. He didn't bother to sniff a single blade of grass. As Lucy struggled to be free from her hold, Scottie mentally slapped herself for forgetting about them.

She walked them out to the highway. Hot tears stung her cheeks, and she cradled her anger in her chest, swallowing the bubbles of sadness as they rose in her throat. By the time they turned to go back, there was a little slack in the leash and Scottie turned her focus from the dogs.

To the south, not a single light glowed as far as she could see. Peace washed over her. She wished she could stay here and stare at the night sky forever, the chilled air numbing her rage. Alone, there would be no chance of letting anyone down. She could just be. And what she would be was right for a change. No need to monitor every cue. Just be. Maybe with twenty dogs, though.

She wept for the loss of the illusion that she shared an honest place with Molly. It was what she deserved, though. After all, she hadn't shared all her feelings. And then, there was the biggest lie. Not even Molly knew about that. That would be the straw that drove Molly from her, though it hardly mattered now. While Scottie had not outright lied, she omitted and she hid, and that was as good as lying.

Once the dogs had eaten, she loaded them up. Her back was screaming from the drive, and she was too tired to make it all the way home. It took a couple of calls, but she found a motel that would take the dogs. Since her only interest was sleep, nothing else about the room mattered.

Despite her bravado, she turned the volume up on the phone and set it on the nightstand. She'd written Penelope off when she hadn't answered her second call. But she would give Molly the night to come to her senses.

She kicked off her boots and lay on the bed. Burnie jumped up. His weight sent a wave across the budget mattress. The muscles in her neck reached up to clench her head against the motion. Scottie pressed her chin toward her chest. The grit between her vertebrae rasped in her ears. Slowly, she turned her head side to side. With each pass, the bones quieted. *I'll be lucky if I can walk tomorrow after a night on this sponge.*

Lucy yapped from the floor on the side of the bed. Scottie looked over in her direction to see a plume of white fur bouncing in and out of sight. Letting her arm fall off the side, she made a half-hearted effort to reach for the dog.

"If you want up, you're going to have to come closer. I don't have the strength to come get you."

It took five more bounces before the little dog figured it out. Scottie scooped her up. Lucy circled the mattress, burrowing into Burnie, who had already attached himself to Scottie's side. Together they fell asleep to reruns of *M*A*S*H* until the phone rang.

Chapter Thirty-Two

Penelope

For the tenth time, Penelope jabbed her finger at the hands-free button on the dash and barked the order, "Call Scottie. Dunn." She tapped her forehead as if that would shake loose a map with a thick red cross marking Alturas. She had slept through the town on the way down, and her old images were incomplete.

More than three decades before, Alturas had been the terminus of their last family vacation. The memory of that trip soured the enchiladas, which, thanks to Hank's need to air four decades of hurt, had congealed in her stomach. *Great. Straight to voicemail.* She waited for the beep.

"Scottie, you can't nine-one-one me and then not answer. Where are you? Is Molly OK? I'm booking a flight to the nearest airport. Hopefully, there's something close. With the way this day is going, I'll have to go back to Reno and rent a damn car. OK, call me. And do not leave until I get there."

She flogged herself mentally for running out on them. Scottie flashed in her mind. The look on her face when Penelope opened the bathroom door to see the naked scar in the mirror—pain, embarrassment, and anger? With that one careless action, she'd shattered the mask that concealed decades of jagged feelings.

Unbidden, six-year-old Scottie appeared from the recesses of Penelope's memory. Standing on the side of the road, her hand rested on the liver-spotted head of their comically named Brittany Spaniel, Gooçois François. Even as young as Penelope was back then, she could see Scottie turning inward as their parents' fight climbed toward its inevitable crescendo. Tethered to that moment only by five tiny fingers in a tuft of silky fur, she watched Scottie slipping inside herself.

Penelope collected Molly first. Scottie would follow her anywhere. She never told Molly *you're not the boss of me*. Penelope knew not to add fuel to their parents' fire, and Scottie attaching herself to their dad's leg would do just that.

She walked Molly by, and Scottie grabbed her hand like it was a magnet. The dog followed. They wandered to the enormous rock that had been the whole point of the trek. This mess was all her fault. She'd insisted they take a family holiday under the guise of her school project. She had fantasized that they would remember how much fun they had together before the fighting started. They would have ice cream cones after dinner and hot cocoa with breakfast. In between, they would stop at all the landmarks, and Penelope would read the brass plaques to everyone. All the meanness would heal over and not even leave a scar.

Instead, she'd opened the wound between her parents so deep they were standing in a parking lot screaming at each other for the whole world to see. Penelope had tried to drown out the hateful words, reciting all the facts she'd learned for her report on Chimney Rock. Scottie stood expressionless, one hand in the dog's fur, staring at the massive boulder.

The man who'd built it over a hundred years before had come to this spot just one year older than Penelope. "He was so brave to travel across the frontier," she'd told her sisters. "There were snakes and wolves and no bathrooms or restaurants." Penelope glanced back at her parents stomping toward them, mouths pursed. She wondered if that twelve-year-old boy wasn't brave at all. Maybe he just wanted to escape his mother and father.

Penelope's foot pressed on the gas harder each time the disembodied voice on her cell offered a phone number for the hospital in Altoona.

"Al-tur-as Ca-li-forn-ia!" She pulled off the highway and picked up the phone. "Lot of damn good you do. For what this car cost, you should read my mind. Dammit."

Angry tears seeped out. Maybe Michael had been right. She made a mess of everything. She didn't know how to love someone the way they needed her to. A sob racked her body. *Pull your shit together, Penelope.* She searched for the number to the hospital, resolving to find a way to steal Victoria when she found a new job. She would have already booked a flight that would have landed practically on the lawn of Alturas General, or whatever the hell they called it, and had a full report from the emergency physician who, though reluctant at first, would have spilled the private medical records of the president himself to make Victoria stop coming at him like the matronly pit bull she was.

She punched in the number and, before the receptionist finished her practiced greeting, Penelope cut in. "Yes. Hello, my name is Penelope Casey. My sister Molly is there in the emergency room. Could you tell me her condition or put me in contact with someone who can?" She tapped the steering wheel.

"I'm sorry, but you're not on any of the patient contact lists. I'm not able to share any information unless a patient has put you on their list." The message was rehearsed, a sure sign of a complete lack of authority.

"I understand patient confidentiality. I have a text from my sister, Scottie, saying Molly had a seizure. So, she is either unconscious and cannot give consent, in which case you can talk to her family, or she is conscious and you can ask her for permission to talk to me. Which is it?" Penelope's voice slowed with each word as her fingernails tattooed the leather.

"Perhaps you could call your other sister and ask for information."

"Of course. I tried that. She's not answering. I assume she turned her phone off because she's in the hospital. Can you page Scottie Dunn?"

"I'm sorry, but I can't page visitors. And visiting hours are over."

"Is there someone else I can talk to?"

"I'm sorry. I know this is difficult . . ."

Penelope disconnected. *I'm sorry. I know this is difficult.* All the moments marched by. Clinging to her dad's neck, hoping he would let go of the big blue suitcase her mom only packed when the whole family was going away for an entire week. On the way to the school bus, dragging Molly by the hand so she wouldn't slip from her grasp. Pulling her up the steps as she cried, *No! Scottie can't just leave. She's our sister! Sisters live together.* Staring at the ER doctor through the slit in her blackened eye, refusing to admit what they all knew was true. Patting her mom's hand as she took her last breaths. Feeling the warmth of her dissipate.

No one is ever really sorry. Just socially expected words you say when you mean there's not a damn thing you can or will do. This is difficult, as if it were an algebra problem or a crossword puzzle and not your heart being ripped from your chest while everyone stands by and pats you on the head.

Hank, Mary, even Michael, though he was a bastard, and now Molly. That moment will be eviscerating. And then she will be alone. And people will say, I'm sorry. I know this is difficult. They will share how they felt when their sister died, or mom, or dad, or favorite dog. They will say there is no comparison, of course, but in their hearts, they don't believe that. Yet it is the one true thing they will say. There will be nothing that compares to losing Molly. She will be alone in her tidy condo, wearing winter white, with only Lucy to console her.

She punched in the number again. This time, it rang.

"Scottie, where have you been? I've been calling for an hour. I left you a voicemail."

"They don't allow phones in the ER." Scottie's words came out in forced staccato. "I didn't check my messages. I was a little busy."

"Look, I'm sorry. I'll be there as fast as I can. Please don't leave until I get there." In the background, she could hear a TV, but Scottie didn't make a sound. She was angry. "I'm sorry. I'll meet you at the hospital tonight."

"Don't bother."

"Look, I shouldn't have left, but I had to handle something in person. I will drive all night if I have to. I'll sort this out."

"I meant, don't bother meeting me at the hospital. I'm in a hotel on 395."

"Why aren't you at the hospital? Molly shouldn't be alone." *What the hell, Scottie? Can't you just, for once, act like you're a part of this family?*

"It wasn't my choice, Penelope. Molly apparently regained consciousness just long enough to instruct the doctor not to tell us anything about her condition. If that wasn't insulting enough, she told him to tell us she will call when she is ready to have visitors."

"What?" The words made no sense to her. Why would Molly not want them there? Maybe she deserved to be shut out after she ran out on them. But Scottie? She didn't.

"You heard me." Scottie paused. Penelope could hear the bedsprings creak. Scottie blew her nose. Her anger dulled to an aching sadness. "So, I'm at the hotel with the dogs. I'll text you the address. I'll wait until you get here to pick up Lucy. Then I'm out. You two can deal with this without me. It'll be like the old days."

Cars raced past her, and her mother's words echoed in her head. *You are the oldest. It's your job to take care of them. It's your job to be the grownup.* She'd had enough of that burden.

"You don't know a thing about the old days. We didn't shut you out. You refused to engage. You never visited one time after you left. We had to come to you."

"First, I didn't leave. I was kicked out. Second, you were court ordered to visit. It was clear you didn't want to see us."

There it was again, self-pity. As if they'd had the perfect life. As if they were some exclusive club she couldn't get into.

"Not us, Scottie. Him. I didn't want to see Dad. And I had very good reasons. Look, I'm not going to sit here and argue about a past I cannot change. Bottom line is, if you care about Molly at all, you'll stick around and help me figure out how to get her home before she gets any sicker. I'll be there in a couple of hours, tops. Send me the hotel address." It was a lie. She didn't know how long it was going to take. She was banking on finding a flight when she got to the airport, but with her luck, it would be routed through Louisiana. Penelope heard the faintest sniffle and wondered if Scottie had put down the phone.

"Are you still there?" she asked. The only response was another sniffle. "I'll be there as soon as I can."

Scottie disconnected.

Chapter Thirty-Three

Molly

MOLLY STARED AT the ceiling tiles and began counting the holes—a strategy she'd developed as a child to drown out the shouting voices and help her think. After an hour of poking and prodding, the nurse had drifted out of the room silently, save for the squeak of her rubber soles.

Fifty-six, fifty-seven, fifty-eight. Her plan was falling apart. Scottie and Penelope weren't even in the same state now. Being within six feet of each other was critical. *Seventy-two, seventy-three.* Scottie was digging her heels in. Dislodging that mule was not going to be easy.

Ninety-six, ninety-seven. A seizure wasn't part of the plan, but if it brought Penelope back, then more drastic measures might not be needed. It pained her to think she'd hurt Scottie, but she needed time to put this train back on the tracks. Scottie would forgive her. She always did, no matter how self-serving the offense. She wouldn't be able to salvage the plan if Scottie knew the truth. She would not support her decision in the way the doctor had been compelled to.

Molly's visions of laughter and healing were replaced by that of three women and two dogs ignoring each other for ten hours with roughly three stops for food and the bathroom. The way her luck was going, the silence would only be punctuated by growled recriminations precipitated by one of them chewing too loudly. At least then they would be talking, though. Molly hated fighting, but she also regretted the times she ran away from it. Her sisters would regret it too someday, if something didn't change.

For the life of her, however short that may be, she could not remember when they'd stopped talking to each other. Scottie had stopped talking altogether, it seemed, when they got back from the trip to Chimney Rock. Molly tried to cheer her up, but she could tell Scottie was just going along. Even when she smiled, her face had a sadness to it. Molly could see it in the old photographs. Scottie's eyes would dart around like she was trying to keep track of everything, all at once. But her face showed no emotion at all.

After their father left, Penelope had attached herself to her mom. One night, Molly had snuck down the hall and found her on the sofa, hugging Mary's neck as she cried. In the morning, Penelope woke them for breakfast like the TV mothers who sashayed into their beloved offspring's bedroom, whisking the curtains open to reveal another perfect sunny day. She acted as if nothing were wrong. Their mother was still asleep. If history was any indication, she would awaken with yesterday's makeup smeared across her face. Molly longed for Mrs. Cunningham or Mrs. Brady with their unwavering smiles, stylish coifs, and unwrinkled dresses.

Penelope had set the table like they were having company over. Proud as can be, she scooped up the mush and passed around the brown sugar. Molly asked for more, and Penelope dished it out with a smile. When Scottie asked for raisins, Penelope said, "Don't be ungrateful." She sounded just like their mom when she was getting fed up to here and sick to death of them.

She had known Scottie was hurt by the treatment, but she

was so glad to be on the good side of Penelope that she didn't want to risk it by sticking up for her. A word from Penelope and their mother might unleash her silent treatment on Molly instead. Besides, Penelope was older and got to do things they did not. Scottie was practically a baby.

Molly was shamed by the memory. She knew this was where it all went bad. When they got home from the trip, everything changed. Molly felt like the rope in a game of tug-of-war. She wanted to visit Dad, but she didn't want to hurt Mom. She wanted to stick up for Scottie, but she didn't want to anger Penelope. Maybe it was her turn to tug, but from the middle.

She reached up to feel the electrodes affixed to her scalp. No wires were attached. Wondering if they were wireless, she peeled one off and set it on the sheet beside her. She waited thirty seconds for the nurses to barge into the room, crash cart in tow. Nothing happened. The slow beep, beep of the machine trudged on. Her head itched as she picked each one off. Once all were removed, she eased her feet to the floor and padded over to the sink. She ripped the tape from the IV and slid it from her vein. Blood flowed from the hole it left behind. She grabbed a paper towel and pressed it to her hand. The thought she had, whenever one of her life-well-lived-ideas formed in her head, crossed her mind. *This may not be your best idea ever.*

When the bleeding subsided, she moved to the closet, where her clothes were unceremoniously jumbled in a white plastic bag. She was relieved to see her purse and, inside, her cell phone. When she pressed the power button, nothing happened, and she thanked the universe. With the sink to steady her, she dressed. Her body was sluggish, and she tipped over while putting her leg into her jeans. She tested her legs with a couple laps around the room. Satisfied no one would find her unconscious in the middle of the street in day-old underwear, looking like an extra in a zombie movie, she left a note on the tray and snuck away.

Chapter Thirty-Four

Scottie

Scottie turned off the TV and rolled to her side. Lucy burrowed into the crook of her hip. The dog's long hair was cool against her belly. Burnie lifted his head just enough to check on the small dog. His face invited deep conversations with his eyes drooping ever so slightly toward his mouth. He reminded her of the counselor who tried to get her to talk after the accident. Scottie didn't see much point in talking about it. The past couldn't be changed. The only thing she knew about the future was that crying wouldn't change that, either. The pain couldn't be this bad forever, and either way, she would survive it. Besides, the counselor wasn't the one who had to learn to walk again. What did he even know about it?

She reached out and scratched Burnie's head. "We're heading home, just you and me. You can sleep in your own bed tomorrow. Your dad's right. I have a family. I don't need this BS. If she doesn't want me here, that's fine." He let out a deep sigh. "I'm thinking about calling Grandpa. You want to weigh in on that, big guy?" Burnie turned his eyes up to her but, otherwise, didn't move a muscle. "I'll take that as a no." She patted his head. "You are a wise dog."

What would she even say? *Dad, Molly's in the hospital. She had a seizure. Don't ask me why, because she forbids the doctor from telling me. I'd ask her myself, but she doesn't want visitors. So, I'm just going to leave her there. Penelope's on her way, and I'm sure she'll let her visit. She can just take care of it herself.* Damn. Damn. Damn. Penelope is coming. She must have picked up her car at the kennel. Great.

Scottie hadn't told the whole truth about the trip. To Hank Casey, half-truths and omissions were lies, plain and simple, and he hated lies. There would be no skirting the consequences of this one. It could only end one way. This wasn't the only lie between them, though. Festering just below the surface, since she was nine years old, was the lie that would infect their relationship with such resentment and distrust it would never heal.

One fall day, not long after they'd moved to the kennel, she found the letter on her way home from school. It was camouflaged among the bills. Scottie might never have seen it had she not lost her balance as she swept the letters from the mailbox.

When she retrieved the pile from the gravel road, one stood out. She ran her fingers over the return address which had once been hers. On the front, it announced Hank Casey, not Hank and Scottie, not Scottie Casey. She wanted to tear it into a million pieces. Her mom had made no attempt to see or talk with her. Every week, they picked up Penelope and Molly, but her mom never asked her to stay over. Her mom was probably writing to ask to un-adopt her. Maybe she didn't want her sisters to visit them anymore. Maybe her real mom showed up and wanted to take her away from Hank. The letter pulsed with the ominous possibilities.

She slid it beneath the front cover of her notebook. She thought about burying it in the middle but knew that would be harder to explain when she gave it to him. One night when she was doing her math homework at the kitchen table, she'd say, *How did this get in here? Dad! I found a letter for you. I don't know how that happened.* Her fantasy of steaming the glue off the envelope flap and resealing it to avoid discovery was quickly discarded as impractical as she wasn't yet allowed to use the stove alone.

Slowly, she slid one side of her scissors between the envelope and the flap and carefully broke the seal. At the halfway point, though, the scissors caught on the seam of the envelope and shot outward, cutting the flap in half. She could glue the flap down, but hiding the slit was not going to be easy. She carefully pulled the letter through the opening.

Hank,

I hope you are well. I miss you dearly. I know I acted rashly and I am sorry for that. I really did forgive you. Can you understand? Every day, she looked more and more like her mother. I wondered how many other people could see it too. I know I shouldn't have worried about that. I'm not proud of it. She's only a little girl. But I was shamed. Can you imagine how that felt? I know I was wrong. It wasn't her fault. I think I can look past all this. I will do my best to love her. Molly and Penelope miss you. They miss Scottie too. I know it will take some time, but I hope we can be a family again someday. If you can forgive me, I can forgive you. Maybe we could start with dinner, just the two of us. If you want this too, please call me. If you don't call, I will know that is your answer.

Love,

Mary

She was filled with anger and sadness. Mary's words pelted her chest with shame so molten she thought she might explode. Her dad could never see the letter. He too might be persuaded her looks were too hideous to bear. He might think she was the reason they got divorced. She couldn't let those words near his head. Like a weed, they would take root and choke out all the good things he thought about her. Scottie buried the letter in the one place he never wanted to help her organize—the back of her underwear drawer.

She got lucky with that lie. She wasn't going to be with this one.

Chapter Thirty-Five

Penelope

P ENELOPE KNOCKED ON the door. The duet of yipping and barking told her she was in the right place. She'd considered waiting until the sun came up, but she'd been wearing the same clothes for over twenty-four hours and couldn't bear to meet another stranger in this condition. Scottie cracked the door in much the same state, which made her laugh.

"What? You don't look much better."

"And hello to you, Scarlett." Penelope pushed past her and scooped up her dog. "Did you miss me?" Lucy's matchstick legs windmilled until a paw caught on Penelope's jacket. That was all the purchase she needed to close the distance to Penelope's cheek. "You did miss me. I'm back. OK. Settle down. I promise I won't leave you again." The muscles in her neck relaxed, and her shoulders dropped at the feel of fur against her face.

"Did you get any further than me at the hospital?" Scottie asked.

"I haven't been." She placed Lucy on the floor, who pawed to get back up as Penelope unbuckled her shoes. "I look like I was recently rolled out of a drunk tank and deloused. I need a shower and coffee before I have words with Miss Molly."

Scottie tipped back to lean against the door. "Assuming you can get past Nurse Ratched."

"Oh, I'll get past her." She narrowed her eyes and pointed at Scottie. "And you will too. We need to be on the same page."

"I told you I'm not staying." Scottie pushed off the door and strode over to the table. She picked up a leash and looped it in her hand. "Clearly, she doesn't want me here."

Penelope kicked off her shoes and sat up to face her sister.

"That's ridiculous. She's not thinking straight. Cut her some slack. You're being a brat." Penelope said it without malice. When Scottie crossed her arms over her chest and set her jaw, she realized her mistake. She didn't know her well enough to use the jab she'd thrown at Molly a million times.

"Screw you. I dropped everything and drove over a thousand miles to help her out. Now she's icing me out. I'm pissed."

"I get it. I'm pissed too. But we're not leaving until we get some straight answers. She won't be able to bulldoze or bamboozle us if we stick together. One way or another, I want the truth about what's going on."

"She probably doesn't even have cancer."

Though nearly whispered, Scottie's words punched her in the gut.

"Jeez, she wouldn't lie about that. Why would you even say that?"

Scottie shrugged. "She's lying about something."

"Everybody's lying about something." Penelope lifted her suitcase onto the bed and pulled out her bag of toiletries. She avoided Scottie's eyes but could tell in the periphery of her vision she was waiting for her to say more. "Let me get a quick shower, and then we can go to the hospital." She left her sitting on the only chair in the room clutching the leash, staring at the floor.

By the time Penelope was ready, Scottie was gone. Lucy was sitting in front of the door like she expected it to open any minute. "Don't hold your breath." The dog turned her head and looked upward at Penelope. "Scottie has an iron will, and no matter how much Burnie likes you, she's not coming back. When she leaves, it's for good." Lucy turned her head back to the door. "Well, I see she's rubbed off on you too. Great."

Next to Lucy, Molly's suitcase stood, its handle still extended. It was red. Of course she couldn't get a black one like everyone else. Penelope lifted it onto the bed and unzipped the top compartment. Molly had affixed a luggage tag with her business card. Surprised that she had one, Penelope slid it out. The paper was thick and matte black. On one third, Molly's logo stood centered by height. Bold letters overlapped in triangle formation, MMC. Molly Molloy Casey. The letters were partially encircled by a jagged swath of red ink. A tiny TM sat in the corner and Penelope wondered why Molly hadn't asked for help to get her logo trademarked. A line separated the other two-thirds where Molly's contact information was listed. The fonts were a combination of solid dependability and unrestrained creativity. Penelope approved.

A tinge of guilt pinched her heart as she opened the main compartment and rifled through the rest of the bag. She wasn't sure what she was looking for, but she knew there had to be a clue in there. Under a pair of jeans, she found two manila envelopes addressed to her and Scottie. They were thick. Beneath them was a printout with directions to a scheduled appointment at the Cancer Center in Seattle, dated the week before she'd called Penelope.

She heard the card slide into the lock and the click as it opened, but she was not fast enough to close the case.

"What are you doing?" Scottie balanced a coffee tray in one hand and Burnie's leash in the other.

"I thought you'd left."

"I did. I went for coffee." She held the door open with a shoulder as the dog rushed by, pulling her off balance. "Stop, Burnie! Why are you going through Molly's things?"

"Because I'm trying to figure out what is wrong with her so I can help her."

"You can't go through her stuff. It's a total violation."

"I'm not robbing her. Lighten up."

"You are robbing her. She has a right to keep this to herself."

"A minute ago, you were walking out because she wouldn't share what was going on. Now, you're her civil rights advocate?"

"Just pack her stuff back up."

"These are addressed to us." Penelope held up the envelopes. "Don't you want to see what's in them?"

"Put them back. She didn't mean for us to have them now. Nothing good ever comes in a sealed envelope."

"How would you know? I think I know her a little better than you." Penelope wanted that to slice her. She was itching for a fight.

"Whatever. I'll meet you at the hospital." She put Penelope's coffee on the table.

"Wait. I'm going with you. We have to drop my rental off."

"You should probably keep it." Scottie whistled for her dog, threw her bag over her shoulder, and walked out the door. Penelope shoved the letters back into the bag and grabbed the coffee Scottie had left behind. It was exactly how she liked it. That made her mad too.

~

Scottie was sitting in her truck when Penelope drove into the hospital parking lot. She knocked on the window, startling her.

"Thanks for waiting," Penelope said.

"I figured you wouldn't want to leave Lucy in the rental." *Of course she's waiting for the dog.*

"You're not staying in the car. Let's go." Penelope waved her out, backing up to give her room. Then she waited until Scottie shoved the door open and stomped, sulking, across the parking lot.

Penelope took the lead as soon as they entered the hospital. She lifted her chin and waltzed in like she owned the place. *Watch and learn, Scottie.* "Molly Casey was admitted last night. We are here to see her. What room is she in?"

The woman looked at her computer. "Excuse me for a moment. I need to check on something." She forced a smile, which gave Penelope a sinking feeling. It wasn't an *I'm sorry I have to disappoint you* smile. It was more of an *I hate to give people bad news* smile. She pushed a button on her phone, tipped her head downward, and spoke into her headset. "I have some people to see Molly Casey. Yes. OK. Thank you." She looked at Penelope. "Someone will be out to speak with you in a moment if you'd like to wait over there." She pointed to a couch across the room.

"We wouldn't like to wait." Scottie pushed past Penelope and placed her hands on the counter. "We would like to know what's happened to our sister." Her face reddened. Penelope could see the terror in her eyes.

"Scottie, let's go sit down." She reached for her arm, but Scottie yanked it away at the touch.

"No." The look of pain was so young and raw on her face. Penelope swept her up in a hug without thinking. Scottie's arms went slack, but she did not pull away. "She can't be dead."

"She's not dead. I can feel it," Penelope said.

She pressed Scottie's body to hers and felt the strength of the two of them together. Though despondent, she was solid, and Penelope drew it into her. Scottie let loose her breath and leaned into Penelope, not yielding but offering. Looking past her to the security door beyond them, Penelope prayed she was not lying.

A diminutive woman in sensible shoes opened the door. She held a file folder in one hand. In one sweeping motion, she introduced herself and moved them all to the waiting area.

"It's my understanding that, Scottie, you met with the doctor last night who explained your sister's wishes." Scottie wiped her tears and nodded. The woman continued. "So, that has not changed. I cannot talk to you about her condition. However, she did leave a note addressed to the two of you when she left." The woman opened the folder.

"When she left?" Penelope, the outraged lawyer, reared her head. "You discharged her without a ride, after having had her first ever seizure, knowing she was from out of town? Do I have that right?"

"We did not discharge her." The doctor straightened. "She left AMA. Against medical advice. And she must have some experience with that as she left us a note too, thanking us for her care and taking responsibility for any repercussions that might arise as a result of her decision to leave, given her condition."

"She left? Just like that?" Scottie raised her face to the rafters and stomped a boot to the floor. The woman nodded and then handed her the note which read, *I need coffee.*

Chapter Thirty-Six

Molly

MOLLY PUT HER hands on the leather-clad shoulders of the man in front of her. Pushing herself up, she swung her leg over the motorcycle. She asked the driver if she could buy him breakfast. He politely declined and told her to take care of herself.

It was early, but the waitress took one look at her leaning against the cold stone wall, arms crossed against the chilly morning air, and took mercy on her. The waitress spoke into the door as she unlocked it. "Well, you better come in. I'll put some coffee on, but the cook doesn't get here too early, so you'll have to wait for food. He's not suited for the breakfast shift, because he likes to party." She leaned one knee on the first booth and pulled the blinds open. "Come to think of it, he's also not suited for dinner because he likes to party." She shook her head and went into the kitchen.

Molly took a table by the window. She could tell the waitress was going to suggest the counter. "My sisters are joining me."

"Will they be here soon?" She set down a glass of water and a menu.

"Soon as they figure out where I went." Molly flashed her a sheepish grin.

Well-seasoned, the waitress didn't ask any more questions.

Molly ordered French toast with extra butter and extra crispy bacon after the cook stumbled in. She'd never be able to eat it, but she needed an excuse to leave a big tip to repay the woman's kindness.

She drank her coffee with real cream. It was old-fashioned coffee made in a pot from coarse grounds. The smell of it reminded her of the every-other-Saturday mornings, checking the dogs with her dad and Scottie while Penelope pouted in the house. He always had a mug in hand. The smell made her feel warm and safe. When he was done, he'd balance the mug on the top of her head and say, "Can you watch this for me?" She would giggle until it slipped off into his waiting hands. It was a scrap of normalcy in an otherwise chaotic childhood.

The doctor had told her she needed to eat more. Even small amounts all day long were better than nothing. She nibbled at the bacon as she waited. It took an hour, and though the restaurant filled with regulars, the waitress didn't rush her.

They pulled up in two vehicles. Not what she had hoped for. Still, Molly considered it a good omen that both showed up at all. Penelope was the first one to reach the restaurant. She swung the door open with such panache that a wind blew through the place. The din muted. She lifted her chin and headed for the table, oblivious to the fact she had closed the door on Scottie.

"What the hell, Molly. You scared the bejeezus out of me." Penelope pulled the napkin from beneath the silverware. She brushed the plastic-covered seat off and plopped down.

"Good morning, Penelope. It's nice to see you too. Would you like some coffee?" Molly wrapped both hands around her mug and took a sip.

Scottie took her time getting to the table. She sat and flagged down the waitress. "Two coffees, please, and I'll have what she's having."

"I don't want coffee, Scottie," Penelope said. "And cut the crap, Molly. This isn't funny."

She thought it was funny, though. Funny that after all these years, Penelope still saw her as a little kid she could boss around. Funny that Scottie thought she could ignore her and pretend like nothing happened.

"That lady works for a living, Penelope. You can't sit here and not eat or drink," Scottie said as she poured cream in the mug.

Penelope reached for Molly's hands, but she sat back and tucked her hands beneath her legs. Accepting her comfort was tempting, but her gut told her that was the last thing they needed. It was like every part of their past was a boulder in the middle of a landslide. The only way to clear the road and move forward was to bulldoze through it. Penelope did not disappoint her.

"Molly, I saw the notice of your appointment in Seattle."

"You went through my stuff?" Molly pushed her plate away. *Well, you wanted discomfort. You better get used to people taking over like you're dead already.* "You didn't have any right to do that."

"I told you it was wrong," Scottie chirped.

"You didn't leave me much choice, not allowing us to talk to the doctor. Not allowing visitors. We drove over a thousand miles to bring you home, Molly."

"Well, counselor, if that's your idea of a compelling argument to justify illegal search and seizure, I'm surprised you have a job."

"As a matter of fact, I don't."

Scottie and Molly put their cups down in unison. Molly jumped in. "Did that asshole fire you?"

"No. I quit."

"Because of me?" She leaned in, worry lining her forehead.

"Of course not, and don't try to change the subject. You need to come clean about what's going on with you."

Scottie looked at Molly and pointed to Penelope with her fork. A piece of French toast fell on the table. "I told her you made it all up." Scottie dared her with a forced grin and then reached over and swiped the extra butter off Molly's plate. She smeared some on her French toast.

"That was uncalled for. I'm going to let that go, though, Scarlett, because I can see that I hurt your feelings by not letting you visit me in the hospital. I was wrong. I apologize. I just needed a little time alone." Molly turned toward Penelope. "Are you OK? Why didn't you tell me things had gotten that bad at work?"

"It's fine. I've survived worse."

"Well, I think you're a badass," Scottie said, still chewing. Molly smiled in approval of her assessment of Penelope.

"If I were a badass, I wouldn't have stayed so long. A lesson I should have learned from Michael." She looked out the window. "Anyway, we need to get moving. You have a doctor's appointment, and I have to look for a job."

"Can't you just do your job? Do you have to work for someone else?" Scottie asked.

"That's really hard. It takes capital to start your own firm."

"If anyone can do it, you can. You put yourself through law school while grieving the death of your husband. You've done really well." Scottie raised her coffee mug to Penelope.

"I wouldn't call it grieving." She smirked at Molly.

"Is this another one of your inside jokes?" Scottie directed her comment to Molly, who was suddenly weary of her martyrdom.

"No. It's not an inside joke. Michael was abusive. There's nothing funny about it." Penelope opened her mouth, but Molly held up a hand. "You weren't around, Scottie, so it's not your fault for stepping in it now. You somehow think you're the only one who's suffered. You're the only one who had it bad. You don't know the half of it. Yes, Penelope and I share a lot of history that you don't. The truth is, you and I share a lot of history that Penelope doesn't know about. It's time to get off the cross. Someone else needs the wood."

Scottie's cheeks reddened. She called for the check. "It's time for me to go."

"Don't be like that." Molly put a hand on her arm. She ignored it.

"No. She's right. We need to get going. And we're going straight home," Penelope said.

"No, we are not, Penelope Casey. We are going to Chimney Rock." Molly sat back with a grin that spread across her face.

"You all have fun. Burnie and I are going straight home." Scottie took one last bite and signed the check. "I'm just here to refuel and say goodbye." She was halfway to standing when Molly stopped her in her tracks.

"Don't you take one step, Scarlett Ann Casey Dunn. Sit your ass back down. I'm not nearly through with you."

Chapter Thirty-Seven

Scottie

Scottie froze. She waited for Molly to crack a joke, but her eyes were angry. Her mouth was pursed in a tight hyphen separating her nose from her chin. Scottie sat.

"We are all going to Chimney Rock." Molly held up her hand when Penelope tried to speak. Scottie admired that. "We're going together in Scottie's truck. I haven't asked for much from you. I suppose we haven't asked much of each other. This is important to me. If you love me, you will do this." Molly pulled a twenty out of her purse and tucked it underneath her plate. She stood and looked down at them. Her expression invited no discussion. Without so much as a glance backward, she walked out. Scottie turned to Penelope, who stared at the closing door.

"What just happened?" she asked.

"I have not one clue." Penelope rose and hefted her bag over her shoulder. Scottie followed.

They found Molly leaning against the passenger door of Scottie's truck. Her face was lifted to the morning sun. Her eyes were closed, but her smile said it all. Scottie knew that feeling when one simple thing was perfect, and you could forget for a moment that your life was changed forever. The first step she took without anyone's help after the accident came back to her. She remembered standing there, a huge smile on her face, tears streaming down her cheeks from the joy of doing something so mundane—walking. Now, Molly was basking in the delight of this ordinary moment. Scottie wondered if she was cataloging the memory for when she could no longer feel the sun.

✧

They rode in silence as they followed Penelope to the rental drop-off. Scottie had so many questions, but she didn't want the answers spinning in her head for seven hundred miles, so she only asked one.

"Why are we doing this?"

"Going to Chimney Rock?" Molly turned away from her to stare out the window. "Because that's where we were our best."

It was like one of those stories you hear about a robbery where every witness gives you a different description of the culprit. By the time they're all done, the composite sketch is so vague and common that it could be anyone—your grandpa, the clerk at the gas station, you. How could that vacation be Molly's memory of their best? Scottie remembered endless fighting, wave after wave of animosity eroding her parents' relationship. She'd worried that, when they stopped, they wouldn't get back into the car together. Scottie rolled herself up like a pill bug—tiny, still, impervious.

Penelope knocked on the window. Molly aimed a thumb at the back seat. Penelope groaned and opened the door.

"Oh, how the mighty have fallen," Scottie said.

"Cute. We're switching every hundred miles." Penelope tried to brush the dog hair to the floor. "Scoot!" Burnie and Lucy didn't budge. Scottie stifled a laugh.

"We'll see," said Molly. She handed her jacket back to Penelope. "Here. Sit on this. We can't wait all day for you to detail Scottie's ride."

Penelope ripped it from her hands. "It would take all day."

"Thank you, Molly. I appreciate your thoughtfulness," Molly said. "No problem, Penelope. That's what sisters are for."

"You want thanks? Trade me places."

"Not gonna happen," Molly replied.

Penelope slammed the door, and Scottie took that as a cue to get this circus on the road.

※

In Scottie's memory, Chimney Rock was far away, but they barely got up to highway speed when the sign appeared. She slowed down at the turnoff to the parking lot and drove past.

"Hey, you promised." Molly turned to watch it disappear behind them.

"Settle down. I saw a dirt road up ahead on the map. It follows the railroad line. I'm going to see if I can get us closer. I don't want to have to carry your ass on this crusade."

Molly sat back. "Thanks."

Penelope weighed in. "That might be a private road. Maybe you should go back. I bet it's not that far a walk."

Scottie ignored her. She pulled off the highway onto a dirt road and backtracked. Her truck squeezed through unscathed between the rail tracks and the scrub brush. Based on the washboard surface that bounced them along, she estimated it hadn't been dragged since last fall. She pulled off parallel to the tracks, leaving barely enough room for someone to pass, and prayed a train wouldn't come along and wipe off her mirror.

Molly was the first out of the truck. She stepped onto the tracks without looking.

"Molly, you're going to get killed," Penelope said. Her hands snapped to her mouth, but the words were out.

She stopped in the middle of the track and turned back to them. "I'll know when it's coming." With a look, she dared them to scold her.

Penelope stopped to look both ways before she followed. Scottie brought up the rear with the dogs in tow.

Like most of her childhood memories, Chimney Rock loomed much larger back then than in real life. The edges had smoothed from decades of rain and wind. Graffiti memorialized couples who had probably not lasted as long as the paint. The technicolor landscape in her head was sepia-toned now. In place of the waves of wheat whispering in the breeze, misshapen clumps of grass speckled the fields. Dusty from months of dirt, sprayed from the wake of farm trucks and railcars, once-evergreen shrubs sat muted and tired.

"I don't know why I ever thought this was worth the trip." Penelope shaded her eyes as she looked up. "If I'd insisted on Disneyland, we would at least have had some memories of Mickey Mouse and Ferris wheels." Penelope turned from the rock and surveyed the surrounding land.

"It wasn't all bad," Molly offered.

"True. It was the end of the fighting, seeing as they broke up when we got back home," Scottie said.

"Maybe you were too young, Scottie. But I remember Penelope playing with us. She was older, so she didn't play with us much anymore. On that trip, though, we played games. She read us books. We were sisters. Like you're supposed to be. Like on TV. The Brady Bunch before the boys came," Molly said.

"I wanted them to stop fighting and be like they were before." Penelope picked at the earth with the toe of her boot.

"Before what?" asked Scottie.

"Before you, I guess." Penelope said it, staring at the top of the rock, as if it were nothing to say.

"Penelope!" Molly whipped her head around and stared at her sister, eyes and mouth wide open.

Scottie refused to give Penelope the satisfaction of seeing her wounds. "It's OK, Molly. It's true. I don't know why they adopted me at all. Who approved that?"

"Nobody. Not like they do today, anyway." Penelope moved to the rock. She reached out and placed her palm against it. Slowly, she followed the impression carved into the stone.

"How do you know that? Do you know who my parents were?" The weight of that possibility rooted Scottie where she stood. Without responding, Penelope turned and headed for the truck. "Penelope, you can't just drop a bomb like that and walk away." Scottie picked up a handful of dirt and gravel and threw it at Penelope. "Hey, I'm talking to you."

She stopped and turned slowly on her heels. "No. I don't know. Not for sure. But your dad does. You should ask him. I'm surprised you haven't already." She called her dog. Lucy ran into her waiting arms.

Scottie turned to Molly. "Did you know? Do you know who my parents are?"

"No, Scottie, I swear I have no clue." Molly reached for her hands, but she pulled them away.

Scottie turned and looked down the tracks. In her mind, she was tossing her keys in the bushes, calling her dog, and walking south.

"Scottie, she's not right. They didn't fall apart when you came along. They were never happy. Grandpa told me once that he couldn't understand how they ever got together. They were so different and didn't agree on anything. That was way before you came along. Hell, if kids were the problem, they wouldn't have made it past Penelope." Molly moved toward her.

"Do not hug me. I do not want to be hugged." Scottie shook off the thought of it with a jerk.

Molly's eyes drooped. Scottie knew she wanted her to say something that would make it better, but she didn't have it in her. Molly shook her head and started toward Penelope. In the middle of the tracks, she stopped and turned back to Scottie.

"I know you felt like an outsider as a kid. But you're not a kid anymore. If you're on the outside now, it's your choice. I won't be here to reach out forever. If you don't let go of that old bullshit and take my hand soon, it'll be too late." She stepped over the rail. "This was the last spot I felt like we were all connected. I thought you might remember that. I can see we've both painted different pasts." Molly walked away.

Burnie wandered to Scottie's side. She reached out to stroke his head as they watched Molly leave. If the rail hadn't been so close to the ground, she would have sat down right there forever. Funny to think her brokenness was the only thing moving her forward in that moment. Burnie nudged her. "Give me a minute. I'm trying to decide who I'm most pissed off at right now. There's a good chance it's me."

She pulled out her phone and held it at arm's length, as if the two extra feet would make a difference. She wanted to talk to her dad. Penny had to be lying. He would have told her if he knew. She hadn't asked, though. Maybe he thought she didn't want to know. Maybe he was right.

Burnie let out a bark and trotted toward Penelope. Lost in her head, she hadn't heard the farm truck drive up. Though it pained her, she picked up the pace, her walk morphing to a jog and a hop. By the time Scottie got back to her vehicle, Molly was safely inside, but Penelope was toe to toe with a man about her age. His unruly hair snuck out in clumps from a faded baseball cap. His clothes were dusty and worn and his lean face red. Penelope blocked him from advancing. Her delicate hands poised to push him away, like a kitten standing tall against a German Shepherd.

"Nowhere is it posted that this is private property." Penelope raised her voice. "It looks like railroad access."

"It's a private road. There's public parking out on the highway, and it's clearly marked. You have no right to be out here."

As Scottie caught up to Burnie, now standing guard at Penelope's side, she saw an older man get out of the truck. He carried a shotgun like he knew how to use it.

"Burnie, sit. Penelope, get in the truck." Scottie stepped in front of her.

"I don't need your help, Scottie." She made a move forward, but Scottie cut her off.

"I said get in the truck." She didn't like turning her back to the men, but Penelope was out of her league. Burnie stood and pressed his shoulder to her knee, a low rumble in his throat.

"I am so sick of people like her coming out here, ruining the road." He pointed at Penelope, and Burnie growled. "Shut your dog up or I'll shoot it."

"It'll be the last thing you shoot." Scottie took a step forward.

"That's enough," said the old man. He was closer now. Though his face was lined with age and weather, the resemblance between the two men was clear. Where his son emitted waves of fury, though, the old man pulsed with a confident peace that dampened Scottie's fear.

"Look, this is my fault, not hers. My sister wanted to see Chimney Rock. We came here as kids. But she's sick." Scottie's eyes followed the old man rounding the hood of her truck. "I didn't think she could walk that far."

Molly rolled down the window and Scottie prayed she hadn't grabbed her gun from the console. The old man and Molly stared at each other silently. He dipped his chin in a slow nod. Molly returned it in kind.

"I didn't see a sign, so I assumed. That's on me. I'm very sorry. We'll get out of here," Scottie said.

The old man stopped their argument cold. "It's OK, son. They're going to be on their way."

Scottie waited until the younger man relaxed, then wasted no time loading up Burnie.

The old man stayed at Molly's side. When Scottie started the engine, he was still loosely attached to the vehicle with one weathered hand on the window frame. He reached out and patted Molly's shoulder. In a voice that could have rocked a baby to sleep, he said, "You take care of yourself, now."

Chapter Thirty-Eight

Penelope

THE HIGHWAY SNAKED its way through the high desert, past receding lakes. Peaks loomed in the distance, and though the truck was pointed in their direction, they never seemed to reach them. As they moved north, the landscape faded into a patchwork of scrub and pasture. Houses, at first miles apart, became closer and closer until they crowded into small towns and then spread apart again as the speed limit rose.

For the next four hours, they covered two hundred and fifty miles without a word. The dogs' snoring ticked away the agonizingly long minutes. Scottie sat bolt upright, watching the road ahead. Though only a handful of cars passed them, she checked her side mirrors regularly. Penelope was convinced it was Scottie's strategy to avoid making eye contact with her in the rearview. She tested her theory by scowling into it.

Molly sat next to Scottie, an elbow on the door to support her face, which was cradled in her hand and fixed in the distance. Ceding her stint in the front, Penelope lodged herself between the door and her briefcase in the back seat. About an hour in,

Lucy abandoned Burnie for Penelope's lap. She wanted to ignore the dog in punishment for choosing him, but dogs were not people. Penelope knew firsthand that strategy only worked on people who were damaged enough in childhood that the denial of affection reinforced their uselessness and made them beg for the abuse. Dogs simply searched for hands that loved them. Lucy had chosen Burnie for his warmth. Penelope took it personally, but she knew intellectually that she wasn't shunning her. So, when Lucy deigned to snuggle onto Penelope's lap, she wrapped one arm around the animal and gently stroked behind her ears until Lucy fell asleep.

Penelope stared at the heads in the front seat. Scottie and Molly couldn't be more different. Like Lucy and Burnie, they somehow found a way to connect. In many ways, Penelope felt more like Scottie than Molly. Though they had all been given the same X chromosome from their dad. Molly was the genetic wildcard, sampling random combinations of genes from the other twenty-three. Her skin was porcelain and her eyes the color of a silty river in spring. Penelope and Scottie leaned toward olive and tanned at the hint of sun. With a cursory look, their eyes might appear to be the same color, but Scottie's had spokes of gold. Though also brown, Molly's hair was much lighter than Scottie's or her own.

It wasn't just their physical attributes, though. While the chaos of their childhood left them cautious and deliberate, Molly rolled the dice. Her dad was right; Molly was a daredevil. Penelope's therapist would have a field day with this one. *Perhaps your inability to connect with Scottie is really a projection of your inability to connect with yourself. Exploring this relationship could be your path to self-acceptance and self-compassion. No, doctor, this relationship is the path to destruction.*

"I need food, and the dogs need to pee." Scottie's words jarred her from her thoughts.

Molly stretched. "I'm fine."

"You're eating," Penelope and Scottie announced in unison. She didn't respond.

"The silent treatment doesn't change anything," Penelope said.

"What's the point of arguing? It's not like you're going to hold me down and force feed me. Just saying, don't waste your money on lunch for me. I'm not eating it."

Alarms sounded in Penelope's gut. Molly would no longer be moving her food around the plate to give the appearance of eating. She was refusing the plate outright. A heavy weight pinned Penelope to the ground. Her arms and legs buzzed with energy, but she was powerless to move. Scottie sat silently next to her. Penelope seethed at her indifference.

"Are you just going to sit there and say nothing?" she asked.

"Me? What's to say? She doesn't want to eat," Scottie said.

"Do you want her to end up in another backwater hospital where they can't even keep track of their patients? Do you even care?"

"Hey, her is me and I am right here. Don't strategize about me like I'm not even here," Molly said.

"OK, fine, Penelope." Scottie craned her neck and pinned her eyes in the rearview mirror. "Molly, you need to eat. It's clear you're sick, though you don't feel the need to share the specifics of that with us. Sick or not, if you don't eat, eventually it will kill you. And, since you think you have us in check, let me share my next move. I will be stopping in John Day. They have excellent cheeseburgers and salads—assuming you don't leave it in a hot car all day." Scottie glanced at Penelope. "I recommend the burger. You can eat or not eat. However, you are not getting in my car if you do not eat. Perhaps you could call an Uber. Please be sure to warn them that you might have a seizure. I suspect not eating is related, so I think you owe it to the poor SOB who takes your call to forewarn him about what a terrifying experience it is to witness you flopping around on the ground with your eyes rolling back in your head. But by all means, don't eat. As you said, I will not be force-feeding you." She looked back again. "There, Penelope, did I say enough?"

Penelope's eyes slid toward the roof. "God, you're just like Dad."

Chapter Thirty-Nine

Molly

MOLLY STARED OUT the window at the rocky crags dotted with pine. She'd read somewhere that pine trees have a fungus that can break down the rock so they can use the minerals to grow deep roots. That was what she was, a fungus trying to break apart a rock to make room for a tree that didn't want to grow there. Soon, the rains would come and wash the sapling away. Then the temperature would drop and the water in the tiny crack would become ice and expand until it cleaved off in pieces. She had to slow down the predictable course of their nature, even if it meant choking down a cheeseburger.

The diner sat one truck length back from the highway. The parking spots were delineated by fading strips of white paint spanning from the building to the road, allowing patrons to come and go from either direction. It would be impossible to know, when they left, which travelers had changed their minds and which were ever more resolute about their journey. Scottie pulled into the space closest to the door. Before the engine had completely died, she was out of the truck and headed for the dogs.

As soon as she pulled the back door open, Penelope clutched Lucy to her chest and shot out the other side. Burnie jumped down from the truck. Scottie slammed the door. The women stalked off in opposite directions, leaving Molly behind.

Dropping down from the cab, she surveyed the two-lane. Burnie trotted along on his leash, tugging Scottie in one direction. Penelope clutched Lucy in the crook of her arm, marching in the other like she had somewhere to be.

Through the glass door, an elderly woman approached, and Molly hurried to pull the door open for her. She prayed the effort required signaled only a need for food. The pity in the old woman's eyes told her it might be more serious than that, though.

She scanned the room for a spot. A waitress, who was scrambling between tables filling coffee cups, pointed at a four-top by the window. Molly grabbed three menus from the counter and sat down. She looked out the window at the cars passing by. The speed limit was reduced going through town, probably less for safety than to give you more time to think about what you needed before that next long, lonely stretch of highway.

Penelope arrived back at the truck before Scottie. She leaned against the rear door, cradling Lucy like a baby in her arms until the door locks beeped. Molly could tell no words passed between them as they loaded their dogs from opposite sides of the vehicle. Penelope marched to the cafe door ahead of Scottie, letting it slam behind her. Scottie's teeth were clenched so tight she was breathing through her nose. Both sat down without a greeting and buried their faces in their menus.

Molly attempted small talk with the waitress to make up for the hostility her sisters were emitting. Through a seasoned smile, the waitress took their orders and retreated to get their drinks. The food followed so quickly that Molly wondered if the waitress had scrawled a code word on the ticket like "RUSH" or "SOS" to alert the cook to the volatile situation.

"OK. See? I'm eating. Can you two make nice?" Molly bit the tip off a French fry. "We're family. It's OK to fight, but we need to work it out."

"We're not, though. Not really," Scottie said. "A family, that is. Not since Mary kicked me out."

Molly closed her eyes and braced for impact. Penelope let out a low growl that filled her with dread. That sound rarely escaped her, but Molly knew it preceded words that would satisfy her older sister in the moment but haunt her in the future. It was a precursor to a side of Penelope that few witnessed.

"Well, we could have been, if Hank had had the decency to respond to her letter." Penelope dropped her fork on the table, hitting her plate. Customers looked her way, but only Scottie was in her sights. "And I know he lied to me when he said he didn't get it."

Molly cringed when Scottie leaned forward. Not the move for dealing with a pissed-off Penelope.

"When did you talk to Dad?"

Molly expected fury, but she heard only fear.

"When I picked up my car. How do you think I got to the airport?" Penelope picked up her fork and stabbed at her salad.

"Hold on a sec. What letter?" Molly asked. *Mom tried to get back with Dad? When did that happen?*

"The letter Mom wrote him asking if we could all be a family again." Penelope said it as if it were common knowledge.

"Wait. You knew about this, and you never told me?" Molly pushed back from the table. *How did I not see this?*

"What would have been the point? I was sparing you more disappointment. He didn't even call. He just left her hanging there. Heartbroken. She wanted them to get back together. Clearly, he didn't care about her or us."

"That's bullshit. You always hated him. I'm not listening to this." Scottie pulled her jacket on.

"Ask him yourself. I bet he lies to you too." A smug smile slid across Penelope's face.

"I know for a fact it's bullshit. She didn't want us to be a family. She wanted him back. She didn't give a shit about me. The sight of me turned her stomach. She said as much."

Penelope's grin wilted. Her eyes narrowed.

Molly's stomach turned sour. It was spiraling out of her control. She reached for Scottie's hand. "You don't know that."

She jerked out of reach. "I do know that, Molly. I read the letter. Dad didn't lie. He never got it."

Penelope dropped her fork. "You hid it from him?"

"Yes, I did." Scottie tossed her napkin on her plate and crossed her arm over her chest. "How would you feel? I was a little kid. I'd already been discarded by two moms. I wasn't going to give her a chance to do it a second time. She was clear in that letter that I would be something she'd put up with to get him back."

Penelope wiped her mouth. "You had no right. And being a kid is no excuse. You knew better. You knew exactly what you were doing. So, next time you're whining about not being a part of our family, remember that's your fault. All your fault." She shoved her chair away from the table, stood, and walked out.

Scottie let her go without a word. She didn't even watch her leave. She picked up her burger and took another bite. Molly stared at her, mouth agape.

"That's it. You're just going to sit there and eat your burger like nothing happened?"

"What should I do? Run after her? Beg her forgiveness? It wouldn't make any difference. She's not even trying to understand me or what I went through."

Molly took in Scottie's hurt and resentment like she'd always done. Maybe excusing it all these years wasn't an act of compassion. Maybe she had to take some responsibility for Scottie and Penelope never having to work these things out. She wanted to hold on to them both so badly that she didn't realize she was the link keeping them apart.

"Look, I get why you hid the letter. I don't agree, but I get why. But did you have to tell her? Can't you see it hurts her too?"

"You want us all to be sisters again. But you don't want us to be honest."

"That's not true. I think you can be honest without being hurtful. That was just plain mean."

"Honest? How about you? Are you being honest? No. You haven't even told us the truth about what's wrong with you. Walk your talk, Molly."

Molly shook her head and walked out.

Chapter Forty

Scottie

SCOTTIE STARED AT the table full of half-eaten food.

"Do you want me to box this up?" the waitress asked.

"No thanks. I think we all lost our appetites." Scottie dropped three twenties on the table. "Keep the change." She knew every person in the place had heard their fight. It didn't matter. She was never coming back here. Their little show would be the cautionary tale these strangers shared when family feuds threatened. *It could be worse. One time I was sitting in a diner and these three chicks walked in. Man, were they screwed up.* This was nothing. Strangers had been witness to far more intimate pain in Scottie's life. What did she care? She stood and looked around the room. Eyes darted to plates as she scanned the place. These people couldn't even scratch the surface of the walls she'd built. She turned and strode out.

Molly and Penelope were nowhere in sight. She should have kept her mouth shut. One of them would tell her dad. That eventuality was the best-case scenario. Penelope was so pissed she'd left her dog behind. With her luck, she would get picked up hitchhiking by a serial killer. Molly would probably cross the road without looking and get hit by a semi. Losing both of his real daughters and learning of her betrayal would be the end of their relationship for sure. Hank would understand why Mary found her so abhorrent.

Molly was right. She'd dug up all the bitterness she'd buried and thrown it at Penelope. Scottie had been telling herself for so many years that she didn't care one bit about Mary—like she'd ceased to exist the day she sent Scottie away. That was a lie too. Mary was a poison inside her, tainting every feeling, every decision, every relationship.

She needed to find them. The next six hundred miles in angry silence would be her penance. It would take that much time to figure out how to apologize to Hank for ruining his life by being born.

Scottie looked north. The road was flat and empty, save for the occasional car. She looked south. In the distance, she saw two figures. One was marching down the east side of the road. The other was on the west side, leaning on a road sign with her thumb out. Both were pointing in the wrong direction.

Scottie rolled up to Molly first. There was a greater risk of losing her, as she had no fear and was more likely to hop onto the first motorcycle that stopped. Pulling to the left shoulder, Scottie rolled the passenger window down. Leaning over the console, keeping one eye on her limping quarry ahead, she said, "Get in."

"I can find my own ride." Molly extended her elbow and lifted her thumb to make her point.

"That may be, but you're going the wrong way. Are you hitching back to Reno?"

Molly walked in front of the hood and stepped out just as a car flew by. The driver laid on the horn. Molly flipped him off. "Screw you. Watch where you're going."

"Molly, get in the truck. You're going to get killed out here."

Molly looked down the highway. "I don't want to talk to you right now."

"Fine. Don't talk. Just get in and I'll take you to Seattle."

Molly put her hands on her hips. "What about Penelope?"

Scottie looked through the window. Penelope had stopped moving. "We'll go get her. She might not want to ride with me, though."

Molly opened the door and pulled herself up. Scottie could tell it took all the effort she could muster. She waited for Molly to buckle in and then drove past Penelope. Though she said nothing, Molly's eyes grew large as they went by. Scottie made a U-turn and met her head-on. They stared at each other through the front windshield. Penelope pivoted on one heel and walked the other way.

Molly rolled down the window and hung her head out. "Penelope, get in." She threw back her shoulders and picked up her pace. "You're being an ass."

Scottie rolled forward until they were nearly alongside her. Lucy chimed in from the back seat, yipping and clawing at the window.

"I don't want a ride," Penelope said.

"Oh, my God. Get in the damn car." Molly unbuckled and leaned out the window. "I don't have the energy to fight with you. We're not leaving without you."

Penelope's face softened to Molly's words. It bit at Scottie's heart, and she had to look away.

∽

They stopped twice for gas. Penelope bought snacks. Molly picked at the bag of Bugles. They took turns letting the dogs out, which Scottie took as a truce of sorts. She gauged their distance from home by the changing landscape. Wheat fields were replaced by wind farms, hills by peaks. Scrub brush turned to ponderosa pines. Farmhouses became towns and then cities. It was late when they hit Snoqualmie Pass.

"We should stop and see Dad," Molly said as they made their descent.

Penelope said nothing.

"I'm tired, Molly. If you want to come out and see your dad, I'll come get you next week. I still have to drive you two into the city and come back out." Scottie didn't want to face her dad in front of them.

"Why do you say it like that?" Penelope asked.

"Like what?"

"Your dad." Penelope's tone morphed from curious to mocking as she punctuated *your* with an angry exclamation point.

"I don't know. What's the big deal?"

"You're always making the point." Penelope sat up. She grabbed the headrest and pulled herself forward. Looking at Scottie in the rearview mirror, she said, "There's us and there's you."

Scottie refused to meet her eyes. Penelope was right. Molly was right. She made herself different. She could have tried to fit in. That would have meant changing, which would be solid proof she was wrong. Inherently wrong. All these years, Molly had been connecting over and over. Scottie treated each time as if it would be the time that the truth would come out—Molly was doing it out of pity and obligation, not the bond real sisters had.

"There's no you and us. We're sisters," Molly spoke for the first time in five hundred miles.

"She doesn't believe that. You should quit wasting your time," Penelope said. She dropped back on the seat and turned to the window. "Ironically, it's true, though."

The words hung there, thick and cold. Scottie's voice was quiet and measured. "I'm not a waste of time." She met Penelope's eyes in the rearview mirror.

"No. You're not a waste of time, Scottie. That's not what I said. I said Molly should stop wasting her time because you refuse to believe the truth. And I can understand why. Everyone has lied to you your whole life. I can even understand why they did that. People are all about self-preservation. Only we didn't know that, did we? We thought everything was our fault. Their fighting. Their sadness. Their worry. All of it caused by three little girls. And we've all carried that with us. I married an abusive asshole and replaced him with an all-consuming job. Molly avoids responsibility and attachments. You have a wall of protection so thick I'm shocked you were able to produce two children. The irony is our whole lives have been a reaction to these beliefs. It's why we aren't closer. We would have to be honest and see the world through each other's eyes. We can't do that though, can we? We'd have to let our guard down. We'd have to stop keeping our parents' secrets."

Penelope's words sucked all the air out of the cab. Molly leaned against the door and started to cry. Lucy climbed over the console into her lap. Scottie reached for her shoulder, but Molly shrugged it off.

"Nice. Look what you did," Scottie said. "So, Princess Penelope, what is the truth?"

Chapter Forty-One

Penelope

"THE TRUTH? You aren't different or separate or whatever story you tell yourself. The truth is, you weren't even adopted. Not really. Not fully." Penelope's heart pounded as the words tumbled out. This secret, that made her feel so special with her mother as a child, had ruined every other relationship she had in her family. Though she could not admit it out loud, anger for Mary glowed like hot coals inside her.

Scottie's eyes jerked into the rearview mirror, wide and seeking. The vehicle swerved, and a horn blared next to them. "What are you talking about?" she demanded.

Molly sat up, dislodging Lucy, who scampered to Burnie for safety. He rose on all fours, looming over Penelope.

"Penelope?" Molly asked.

Scottie pulled off on the shoulder and put on her hazard lights. She unbuckled and turned to Penelope. "What the fuck are you talking about?" Burnie turned to her, and Scottie commanded him to lie down.

Penelope remained fixed on the window. She knew she had

gone too far, but there was no turning back. "We all have the same dad."

Scottie's mouth dropped open.

"Hank's your real dad, Scottie. He had an affair, but he wouldn't leave Mom for that woman when she got pregnant." Now that the story was out, she needed her to understand it all. "Just after you were born, the woman showed up at the house and dropped you off. And so, Mom took you in and loved you like you were her own."

"Yes, that was obvious the day she kicked me out." Scottie lifted her chin. Tears washed across the defiance on her face.

"You always focus on the bad stuff."

"Tell me, Penelope, what is the good stuff? Because all I can think of right now is that the one parent, who I thought really loved me, has been lying to me my whole life. Apparently, you knew. That's great." Scottie turned to Molly. "Did you know as well? Have I just been the family joke all along?"

"No, Scottie. I didn't know. You're not a joke."

The hurt in Molly's eyes stung Penelope, but she couldn't stop herself. It was high time Scottie understood Mary had done the best she could with what Hank had brought down on them all.

"Maybe you were just too young to remember. Maybe you want to hold on to your anger. But there was good stuff. She took care of you. She protected you from that horrible woman." Scottie jerked back at the words. Penelope hadn't meant to spit them out, but years of controlling her rancor had made the dam weak. It all gushed out. "Yes. Horrible woman. She gave you away in exchange for the satisfaction of hurting Mom. And when she came back for you years later, she didn't really want you. She wanted money. Mom protected you from her. She never even told Dad about that. All Mom asked for was to not be humiliated by his affair. It wasn't meant to hurt you. She adopted you willingly. She didn't want people to know Dad cheated on her. You can understand that. You're a wife."

"Why didn't she just give me back to my mom?"

"Are you even listening? Mom loved you. That woman didn't really want you. She wanted money. Five hundred bucks. I was there. That's what that bitch wanted. Mom knew it. She didn't want to give you up."

"Maybe not then." Scottie turned back and started the truck. "But in the end, she did it."

Penelope felt like a wrecking ball moving under the indiscriminate force of gravity. Swinging back and forth, destroying everything until it came to rest. "You look like her."

Scottie put the truck in gear and checked her side mirror.

Penelope could tell she was shutting down. Scottie wiped her eyes roughly with her sleeve. Her face lost all expression.

"Stop," Penelope said. "You have to understand. See it from her eyes. You started to look like that woman. Mom tried to ignore it, but there you were with her face staring back. A constant reminder of Dad's affair. She snapped. She tried so hard. She cried about it for days after Dad came to get you."

"Stop defending her. You make it sound like Dad was taking me away from her. That's bullshit and you know it."

"Don't be a hypocrite. You're the reason we didn't get back together as a family. If you hadn't hidden the letter from Dad, things might have turned out differently."

"Mary didn't want to get back together as a family. She wanted him back. I was something she would tolerate to get him." Scottie forced the words out through her sobs.

"Scottie." Penelope reached forward.

"No. We're done talking." She punched the hazard lights and accelerated onto the highway.

"Great work, Penelope," Molly said. "Are there any bombs about me you want to drop on my life?"

"Don't be so sanctimonious. You dropped a bomb on both of our lives. As usual, we came running. You have your own secrets and you're happy to ask for our help, but you aren't being honest with us, either."

Chapter Forty-Two

Molly

MOLLY HUGGED HER coat around her body. The heat was blasting in the cab, yet her bones were chilled. Not quite the fairy-tale ending she'd had in mind. She'd been stupid to think that they would connect after all these years. Stupidity was the least of her sins. She'd been careless with their lives. Her plan made her feel better about leaving them. She'd convinced herself she was filling the brokenness in their lives, but she'd just shoved the wedge in deeper. It hurt her heart to imagine them never speaking again.

She turned and pressed her back to the door. Scottie was looking straight ahead. A stranger might think she was merely focused on driving. Molly had seen this look a hundred times in the hospital, though. A nurse would come in with a bounce in her step to assault Scottie's body with yet another needle. She would refuse to cry or scream. That was what she was doing now. Scottie was shoving down the pain, like her heart was a suitcase overflowing with clothes and she had to cram them all in there and zip it shut.

Molly looked back at Penelope. Her right hand gripped the door handle. She wondered how she had missed it all these years. What she had discarded as a vague coincidence now glowed like a neon sign. Perhaps because she always considered them sisters, she hadn't really thought about the physical similarities of Scottie and Penelope. After all, they were alike in about the same measure as she differed from them both.

They had kept such big secrets from her and not for a moment, but for a lifetime. She'd thought she was close to both of them. Apparently not that close. If she were honest, she'd kept secrets too, though. She'd never shared any of her relationships. She hadn't told them she was dying. She hadn't told them she had chosen to die rather than fight this thing growing inside her. She hadn't said she was scared or asked them for comfort.

"I'm a lesbian," Molly announced.

They looked at her.

Scottie said, "Duh."

Penelope said, "That's your big secret? I don't think so."

Molly did not give herself time to process this revelation. "Fine. I'm dying."

"Again," Penelope said.

"No. I mean, I am not going to have treatment. I am choosing to die."

Scottie turned to her. Her stoic face heightened in alarm.

"There's no doctor's appointment. Well, there is. But I will not be attending." She cocooned herself in the coat.

Penelope stared at her, stunned. "How can you do this? You didn't even talk to me."

"I knew you'd try to talk me out of it." Molly could not meet her eyes.

"Of course I would. This is asinine. You're young. So, you would have a few months of chemo or radiation, but then you could live a long time."

"A few months of chemo isn't going to cure this. I'm not going to waste away in pain like Mom did. I can't go through that."

"At least go to the appointment and hear what the doctor has to say. Scottie, for Christ's sake, engage. Help me out here," Penelope begged.

"It sounds like her mind is made up." Scottie's words were low and quiet.

"That's it. That's all you're going to say? Do you care if she lives?" Penelope threw her phone on the floor. Burnie curled around Lucy.

"Penelope, I know you're angry. But it's too late," Molly said.

"You can change your mind."

"But I can't turn back time."

Scottie looked at Molly. She could tell she understood. There was no fight left in her. "I wish you had talked to me—or Penelope."

"Penelope, I was sick when I left for Reno. I knew what it was. I wanted one more winter in the snow. One more season with my friends. I couldn't bear the thought of waiting around to die. Watching all of you suffer. For what? Nothing is going to change this."

Molly turned toward the shoulder. For the next hour, she listened to their muffled tears. She watched the mile markers fly by and prayed to a God she no longer believed in that they would forgive her before she passed. She prayed they would forgive each other and themselves.

※

Scottie pulled in front of the condo and slid down to the pavement. Molly could tell by the groans that the trip had been too much for her. Though she limped with every step, Scottie hauled her bags to the foyer. Penelope, clutching Lucy to her chest with one arm, pulled her bag from the back.

"You don't have to stay with me," Molly said.

"I'm not. I called a taxi."

"Oh." Molly's relief turned to regret. She swept her up in a hug. Penelope did not hug her back. "I'm sorry. This isn't how I wanted this to end."

She wanted Penelope to tell her everything would be OK, but she said nothing. Molly turned back to the truck, and watched Scottie pull into traffic.

Chapter Forty-Three

Scottie

S COTTIE HELD THE secret inside. It wasn't hard. She'd had a lifetime of keeping things hidden, and she'd surrounded herself with people who didn't push her. Even her closest friend, Molly, had respected those boundaries. Penelope was the only one who barreled through them. She wouldn't have to worry about that much longer. Once Molly was gone, she doubted they'd ever see each other again.

She avoided Hank as best she could. Every time the urge to confront him arose, she reminded herself she had betrayed him too. One could not be addressed without the other. What would it accomplish anyway, except to sever the only tie to her childhood she had left? As much as it pained her, it defined her.

With the exception of her toothbrush, she left her duffle at the bottom of her closet, still packed with dirty clothes. Each morning, she'd kicked it farther in until it lodged in the corner, hunched but unsubstantial. The form reminded her of a huddled child. That was what she'd been carrying with her all this time—the child hiding in the corner.

Scottie wrenched the bag from the floor and tossed it on the bed. At the sudden movement, Burnie rose from where he lay to stand in the threshold of the door. She tore open the zipper and scooped the clothes into her arms. Among the soft folds of socks and T-shirts, she felt a sharp corner of heavy paper. She released her grasp and watched as a manila envelope dropped to the floor among the clothes. In block letters, her name was written on the front.

A beam of morning sunlight climbed up her body as she slid to the floor. Early spring yet, the light did little to warm her. Still, she lifted her face to the sun as she reached for the package and pressed it against her chest. *Molly, what have you done?*

Scottie tore the flap open and spilled the contents on the carpet between her outstretched legs. A cluster of photographs and a single sheet of paper fluttered to the ground. Though faded, she made out the top half of Chimney Rock and slipped the picture from the pile. In high-waisted jeans and a striped T-shirt, a scowling Penelope looked like a sailor saluting the monument. Reaching her index finger out, Scottie outlined the figure next to her. A little girl, with a broad smile, is poised to jump into the older girl's arms. There it was in black and white, unfiltered by resentment. In that moment, her love for Penelope shone in her smile.

Scottie held the picture in her hand. She was frozen in the sharp pain of loss. Barely registering his motion, she sat staring at the photo until Burnie broke the spell, putting his nose to her neck. Leaning into him with closed eyes, she rubbed her face against his as if she could soak up his courage. When she stopped, he lay down by her side, pressing his weight against her thigh.

Scottie spread the photographs out and turned them right side up. A flash of orange caught her eye. Mary sits in an armchair. Beneath her rust-colored vest, an enormous white collar points toward each shoulder. Mary's smiling face is tilted downward as five tiny fingers reach up to her. Next to her, Hank crouches with one arm around Penelope and one around Molly. Even in the flat and dusty photograph, joy sparkles in their eyes.

Scottie shuffled through the stack three times, searching for the moment all this love turned to disdain. *You didn't include that, Molly. Of course you didn't.* She swiped the note from the floor and crumpled it between her hands. Startled, Burnie scrambled from the floor.

"Sorry. Sorry. It's OK." She reached out for the dog, but he retreated to the doorway. As her tears began to fall, she flattened the paper against her thigh and read.

> *Scottie,*
>
> *I bet you're pretty mad at me right now. I hope you're getting this in time to stop being mad at me before I go. I know you don't want me to spend eternity with that on my conscience. At the risk of making things worse, I have some things I need to say to you. If you have this letter, it means that I didn't get to say them in person. The only upside to that is that I get to say what I want without being interrupted which is a nice change for a second born. :)*
>
> *I know you've always felt like you don't quite belong anywhere. I've watched you and, even with Dad who adores you, you always seem like you're waiting for the other shoe to drop. I know you want to tear this letter up right now, but please let me finish. I don't know what all happened between Mom and Dad or even what happened to you. Not the whole story, anyway. I do know I have always loved you as a sister. A real sister. Your being adopted does not matter one bit to me. You can believe me or not, but it's the truth. You are perfect exactly as you are. Just like everyone else, you do not have to do, or*

be, or give anything to deserve to be loved. And I love you the same as I love Penelope. Exactly the same.

I also know that whatever messed up stuff happened, it wasn't your fault. It wasn't my fault or Penelope's, either. Mom and Dad had their issues. We all got caught up in that. I'm not saying it wasn't hard on you. What Mom did was awful. But she didn't just do it to you. She did it to all of us. We were too little to fight back or change the situation. Losing you hurt me, and it hurt Penelope too. We were all just kids. We are not kids anymore, though.

Time is running out for me. You and Penelope still have time, though. Before you discard that idea, she was just as much a casualty of their issues as you were. If you think about it, whatever it is you two are holding against each other is not in the present. It's in the past. I know that because you rarely even speak to each other. That means all those hurts are old and childish. You might be old, but you don't have to be childish. The way I see it, you're punishing Penelope because you can't punish Mom. Penelope is not Mom. You made your mind up a long time ago, and then you lined up all the evidence against Penelope to prove yourself right. But ask yourself, has she been excluding you or is that just your excuse so you don't have to put yourself out there and engage?

It's time to let go of all this resentment and animosity toward her. Sure, you'll still have Dad, but not forever. Think about this. Without you, when I go, Penelope will have no one. Maybe you want that. Maybe you want to keep punishing her. But remember what it feels like to be alone. You know how awful that is. You didn't deserve to feel that way. Neither does Penelope. Don't wait for her. It's time to reach out and make things right. Trust me, when this whole ride comes to an end, the only things you will regret are the things you should have *said, the forgiveness you withheld, and the time you wasted on anger and fear.*

I love you. I know you love me too. If you forgive yourself and Penelope, you'll be able to love her the way that little girl in these pictures did. Make things right, Scottie.

Molly

Scottie eased her back to the floor and let out a groan. The carpet did little to soften the hard floor. Her hips and shoulders ached where they met the ground. Burnie flopped down alongside her. With one hand in his fur, she stared at the ceiling and thought back to the nights in the hospital when she'd felt so alone. She'd never told anyone how frightened and empty she felt, but Molly knew. Not just Molly, though; Hank and Jason, even Mary knew. They hadn't respected her boundaries at all. They let her push them away, taking care of her without taking her power away. It was dishonest on all their parts. But it was a truer version of the story than Scottie had been carrying around all these years.

Molly was right. Scottie knew where she had to start.

Chapter Forty-Four

Penelope

PENELOPE TURNED ON the shower. After two days of binge-watching crime shows and eating takeout food, her pajamas were probably a complete loss, but she threw them in the hamper anyway. Lucy sat on the bathmat staring at her.

"Go. Get in your bed." The dog didn't move. "You know I picked you, instead of a cat, because your species is known for unconditional love and forgiveness. You might want to ease up on the disappointment. Cats don't have to be walked." Lucy lay down, resting her head on her paws with a sigh. "I'm well aware that I have managed to screw up my whole life in one week. I don't need your judgment. I bet you are laughing your ass off at the mess I've made, Michael, wherever you are. Hell, if there's any justice in this world."

The only time she hadn't had a job since eighth grade was when she was married to Michael. At first, it was such a relief to have someone else take care of her for a change. She thought he would provide what she needed. In the end, the cost was all her power. He controlled the money, so he determined what she needed.

There wasn't anyone to ask for help from, even if she could force herself to do it. She'd burned her bridge clear through with Hank. Mary was gone. Molly soon would be. She couldn't face her anyway after the bomb she dropped on Scottie's life. And then there was Scottie. She'd hated Penelope her whole life. She didn't think they could go backward from that, but Penelope was apparently an overachiever in destroying relationships as well.

Though she had nowhere to go, she couldn't face rebuilding her life in her current disheveled state. She took a shower, fixed her hair, put on her makeup, and dressed in business casual. Lucy pattered after her, from room to room, periodically letting out a yip to spur Penelope on.

While she sorted out what the world could see, she also set about cleaning up what no one else could see. Penelope made a mental list of the things that had to be done to get her life back on the rails. *Find a job.* When a thought arose that interfered with forward motion, she squashed it. *You're probably already blacklisted. You'll have to move out of state to get a job.* No. *Find a job. Evaluate my assets. Get ready to sell them off to survive.* Stop. *Evaluate my expenses. Thanks to my bitchy outburst, I won't be paying for an extended houseguest.* Stay on track. *Find a job. Evaluate my assets. Evaluate my expenses. Three things. Move forward.*

Penelope sat on a stool at the bar that bordered the kitchen. She slid her laptop out of her briefcase, and with it came a manila envelope. In Molly's hand, Penelope was scribbled on the front. The sight of it slammed her back against her seat. With one finger, she pushed the package away. *Do not open that. Find a job. Evaluate your assets. Evaluate your expenses. Deal with Molly after.* She had one wheel on the track. Reaching for the laptop would put the other one on too. Reaching for the envelope would knock her off.

She picked it up and tore off the top. With one shake, photographs scattered across the counter. Gingerly, she separated them with her fingertips. A kaleidoscope of images pointed in every direction. Lucy jumped against her leg, begging to be held. Penelope scooped the dog into her lap and busied her hands stroking her head. When Lucy settled, Penelope reached out a finger to slide a picture from the stack.

On a rocky beach, Hank leaned over Penelope. His hands cocooned hers on a fishing rod. Her face was turned up and back, directing a smile to her father. He returned the same. She remembered the trip. The other girls were too small for a proper rod and reel. They were left to dip their toy rods in the water off the dock with Mary. Hank and Penelope had snuck away when they weren't watching. Though she didn't recall catching a fish, she did remember him telling her she was a natural.

Lucy snaked her head onto the counter, resting her chin on a photo. Penelope slid it aside. She couldn't recall this one at all, but she guessed it was Easter from the matching pastel dresses. Penelope was in the center. On either side, Molly and Scottie were holding her hands. Molly was hamming it up for the camera. Scottie, standing close to Penelope, looked up in awe at her sister. She couldn't remember either of them adoring her, but there it was in living color.

Buried, but for a flash of her striped shirt, was a picture of their trip to Chimney Rock. A stranger looking at it might think Penelope was concentrating on the monument. She remembered clearly what she was looking at. They'd argued the whole way to California. Maybe Molly and Scottie were not aware. Mary had mastered the whispering fight, tossing venomous words in hushed tones at Hank. Penelope knew as soon as the car stopped, the volume would increase. She'd taken her sisters in the opposite direction, distracting them with facts about the historical site. By the time their parents headed back, they were all exhausted.

Penelope shielded her eyes to watch them approach, ready to whisk the girls away if they were not finished airing their grievances. Hank, it seemed, was done. He stopped to photograph the sisters. Penelope wilted at the sight of Mary. Even from a distance, it was clear she was still mad. This picture was what she remembered, always three girls clinging to each other and the two of them breaking apart. Until Scottie left.

Penelope picked up the envelope to see if she had missed any pictures. Inside was a handwritten note. She wanted to pretend she hadn't seen it, but who was she pretending for? Lucy? She shook it onto the counter.

Penelope,

Well, my brilliant plan must have flopped, or you wouldn't be reading this letter. If this wasn't so damn tragic, I bet you'd be rolling your eyes and laughing at my feeble attempt to manipulate you. Seriously, though, I am sorry for putting you through this. I hope you will forgive me before it is too late. I would hate to spend eternity atoning for destroying decades of our friendship in a single weekend. (That has to be a record, even in our family.) Given that you might not get over this debacle in time, I am going to have to risk our potential reconciliation because there are things I need to say. While you might not be watching the clock, I am.

I hope you know I love you very much, and I have always admired you. I feel blessed we were born sisters. Doubly so that we are friends. I know you shielded me from a lot when we were growing up. If I have never said it, thank you for taking care of me. That must have been a huge burden, seeing as you were just a kid yourself.

I know I tease you about taking vacations, getting laid, and generally having some fun, but I know how important your work is to you. I'm really proud of how hard you've worked to become a lawyer. I'm glad you found your passion. Just remember, you earned it. I hope whoever is in charge knows you could work anywhere you want to. You deserve the best. Don't settle.

I wish I could be around longer to cheer you on. Let's face it, you've been working so hard, you're a little short in the friend department. Lucky for you, you have another sister. Before you jump in with all the reasons that's not going to work, I am just going to say—you have never really tried. Yes, I know she hasn't, either. She's getting a letter too.

I don't know all the details, and I don't need to. The way I see it, you two have been punishing each other for decades for nothing. She punishes you for what Mom did. You punish her for what Dad did. You are both old enough and smart enough to see this. It's stupid if you ask me. It's like your hurt is a treasure you want to sit around and polish and admire. It's not a treasure. It's a curse. Get rid of it. By the way, at least Dad is still around so you could have it out. Scottie will never get that closure with Mom. Think about it. She'll never get resolution. Mom is never going to accept responsibility, or apologize and tell Scottie she is a fundamentally loveable, worthy human being. There's still time for Dad to make it right with you. If he doesn't, let me say right here and now, you are good. You are smart. You are worthy. You are strong and brave. You are enough.

Here's the irony. You two are a lot alike. She won't ask for help because she assumes no one will be there. She expects to be disappointed. She thinks there is something fundamentally unlovable about her. You won't ask for help because you think it makes you weak. You worry about being a disappointment. You think you can never be enough. You are two sides of the same coin.

When we were little, I was the one who always felt like the third wheel. Scottie was the baby, so you looked after her. You were the big sister, so she looked up to you. I can't tell if you forgot all that or if you just painted over it to match the story you tell yourself. From the outside looking in, it's pretty clear.

Be the big sister again. Put your hand out and take hers. From where I am sitting, there's nothing in the last four decades left to hold against each other. Forgive yourself. Forgive her. Have it out with Hank. Don't spend the next forty years—or forty minutes, for that matter—alone. Loneliness is not a sentence. It's a choice. My biggest regret is not saying these things to you both years ago. I traded temporary peace for long-term love. I am sorry for that. I love you. Don't be a mule. Make things right.

Molly

Penelope cradled the dog against her chest. She let her tears fall, flattening the dog's hair. *Find a job. Make things right. Evaluate my assets. Make things right. Evaluate my expenses. Damnit, Molly. Fine. Make things right.*

She knew exactly what she had to do.

Chapter Forty-Five

Scottie

Hank handed her a mug. "Penelope called me this morning," he said.

Scottie grunted her reply. *She couldn't just let it be.*

"I wondered why you'd been so quiet since you got back." He leaned against the counter. They'd had so many talks over the years in this space.

Scottie saw no point in sitting through a scolding she'd already given herself. She knew an apology could not fix this, but a preemptive one might shorten it, and then she could get on with the business of figuring out what to do with the rest of her life. It was time to make things right regardless of the cost.

"So, you know. Well, what can I say except I'm so sorry." She couldn't meet his eyes. Burnie was sitting at her side, leaning his head against her knee. Reaching out her fingertips, she grazed the ends of his fur. The truth she had packed so carefully away, all the boxes of fear and anger she'd stacked in her belly, threatened to burst open. She wanted to sit on the floor and take Burnie in her lap, but she knew even holding him against her would not shield her from the rage she deserved. Seconds passed. In the silence of those moments, her words bubbled up and broke the surface.

"I was young and dumb, but that's no excuse for not coming clean. I wish I could say I want to go back and do it over. But I can't. It hurt so bad back then. To know I wasn't wanted. That she would only take me back because it meant getting you." Her sisters were right. She hadn't been honest even with herself, certainly not with Hank. "I was so scared you wouldn't want me around, either. I had this thought that if you read the letter, you'd see I was the problem. I just loved you so much and I needed you so much. I couldn't lose you no matter the cost."

Hank was still, and Scottie's heart pounded, grabbing her throat with every pulse.

"That's not what Penny called to tell me." He sat down. "Since you brought it up, I knew about the letter." Her face must have betrayed the question in her head because he answered it before she could ask. "When you were in the hospital, I had to pack your clothes. I found it in your drawer."

Scottie's face reddened. "Why didn't you say anything?"

"What did it matter? I thought you were going to die. What difference did anything make at that moment? I'm so sorry you've been carrying that around all these years. I wish you had told me. I wish I had paid better attention. What did I know about raising a little girl? As time went on, I just convinced myself you were fine. You were such a determined kid. Stupid to say it now, but I thought you worked it all out in your head and were fine. I should have seen the signs. Especially with your sister. You stopped connecting with Penelope right away. I had hope for you and Molly. I should have known you were holding back." He stood and crushed her in a hug. "Please don't carry this around anymore."

She let him hold her. Once the tears of the present stopped flowing, ancient ones took their place. All the hurt she'd held in, for fear she was too burdensome, flowed in salty drops.

Hank pulled back. "That isn't why Penny called. There's something else we need to talk about."

Taking her hand, he led her to a pair of chairs, and they sat. He leaned across the table where he had told her about the birds and the bees, where he had told her Mary had died, where he had explained the next surgery, and the one after that.

"Penny called to apologize to me for announcing I'm your biological father. I told her she was apologizing to the wrong person."

Scottie felt inside for the anger that always floated in the background, but there was none. Only love and gratitude washed through her. "It's OK. I've always thought of you as my dad. Even when I didn't know the truth," she said.

"It's not OK. And you can be angry with me. You should be angry with me. Even if you are, I will still love you and you will still love me." He squeezed her hands. "I thought I was doing the right thing to make up for all the wrong things I'd done. I wanted you to be safe. You were a baby, not a sin. I couldn't give you to a stranger. I also couldn't hurt Mary anymore. You're a wife now, so I know you get it. Sometimes doing the right things by your kids has a cost. I thought I could have it both ways. If you knew the truth, though, everyone would. Mary could not bear the humiliation of my adultery. That's what ate away at her—my affair, not you."

"I ruined your marriage."

"No. You did not. Lots of things ruined it long before you existed. I'm not making excuses. I was wrong to cheat. Mary didn't deserve that, but we were unhappy from the start, it seems. I never wanted to live on the west side. I never wanted to work in your grandpa's business. I did that for love. In the end, though, I was staying for the penance, not love." He let loose her hands, but she did not move. "Hey, kiddo, I should have told you that you were my daughter. I could not be prouder to say those words.

I had planned to when I thought you were old enough to understand, but then you had the accident." Hank looked like he might cry. Scottie'd never seen him cry. Her heart raced. She looked for an escape route. "That was my fault. I just couldn't make it worse by dropping that bombshell on you."

"It was an accident. If anyone's to blame, it's me for screwing around. You warned me to be careful."

"No. The ATV had been recalled. I thought it was safe to use, just to haul things back and forth to the kennel. I should have known better. I felt like hell watching you suffer. I knew you'd never be the same. I didn't want you to hate me. So, I told myself I should wait until you healed. Every time I thought about telling you, I found a reason not to. I told myself it didn't change a thing. I couldn't love you more. It was a chickenshit thing to do. I knew it would come out someday and hurt you."

The lines on his face deepened. Even as a mother, she hadn't stopped to think of how he might have felt. His child was rejected. His child was broken and bruised. She knew the lengths she would go for her kids. Surely Hank would do no less.

"I love you." Scottie took his hands. Her words came with a healing pain. "The funny thing is I don't love you more or less than I did before Penelope told me. I'm not saying it's not important, but the truth is, you've always been my dad. Adoption papers and DNA have nothing to do with that." She leaned in and hugged him. Relief flowed with tears. "It is shocking, though, that I'm biologically related to Penelope." She laughed as she wiped her nose.

"You need to cut your sister some slack. None of this was easy on her or Molly, either. What happened to us, happened to all of us."

"Well, since we're coming clean. Did Penelope tell you about Molly?"

"No. Molly did." He took a drink of his coffee. "She called this morning too."

"I'm sorry, Dad." Scottie's eyes welled again with tears.

"Not your fault. Not your responsibility, either. I'm going to see her today. You should too."

"We all said some awful things to each other." Scottie closed her eyes. "I don't know how I can be so angry at her one minute, but the next minute, I can't breathe thinking about her gone."

"Why are you so mad?"

"Are you kidding? She didn't even try to survive."

"Maybe it's not her you're mad at."

"Who then? Penelope?"

"You need to get a mirror, kiddo."

"What the hell, Dad?" Scottie searched his face, sure he must be joking.

"Seems to me you're taking her decision personally. She's not doing it to you. She's got her reasons, and she doesn't owe us an explanation. I think we owe her some compassion, though." He stood and looked down at her. "I love you. And I'm saying this from love. You're missing your chance to give back to her what she's given you all these years. She loves you so much. Every evening, she would come to the hospital. Did you know that? Every night. It wasn't easy on her. You're avoiding her to keep your heart safe. No matter how this plays out, your heart's going to break some. Do you want that break to be filled with regret for what you should have done? Or do you want it to fill up with the good stuff? 'Cause it seems to me there was a lot of good stuff between you. And while I have the floor, let me remind you that you have not one but two sisters. It might take some work, but you need to see what you are missing." Hank held up his hand when Scottie opened her mouth. "And before you say it, Penelope is missing out too. I told her as much this morning."

She thought about seeing Molly again after all that had happened. "I don't know if I'm ready. What would I even say?"

"Well. That's your decision. You need to figure it out. If you're planning to make it right, you better get on it. She's going into hospice today." Hank patted her shoulder and walked away.

Chapter Forty-Six

Penelope

"Penelope Casey, Attorney at Law, how may I help you?"

Penelope smiled every time she heard Victoria say those words. She thanked her lucky stars Victoria had taken a chance on her new venture. The firm made a last-ditch effort to get her to stay as she picked up her meager belongings. News of her departure spread like wildfire. They'd underestimated her popularity with their clients. She considered their offer for about a minute before declining. Life was too short.

Penelope had been right. Going out on her own was not a simple task. They set up a makeshift office in her dining room as they looked for office space. On the first day, Victoria had carried in a box of her personal items and set it on the island in Penelope's kitchen. She announced it would remain there until they moved into their new offices. As her family picture and the smooth stone from her husband were in the box, she informed Penelope they needed to get this show on the road.

She hadn't talked to Molly in the days since they dropped

her off. Every night at 6:00 p.m., she thought about calling her. The break in that connection made her heart hurt. She thought they would have time to hash it all out. Molly would give it a few days and then call and ask her to take her to the doctor or the grocery store.

Ironically, she'd had no trouble finding the words to say to her father. By the time she'd picked up her car at SeaTac and made it back to her apartment, the fury she felt for her sisters had grown to a bonfire. She let it smolder, and then she'd picked up the phone. She wanted him to take responsibility for screwing them all up. As the words broke through the ragged sobs, he listened. All the blame of forty years spilled out. *You didn't even try. How could you just leave us? Scottie was more important. You cheated on Mom. You destroyed her.* She'd thrown it all at him, and when her tears ran dry and her words ran out, he was still on the line.

"Penelope, I'm so sorry. If I could go back, I would. Believe me, I would. I know you hate me right now. I understand if you can never forgive me. But you have to let the hate go. It's eating you up. You've grown up to be such an amazing woman. I know I had no part in that. But I'm in awe of your strength and talent. The hate is holding you back. It's like an anchor holding you in this place. There's so much more for you."

All the fuel burned out at his words. Sitting in her high-rise apartment, with her cotton candy dog curled up next to her, Penelope looked around. She'd built an enviable living space, but she hadn't built a life. He was right. Her anger had outlived its usefulness long ago. She wasn't punishing anyone but herself.

"Dad, I did a terrible thing."

"Whatever it is, it'll be OK," he said.

And it was. When she finished apologizing for outing Scottie's parentage, he told her not to worry. Penelope bearing that secret all these years was his only regret.

Victoria stood in the doorway and knocked on the doorjamb to get her attention. She looked to Penelope and then back to the phone in her hand. "You need to take this call."

She listened as Hank carefully meted out the details. Somehow, she knew it would be him to call. With every word that he said, Penelope felt the crush of regret. She'd said terrible things to Molly. She clutched her sorrow like a precious gift, while disregarding the treasure their nightly phone calls had been—could still be.

"I'll be there." She scanned the room. Papers covered the table. Three layers of boxes lined one side of the hall.

Victoria picked Penelope's coat off the chair where she'd discarded it in haste the night before. She collected her purse from the kitchen counter. Then she handed them over and asked, "Do you want me to drive?"

Penelope looked at the woman who had such compassion, such faith in her. "Thank you. You're always taking care of me." She hugged her. "I have to do this alone."

Chapter Forty-Seven

Molly

Hank held her hand.

"I feel silly. I think this was a false alarm. Leave it to me to be dramatic to the very end." She reached for the cup of water on the tray next to her. Hank picked it up and held the straw to her lips. "Thank you."

"It's OK, Mollypop. I have nothing but time." He dabbed her chin with a washcloth.

"I need to give something back to you. It's in a box in my bag. Don't open it here."

Hank unzipped the bag. "What is it?"

"It's your gun."

"I didn't expect you to give it back."

"Well, I won't be needing it." She frowned. "I want you to have it. It meant a lot to me. I know you worried about me."

"Of course I worried. I'm your dad. I never stopped worrying. And I hope you know I never stopped loving you, no matter what happened between your mom and me."

"I know. I'm sorry it took so long for me to see it. Lots of wasted time."

Hank leaned over and pulled her to him. He cradled her head to his neck. "None of that matters. Right now is all that matters." They cried in each other's arms. When the tears subsided, Hank wiped her face and kissed her forehead.

"I forgot to say, the girls are coming." He went to the sink and splashed his face with water.

She shook her head. "I'm surprised. They haven't spoken to me since we got back. Those two can carry Olympic-sized grudges."

"They love you." He reached out and tucked an errant tendril behind her ear.

"I know. I wish they weren't mad at me, though." She looked to her left, where a tall, slender window framed a slice of the city. Searching the cracks between skyscrapers, she found a wisp of the Puget Sound. Memories pelted her heart. Digging for clams on Hood Canal. Hunting for sand dollars on Dungeness Spit. Hiking Hurricane Ridge. Skiing on the pass. Still, she'd held on to that one last trip to Chimney Rock like a tourniquet. She should have picked one before the bleeding started. An earlier one before they started collecting their scars. Maybe things would have turned out differently.

"They're mad at themselves, not you." He patted her hand. His hands were warm and heavy, and she wished she could crawl into his arms like a child.

"I'm pretty sure they're mad at me. FYI, I'm planning to play the sick and dying card when they get here just to break the ice."

Hank shook his head, smiling. "You know I love you. I'm so proud of you." He put his head down. A tear dropped onto Molly's hand.

"I know, Dad. It's going to be OK. Hey, I might get to see Mom soon." She squeezed his hand.

"Might?"

"Well, I haven't always done the right thing."

"We're all just doing the best we can, kiddo." Hank let the tears run down his face. Molly wanted to wipe them away. Her heart tightened at his pain.

"I heard when you die, you end up married again. Wouldn't that be awful?"

Hank shook his head. "No, honey. It wouldn't." He brushed the back of his hand under his eyes and sniffed. "Your mom gave me the three best things in my life. It wasn't always easy. I made a lot of mistakes. We made a lot of mistakes. But you three weren't one of them."

The door opened slowly. Scottie came in first. Penelope followed. The room was small, and Hank had claimed his spot on Molly's left side. He made no move to accommodate them, which forced them to stand together on her right. Like soldiers in drill formation, they stood bolt upright and an arm's length apart.

"I see we're still playing *Family Feud*," Molly joked.

Penelope and Scottie glanced at each other.

"Hey, Dad. Do you remember that thing you used to do where you would make us hug when we were mad at each other? Let's make them do that." She pointed back and forth between her sisters.

"Cute," said Scottie.

"No, really. Isn't there a rule that you have to grant me my last wish?"

Penelope wiped a tear from her face.

"Oh, my God, you two. Get over yourselves. You can't seriously still be angry."

Neither moved. Molly pointed to her water and Hank lifted it to her lips.

"Don't you get it?" She pushed herself to sitting. "It's always over too soon. You always regret what you didn't do more than what you did. I love you, but you're both bullheaded. Well, you're gonna have to figure it out for yourself. You're it. You're all you've got. The end."

Penelope reached out for Scottie's hand. Like a magnet, Scottie grabbed her hand.

"OK. That's a start," Molly announced. "We'll work up to a hug."

Through the night, they held on to her and to each other. Shared memories, like dormant seeds waiting decades for the perfect conditions, blossomed in brilliant hues. Christmas mornings, board games, haircuts, camping trips—every tiny moment was amplified and made present by their retelling. Laughter and tears flowed in equal measure. None were contained. They said what needed to be said. As the hours passed, they took turns holding her hand. Molly knew she could let go when Penelope pulled Scottie close and reached for Hank.

Chapter Forty-Eight

Scottie

Scottie sat on the corner of the concrete box that spanned the length of the plate-glass windows. Her legs were too short to touch the ground from her perch, so she wedged her heels against the brick façade. Though filled with a row of azaleas that would no doubt blossom in identical hues, it was clear to her the planter was an aesthetically acceptable barrier against attack. Scottie wondered if her sister was worried about that.

The box rested on her knees. Her hands covered the top as if it were in danger of floating away without her attention. Black slacks, cuffed and creased, came into view.

"You look like a drifter," Penelope said as she leaned over to scratch Burnie's ears.

"Hey, these boots cost more than yours."

"I was referring to your disheveled appearance and vacant stare. Come on up. Let's get you off the streets before the doorman calls security."

"Are you sure they'll let me in?"

"If I vouch for you and your vicious guard dog." Penelope pointed to the box. "Is that it?"

"Yes. Dad did a nice job carving it." Scottie held the box up. "And no one lost a finger, so that's a bonus."

"He didn't want to come with us?"

"No, he said his goodbyes."

"I wish she was here with us."

"She is." Scottie patted the lid of the box.

"Not exactly what I had in mind."

She put her arm around Penelope's shoulder. "Let's go. One last trip to Chimney Rock."

About the Author

Catherine Matthews is an award-winning Pacific Northwest author. Through her novels, she tells stories of strong women finding the courage to face the storm and live their dreams—usually in the company of a faithful hound.

Catherine's debut novel, *Releasing the Reins*, won the 2024 American Writing Awards in the categories of Thriller/Adventure and Western, first place in the 2024 BookFest Awards for Women's Fiction Thriller and Suspense, and Best Book for Women's Fiction in the 2024 Fall Pencraft Awards.

She is up before dawn to start her day writing—always in the company of her two favorite hounds, Delta and Buttercup. You can connect with her on *Facebook* or *Instagram* or visit her webpage *www.catherinematthewsauthor.com*.

Discussion Questions

1. Why did the author title this novel *Roadside Sisters*? What would you have titled it?
2. Which sister resonated with you the most and why?
3. What scene in the novel had the greatest emotional impact on you and why?
4. Of the themes woven through this novel, which theme does each sister most exemplify?
5. Family secrets are internally destructive forces that can influence future relationships and life choices. What impact did each sister's secret have on their adult life?
6. Though a powerful and supportive experience for many women, being a member of a sisterhood has benefits and costs. For each sister, what cost is so great that it prevents them from taking part in their sisterhood?
7. How did each sister's secret benefit them?
8. Should the sisters have shared their secrets? Why or why not?
9. To heal, who and what does each sister need to forgive? What, if anything, is unforgiveable?
10. What lie does each sister believe about herself? How does that lie keep each from a relationship with her sisters?
11. What purpose do Jason, Victoria, and Angie serve in the story?

12. The author includes two dogs on the sister's road trip: a Bernese Mountain Dog and a Lhasa Apso. Considering their physical characteristics, personalities, and breed group, why did the author pick these two very different breeds?
13. The dogs appear to be characters themselves. Why did the author include them in the cast?
14. Most of the story takes place inside an SUV on a road trip between Reno and Seattle. What impact did this contained setting have on the plot?
15. In the story, Molly wants the sisters to stop at Chimney Rock which was the destination of their final childhood road trip. Why did the author choose Chimney Rock?

THE
TUNDRA SECRETS
SERIES

RELEASING THE REINS

A Novel

CATHERINE MATTHEWS

More by Catherine Matthews

RELEASING THE REINS

Tundra Secrets Series Book 1

In the dawning of summer, the rugged landscape of rural Alaska sets the stage for a tale of determination and dark secrets. Headstrong Bunny O'Kelly arrives on the sprawling expanses of Buck Miller's horse ranch with the fiery ambition to make a name for herself. Against the backdrop of wild horses and unchecked wilderness, she embarks on a grueling journey to prove her worth, not just as a ranch hand, but as a woman in a world that doesn't want her.

But when Bunny stumbles upon the shattered remnants of Katie Miller's life, the ranch transforms into a web of lies. Katie's fatal accident, long unexamined, whispers of hidden truths and cloaked motives. As Bunny delves deeper, she uncovers a sinister layer to the tragedy and finds herself caught in a dangerous game where her quest for justice could unravel the very fabric of her newfound haven . . . yet silence could enshrine a killer's freedom.

Releasing the Reins spurs you to unravel its mysteries. Can Bunny O'Kelly expose the truth when trust shatters and daylight reveals the deadliest secrets?

Be the first to learn about upcoming books by Catherine Matthews. Subscribe to her newsletter, *Books, Boxers, and Big News.*

Acknowledgements

This book was mapped out on a highway between Rome and Calhoun after my sister and I spent a morning marvelling at the miniature Roman Colosseum and Notre Dame Cathedral in the Rock Garden. As all books do, it meandered on from those first ideas and picked up many people along the way. Still, my first thanks goes to my sister Judy whose love of road trips and obscure roadside attractions inspired the setting for this book. Thanks for making every journey an adventure.

Thanks to my husband Scott for encouraging me to chase my dreams. The best miles of my life have been sitting in a pickup truck next to you.

Thanks to my daughter Shannan for your daily support an encouragement, so powerful I can feel it eight states away. You inspire me to live my passion by living yours.

The road to publication is long and riddled with tempting detours. I am grateful for the writers and friends who keep me on course. Thanks to Heather Ewan-Foster Carter for getting up before dawn every day for a writer check in. I am so grateful for your friendship, support, and feedback. Thanks to the Early Birds for creating an uplifting space overflowing with creative energy in which to write every day. Thanks to the WFWA Writing Dates InMates for generously sharing your expertise and encouragement, and for keeping me accountable. Thanks to my critique partners, James Shipman and S.G. Prince, for making me a better writer and *Roadside Sisters* a better book. Thanks to editor Virginia McCullough for your invaluable guidance and wise counsel. Thanks to developmental editor Tiffany Yates Martin for your insightful feedback.

Thanks to my beta readers for providing your critical input to get this book to its final destination: Heather Ewan-Foster Carter, Jamie Edson, Ann Burns, Becky Ballbach, Donna Kaputska, Shelley Boten, Shannon Koehnen, and Carol Whitehead.

Made in the USA
Middletown, DE
29 August 2025

13289837R00191